PRAISE FOR FRASER

All the Swoony vibes I crave with the added level of suspense and chase. I can't wait for the other books in the series to come out.

SHANNON, THE REEL BOOKERY

I inhaled this book and loved every minute of the journey. It was everything I love about Susan May Warren's romantic suspense. Readers can expect heart-pounding action, suspense, twists and turns, the perfect romance, biblical truth, characters you will love and root for until the last page and appearances from many past characters. *Fraser* was an explosive beginning to the Minnesota Marshalls and I can't wait to see what happens next.

KELLY, THE COZY BOOKWORM

I devoured it. Loved it. And want more. Good news that this will be a 5 book series because I am here for it! Now to try and get over this book hangover...

NICOLE AND THE UNENDING TBR

FRASER

THE MINNESOTA MARSHALLS
BOOK ONE

SUSAN MAY WARREN

Soli Deo Gloria

FRASER

THE MINNESOTA MARSHALLS

Let's start with this...

He might be the luckiest guy on the planet.

Creed Marshall stood at the entrance of Gelato Artigianale, the sounds of the wharf in his ears—the listing of sailboats at anchor, music from a nearby club, electronic hip-hop pulsing into the night. Under the star-strewn sky, the lights of Geneva rippled along the water of the massive lake in colors of red, orange, and purple, adding a techno mystique to the evening.

Yeah, he wasn't in Kansas anymore, as the saying went. Or, more accurately, Minnesota.

He checked his watch, a graduation gift three years ago from his adopted father, Garrett Marshall.

Where was she?

They should have stayed at the club, like he'd suggested. Had a good mind to return there, but frankly, the dance floor writhed with bodies. And she'd said she wanted gelato, just a couple blocks away at this place by the lake.

He saw romance, and he'd gobbled up the idea like...

Like he might be a lucky guy. The kind of guy who'd saved—sorta saved, because they hadn't been in any real danger—a pretty girl on a wind-roughened gondola.

Her name was Imani. Cool name. Cool girl. Hazel eyes, dark hair, tanned. American. And judging by the giggle and the way she'd held onto him today, even in fear—yeah, she liked him too.

Or he'd thought so.

And what was it that his brother Fraser always said—you make your own luck?

So he'd taken a chance and, to his surprise, landed a yes when he asked said pretty girl out to go dancing with his friends from the international cross-country competition. A competition he didn't exactly win but hadn't lost either.

He'd counted it as a win because his parents got on a plane and flew to Europe to watch him. That was cool too.

"Can I help you, sir?" A waitress, her accent French, approached him. He'd been standing at a table as if he was holding it.

"No. Sorry."

"Are you waiting for someone?"

Yes. Sort of. "No." He moved away and checked his watch again.

He should have been more insistent when he offered to walk her over, but she said she'd meet him here.

Sure. Whatever the woman wanted.

Maybe she'd had trouble ditching her friend. Or cousin or whoever she was. Pippa. Uptight. Unfriendly, even. But Pippa had come with her tonight to the bar, so maybe she wasn't that stuffy.

He checked his watch again.

Along the boardwalk, sailboats swayed in the scant wind, and farther out the massive water jet sprayed its plume, casting the faintest mist into the air.

She wasn't coming.

And he didn't really feel like going back to the club. Not when he'd made a big deal of leaving his friends for…

Apparently, he wasn't as lucky as he thought. Hoped.

Oh, didn't matter. He was leaving for Minnesota in the morning.

He started down the boardwalk, heading for his hotel, across the street from the Jardin Anglais, not far from the club. People walked hand in hand through puddles of lamplight, the scent of autumn in the air.

He turned and cut down a narrow street bordered on both sides by ancient, tall buildings—clean, as was all of Geneva, and quaint. He'd spent much of yesterday walking around Old Town. Had seen the St. Pierre Cathedral. Stopped at a place to grab a pizza—

A scream cut through the night. Nearby, a flock of pigeons scattered.

He stilled.

Silly. Probably it was a car screeching.

But in his soul, he couldn't shake the fear that— "Imani?"

Except, if she'd screamed, maybe she was scared. After all, she was in a foreign country, alone—

Oh, he should have gone with her—

He crossed the street again and entered the park. Here, the trees gathered the wind, the chill of the night. He tucked his coat around him and headed toward the fountain, still in the distance.

Lights flickered through the trees, the city on the other bank of the river.

And that's when he saw movement. A girl running through the park.

She was being chased. Not closely, but some hundred feet behind her, a man followed, also running.

Probably the victim wasn't Imani. But whoever it was, she was in trouble.

He took off, cutting through the pathways, his eyes adjusted to the dark, and kept his eyes on the chase.

He emerged ten feet behind the woman, pivoted, and put on speed.

He caught up to her fast, and then, just as she reached the edge of the park, he wrapped his arms around her and pulled her off her feet and into the brush.

She whirled and struck him hard in the chest, but he grabbed her hand. "I'm trying to help you."

Imani.

He stilled, his eyes wide, and she, too, just looked at him.

What—

Then his instincts took over—instincts from days way gone by, the kind he had really forgotten but had learned back when he'd lived in inner-city Minneapolis.

Back when his brother was doing bad things.

"Get down," he said, and pulled her to himself, secreting her behind a tree.

She leaned against him, breathing hard.

The feet ran by, then slowed.

No.

He grabbed her hand and yanked her behind him and took off.

She was running in heels. Twice, he nearly pulled her over.

A glance behind him revealed nothing, but it wouldn't be long before—

Suddenly, she gave him a hard tug, changing directions. What—

Oh no—*no*—

Yes. Because before he could stop them, and with what seemed all her strength, she launched them both out and into the dark, frigid waters of Lake Geneva.

The cold sucked him down, pinned him, shucked out his breath, and if not for her hand in his, gripping it, he might have let go and panic-kicked to the surface.

He wasn't a great swimmer.

But she pulled him up, and by the time he surfaced, she had grabbed onto his jacket and was swimming hard for the dock.

Clearly not to climb out of the freezing cold, because she pulled him under the decking, holding on to a pylon in the darkness.

He could barely make out her face, so close to his in the night.

"What's happening here?" he whispered. "Who is chasing you?"

"Shh." Her teeth rattled, and her hair had sprung up, frizzy around her face.

"Why are you running?"

She looked at him then. "I guess because when a guy has his throat slit right in front of you, you don't stop to ask why."

Oh.

A light shone along the edge of the lake front, and she shrank back into the shadows.

"You think that's him?"

"Mm-hmm," she said, and he pulled her to himself, holding on to the pylon with the other hand. Then he moved them back, deeper into the pitch.

But he waited, watching as the man studied the water. A Caucasian man wearing a short coat, in his forties, maybe, although frankly, Creed couldn't get a decent look.

But what he did know was that right now, right here, he just might be a hero.

And that felt a lot like luck.

One

F raser couldn't escape the carnage.

No, the dream—he knew it was a dream, for the screams, his own groans, the taste of blood in his teeth played out just as he remembered.

So rather, it was memories that stalked Fraser Marshall, chased him down, kept him twisting in his sheets.

The kind of memories that left him sweaty, raw, and shaken.

But not tonight.

Tonight, as Fraser woke, a rough, jerky yank to consciousness, his heart slamming against his rib cage, he caught his breath and listened.

Someone was out there.

They'd followed him.

He blinked, just to clear his brain from the raw, feral scents of the Nigerian savanna, the acrid smell of wood fires, and the sharp, raucous arguing between Boko Haram terrorists.

Nope, he wasn't tied up, his broken arm festering, aching, his gut tight with hunger, reliving his mistakes and desperately fighting to survive, to escape with the people he was supposed to protect.

Instead, he was back in his childhood bedroom in Minnesota. With the hockey posters of his favorite Blue Ox players, the inspirational poster about not giving up—written in Latin, featuring a man holding up a massive rock—the few track trophies that cluttered his dresser. Alive and breathing.

Mostly.

He barely fit into the bed, his feet hanging off the end, and the tiny frame groaned as he sat up, the covers falling to his waist. Holding his breath, he listened.

Hard to hear breathing or even a scuff of sound over the thunder of his heart, so Fraser took a deep breath, told himself to calm down, and pushed himself to his feet.

The wooden floor creaked, and he stilled.

Wind sent leaves skittering across the roof, into the gutters. The porch swing whined.

He looked out the window, and his second-story view revealed nothing amiss in the yard, the vineyard spent of its harvest, the leaves drying, barren.

Sheesh, what did he think? That Abu Hassiff would send one of his thugs—or even track Fraser himself—across an ocean to finish the job? Fraser shook himself out of the thought and back into reality.

The nightmare was *over*. Time to wake up and move *on*.

Maybe the itchy feeling in his gut, the hyperawareness of every sound, was simply his father's words, uttered when he left with the rest of the family for Europe, rising to haunt his oldest son. *You're in charge, Fraser. Please don't let anything happen to the wine.*

Like all one hundred and fifty barrels of the wine, both the aging La Crescent Gold, and the deep red Marquette Crimson might get up and sneak away. But after the tornado a few years back that had damaged their fields, Dad had practically hand-nurtured the vines back to life. This year might be award-winning.

And his father had left Fraser in charge.

He'd missed most of the harvest during his hospitalization and recuperation, not to mention a recent op in Florida that Ham had called him in for. But now, with all the grapes picked, squeezed, put through the primary fermenter, then into barrels—aka, the big work done—it was a waiting game.

Which felt a little like being put in charge of watching paint dry.

But maybe that was his life now. His hand wasn't getting better after all. And after his missed shots and a near catastrophic accident on the op, it was clear he had some time on the bench ahead.

Fraser blew out a breath and reached for a T-shirt. Pulling it on, he headed downstairs.

Shadows gathered in the empty bedrooms down the hallway of the old farmhouse, and admittedly, the place seemed a little haunted, filled with voices from his childhood, memories of wrestling with his brothers, or long discussions with his father when he was figuring out if he wanted to be a SEAL.

Yes, ghosts lived here, ghosts of the boy who'd wanted to be the best, to serve his country, to save his buddies, even the world.

Ghosts that lurked even in the daytime, when he'd put all the other nightmares to rest.

He avoided the third step on the way down, just in case there might be a terrorist waiting in the living room, but of course it was empty, save for his parents' new sectional, the overflowing bookcase, the cold hearth.

He flicked on the light in the kitchen area and headed over to the fridge.

Two a.m. on the oven clock. Yeah, that felt about right for his early-morning wander around the house. For him to try and lose himself in a Jack Reacher book, give up, and turn on old reruns of *Law and Order* until he fell asleep in the recliner.

Usually, by four a.m. he slept like the dead.

And lately, had been letting himself sleep in to seven. Maybe eight.

It wasn't like his cell phone was suddenly going to buzz with a callout text.

He pulled a glass down from the cupboard and filled it with water. Leaned a hip against the sink as he looked out the massive picture window to the patio and, beyond, the barn.

Shook his right hand, a habit he'd picked up over the past month, as if trying to wake it up. He watched himself make a fist, and the act felt disembodied.

He could move his hand. He just couldn't feel it.

Which worked oh so well for a man whose job description called for being able to shoot accurately.

He stared at himself in the window—the too-long scruff, unruly dark-blond hair, a pair of pajama pants, a T-shirt, the scars from the surgery still angry and raw on his arm. Yeah, no wonder his parents suggested he stay home from their trek over to Switzerland to watch Creed's international competition.

He probably shouldn't leave the house.

He finished his water, was setting the glass in the sink when a light flashed against the pane.

He stilled, then crouched, a reflex rather than clear thought. But there it went again—light flashing in the barn, aka winery, that housed the barrels.

Hello.

Maybe his father wasn't kidding about the need for secrecy in his recipe.

He reached up and, with his left hand, found a knife from the block.

Except, maybe that was overkill. And besides, what was he going to do—kill someone for sneaking a sip of wine? He put the knife back.

But he hustled through the door and secreted himself behind

a post on the patio, waiting. The late-October wind snaked under his T-shirt, and the scent of rain hinted the air.

Overhead, clouds obscured the stars, but his eyes had adjusted to the thick shadows of the barn, the gazebo where they held events, and the various equipment parked near the machinery shed.

The light flickered again, this time against the glass sliding doors of their tasting room.

Where their premier wine, some bottles up to a decade old, sat in a display case. Some of those bottles sold for up to $750.

He edged out, crossed the darkened yard, then eased open the massive door that housed the barrels, up on tidy racks, placed by a forklift.

Slid inside and hid near a rack. The smell of oak, the yeasty redolence of aging wine permeated the air. The cement floor of the building echoed sound, and now he thought he heard—a giggle?

What?

He was scooting out toward the tasting room when, just like that, the forklift roared to life in the darkness.

Headlights flicked on, and he held up a hand, the light blinding as it saturated the room. Dots formed in his eyes, and he blinked them away, finding cover behind one of the aluminum primary fermenters.

The forklift began to move—jerky, then in a circle around the room.

Was someone stealing a barrel?

Crazy. But not on his watch.

He moved behind the lift, his eyes still trying to adjust in the light. With the driver's back to Fraser, he couldn't make him out.

Didn't matter.

Three steps, and Fraser launched himself onto the forklift,

grabbed the driver by the shoulder and ripped him away from the driver's seat.

They fell off, rolled, and Fraser came up first, pouncing on the driver's back. A man.

"Stop! Please—"

No, a *kid,* given the tenor and fear that rocked his voice.

"Don't hurt him!"

A girl's voice—probably to go along with the giggle—and then light poured over the both of them as she jumped off the forklift and came running toward them.

Fraser looked down at where he'd shoved his arm against the boy's neck, pinning him, his other hand reeled back in a submission hold.

"I was just showing her around!" The kid writhed beneath him.

"You're hurting him!" The girl came up, and Fraser had to give her props, because she leaped on Fraser's back, hitting him.

Aw—

He let go of the kid, turned and grabbed the girl's arm. "Stop."

She jerked her wrist from his grip, but that was no surprise, given his flimsy hold. Dark hair, fiery blue eyes, she glared at him. "Who are you?"

"Who am—I own this place."

The kid had rolled over, kicking himself away from Fraser. "No, you don't. This is the Marshall place—"

"Sheesh, kid." Fraser stood up. "I'm Fraser Marshall."

The kid—Fraser put him at about nineteen, maybe, wiry and cocky and wearing a University of MN T-shirt—backed up, hands up. "Whoa—sorry, man. I didn't know you were back."

"Clearly, but who are you?"

"I'm Neil. I work here on the weekends—"

The sound of splintering wood fractured his words.

Fraser spun and took off for the forklift, now rammed into

one of the tall barrel stacks, wheels turning as it chewed into the wood.

The barrels shook under the onslaught.

He leaped into the cab, reaching for the steering wheel and the gear shift. Slamming his foot on the brake, he then jerked the forklift into reverse, turned the wheel with his good hand to yank the machine from the shelving, then hit the gas.

The lift jerked forward, hard, and the shelving splintered. As Fraser—and Neil—yelled, the barrels cascaded into themselves, bouncing, then rolling onto the floor, five hundred pounds each of lethal bowling ball.

"Look out!" Fraser's voice, but Neil reacted and grabbed his girlfriend and pulled her away, behind a sturdy fermenter.

The barrels rolled out, some slamming against the wall, a few rolling toward the door.

Two split upon impact, the barrels possibly old, but wine spurted out, saturating the floor.

Fraser turned off the motor. One of the barrels landed on the forklift, pinning it. He'd been saved from being crushed by the roll bars.

Neil flicked on the barn light. Came out, wide-eyed. "Someone is going to die."

Fraser glanced at him, his mouth tight. But the kid was right.

Wine, his father's precious Marquette Crimson recipe, flooded the floor a deep red.

A regular crime scene.

He climbed off the forklift, shaking his stupid, prickly, useless hand.

"You okay, dude?" Neil came out from behind the fermenter, holding the hand of his girlfriend.

"Am I—are you kidding me?" Fraser hadn't a clue where or how to start cleaning this up. He shook his head. "What are you doing here?"

Neil made a face. "Sorry. I wanted to show Daisy what we did."

"This is very cool—" Daisy said.

"Get out. Get. Out!"

Neil held up a hand, then headed for the door. But there, he turned. "I'm driving her home. Then I'll be back to help clean this up. The boss is going to be hot."

Fraser just stared at him as wine puddled like blood around his bare feet.

PIPPA HATED TO ADMIT IT, BUT IT MIGHT HAVE BEEN helpful to have *two* people on the security detail of Her Royal Highness Princess Imani of Lauchtenland.

Just so one of them might get a little shut-eye between the crazy escapades of Her Royalness.

Yes, Imani was one headstrong American, and one of these times, one of these pizza runs, someone was going to get killed.

And sure, it might be because Imani didn't even bother to look both ways before she crossed a busy night-strewn cobblestone street in the middle of Old Town Geneva, Switzerland, only to be mowed down by a reckless scooter, but still.

It would be Pippa's fault.

Which was why she just wanted to fast-walk up to the stubborn American teenager-turned-princess, grab her by her curly ponytail, and yank her into a waiting Uber.

Maybe remind her, just for a split second, that she might not be blood royalty to the House of Blue, but as the adopted daughter of Princess Gemma, she had a neon-red target on her back. And she couldn't just sneak out after Pippa had secured her in her room for the night.

But the princess clearly didn't see the danger, because the

girl had spent her epic year-long gap year gallivanting through South America, Africa, Thailand, and now Europe acting like she might be a free-spirited American on holiday.

Okay, in a way, she was that too.

Still, six more weeks felt way too long when Pippa was standing outside some hole-in-the-wall pizza joint or hamburger stand or even 7-Eleven so Imani could tame her junk-food addiction.

Now the girl was laughing with some handsome cashier as she bumbled through her abysmal French and ordered something passing as a pizza from the picture menu.

Poor guy. He looked already smitten with the dark-haired, dark-skinned beauty. There she went again, leaving a trail of broken hearts behind her.

Pippa shook her head and checked her watch—way past her check-in with Gunner. She sent her boss a quick text—

Out with Imani. Will text when we return.

Pippa fully planned on lying prostrate in front of the captain of Her Majesty's Security Detail and begging for a transfer.

Hopefully right into the service of the Princess Gemma.

Like father, like daughter.

She glanced over at the Uber driver, sitting in the darkness, probably tapping his steering wheel, antsy to complete his fare. She'd offered him double his rate as a tip, so hopefully—

Inside, Imani had retrieved her pizza, neatly boxed, and with a laugh and a flip of her dark curly hair, she left the shop.

"Your Highness, your ride is this way."

Imani froze, right there on the sidewalk.

And Pippa couldn't help herself. "Did you seriously think I wouldn't know you sneaked out for some nosh? Ma'am."

"You didn't have to follow me." Her brown eyes sparked.

"Pardon me, Your Highness, but have you given one thought to how dodgy this area is late at night?"

"It's not that late."

Pippa took a breath. "Ma'am. Pardon the impertinence, but please get your queen mum in the car."

Imani matched her breath, and for a second, Pippa thought she might have to—what? Manhandle her into the vehicle?

Pippa's voice softened. "Please, Your Royal Highness. It's late, and you have a busy day tomorrow."

"Fine." Imani shook her head. "You act like someone is going to yank me off the street, sell me to the highest bidder."

Pippa opened the door. "You *are* a princess."

"Whatever." She climbed inside the Uber.

Pippa joined her. "Back to the hotel," she said in French.

The driver nodded, and she closed the door.

"Want a piece?" Imani opened the box. Admittedly, the pizza looked much like the pizza that Princess Gemma occasionally had the chefs make back in Lauchtenland. Round crust, tomato sauce, sausage, cheese. Pippa pressed her hand against her stomach, the smell stirring the hole inside.

"No, thank you, ma'am."

Imani snagged a piece. "Please. For the love, call me Imani. It's been a year. You've seen me naked. I think it's time."

"You screamed."

"There was a roach the size of my foot in the shower."

"I have wiped your royal birthday suit from my mind."

"Thank you. Now, have a piece of pizza. Remember when we were in Morocco, I found that little place in Casablanca—"

"Yes, I remember." And Pippa's stomach had paid the price, had her hugging the loo long into the night.

"I don't get you." Imani folded her pizza in half and bit into it.

"Very good, ma'am." But really, it was Pippa who didn't get Imani. The girl was...

Sweet, mostly. But also independent and without a flicker of common sense, at least when it came to self-protection. She would walk right into a murder and stand there asking who'd done it.

And Pippa would be the one who'd have to step between her and a bullet.

Yep, like father like daughter.

She turned away and watched the buildings slide by. She'd never been to Geneva and wouldn't have minded a walkabout to see the sights. Old Town reminded her much of Fressa, the port city of Lauchtenland. Ancient buildings that crowded narrow cobblestone streets, crests and emblems over the doors, tiny Juliet balconies overflowing with flowers. St. Pierre Cathedral, built in the twelfth century, looked much like one of the cathedrals in the center of Fressa that made up the central square, called the Heart of God.

She would have liked to see the Flower Clock, made from over twelve thousand flowers, and probably just as pretty as the queen's garden.

Maybe even take a day trip to Chamonix-Mont-Blanc, a tiny ski town not so different from one of her favorite ski resorts on the north side of the island.

Pippa pressed her hand to her jacket, drew in a breath. She missed Lauchtenland, despite the grand adventure of the last year.

She just wanted to be back, her feet on her own land, eating dinner at the Belly of the Beast and walking through the queen's gardens.

And for sure, she'd stop by the Dalholm cemetery. Check in. Status report on her quest to prove that everyone had been wrong.

They passed over Mont Blanc Bridge, and in the distance, the Jet d'Eau water fountain sprayed over a hundred meters high, catching the starlight and glitter of the city as it fell in droplets back to Lake Geneva. In the distance, mountains rose to embrace the valley city, and above it, stars sprayed a perfect indigo sky like diamonds.

A beautiful night for a stroll, maybe, so perhaps she shouldn't be so hard on Imani. But if Pippa allowed the woman to get hurt on her watch, her father's name would never be redeemed.

"I don't know why we had to stay at the Four Seasons," Imani said, closing the box on the rest of her pizza. "It's so...ostentatious."

Or beautiful. The magnificent hotel sat at the edge of Lake Geneva, rising six stories to overlook the river connecting the lake, the ambiance of Old Town. The first decent hotel they'd stayed in since leaving Lauchtenland ten months ago.

"We could have stayed at a youth hostel. There's a really nice one right up the road."

"Your parents booked this one for you. They'll be here at the end of the week."

"I still don't know why I had to meet them here. I could have gone to Portofino and met them on the *Serenity*."

Pippa, for one, was tired of managing the danger of sleeping in just barely approved youth hostels, or even the occasional barrack reserved for humanitarian workers. Tonight, thankfully, they stayed at the Four Seasons, courtesy of the Crown, and after she secured the princess in her room, Pippa had just wanted to fall into the plushness of the king bed in her adjoining room, stare at the ornate ceiling medallion, and sleep for a thousand years. Would have if she hadn't heard Imani's door softly close, footsteps down the hallway shortly after she'd bid Pippa good night.

Six. Weeks.

"Can you sneak us in the back? I don't want the press to know I'm here."

Pippa glanced at her. For the first time, Imani was making

some sense. Pippa leaned forward and asked the driver to pull around to the side.

Lights glowed from the main street, turning the side entrance to shadow, but Pippa got out, checked for trouble, then used her key card to hustle her charge inside.

The heady fragrance of the massive bouquet of lilies on the center entry table filled the gilded hallway as Pippa waited for the elevator.

Yes, so much better than a tent in the middle of a South African game park with the sounds—and smells—of lions and hyenas stirring in the night. She hadn't slept for fear of finding the princess dragged out of her bed and into the bush for a late-night snack.

She could already feel the thread count of the Four Season's sheets.

The lift opened on the fifth floor, and she led Imani down to her plush executive suite—one bedroom, with a living room and balcony overlooking Lake Geneva.

Even the adjoining room, a one-bedroom deluxe, had a view with a sitting area.

Please, let them spend a week here. But knowing Imani, she'd be on the internet tonight, signing up for some unvetted, impromptu adventure tour through the Alps.

Six. Weeks.

"Please, stay in your room until morning, ma'am," Pippa said as she opened the door, then stepped inside and did a quick sweep. Imani's backpack lay on the floor, a few clothes strewn on a plush blue velvet sofa in the living room.

She gave the all clear, and Imani came inside. Set the pizza on the coffee table, then walked to the window. "There's a gelato place across the river."

"Good night, Your Highness."

She turned to Pippa. "Fine. By the way, we're going to the

13

Aiguille du Midi in the morning." She held up the pizza box. "It'll be good cold, too."

"I'll order you a poached egg, toast, and tea. Have a good night."

Imani rolled her eyes, but Pippa closed her door, then pulled out her phone. *We're back. I'll meet you in the lobby.*

It helped that her boss Gunner Ferguson, lead officer of Her Majesty's Security Detail, had secured the entire floor and the one above for use by the Lauchtenland entourage. Their Royal Highnesses, Crown Prince John and Princess Gemma, would occupy the Presidential Loft Suite in the penthouse, while the rest of the envoy—including Hamish Fickle, the MP who also served as the liaison to the North Sea Coalition delegates— would fill the executive suites on this level.

She was heading for the lift again when a door opened down the hall. "Pippa."

Gunner stepped out into the hall. He still wore a suit, always on the job, and looked every inch a royal guard with his dark, short-shaved hair, impressive shoulders, and pensive blue eyes. He even wore the distinctive blue suit with the gold gauntlets on the sleeves of the jacket.

"Sir," she said.

"In here." He motioned with his head to his suite, and she stepped inside as he held open the door.

Of course, he, too, had an executive suite—that didn't surprise her. After all, he'd have meetings here with his team every morning of the conference, handing out assignments, giving briefings, and generally keeping the delegation from Lauchtenland safe.

He'd probably brought most of his team. Maybe Fredrik was even around, given that he was on the team for Hamish Fickle and his entourage.

He closed the door behind her. "It's good to see you. You don't look worse for wear during your gap year."

"The *princess's* gap year. There's been no holiday about it."
Although she did sport a nice tan from their last month in
Greece, touring the travels of Saint Paul. "She has too much
American in her to stay put, do something sensible. It's been a
bit of a dance to stay one step ahead."

He walked over to the sofa and leaned against the back of it,
his hands gripping the edges.

"Six more weeks and you'll be home, and she'll enroll in
Haxton University. You'll love the campus—it's quite beautiful.
Old buildings, a quaint pub."

She stilled, and the ex-marine must have caught it, because
he cocked his head. Raised an eyebrow.

"Permission to speak freely, sir?"

"Please, Pippa. We've been friends a long time. And your
father was—"

"I know what my father was. And who I am. I thought after
this assignment..." She swallowed.

"You want to serve on Her Majesty Princess Gemma's
detail."

"I applied to serve Daffy, but that was denied."

"Because you knew each other as children at the castle, and I
thought it might be a conflict now that she's a princess."

"I have no problem serving a princess."

"And her father was one of the inquisitors into Aberforth
Fickle's assassination. He accused your father—"

"My father was serving his country. And he gave his life for
the man. He had nothing to do with the antimonarchy plot."
Her throat thickened at the last of her words.

"I know, Pippa. Breathe."

She looked away, her jaw tight. "I've been with the service
since university, transferring into the Marines for exactly this
detail." She met his eyes. "Nearly ten years, proving myself..."
She drew a breath. "I rode an elephant. And slept in a yurt."

He hid a smile. "And no one appreciates your service more

than Prince John." He rose. "Okay, I'll put it to the prince, with my recommendation."

She stared at him, even as her heart gave a thump. "Truly?"

"Yes. You're right, you deserve a spot on Her Highness's detail. If Prince John approves it, then we'll institute your commission when you finish Princess Imani's gap year."

"Thank you, sir. I'll make you proud."

He gave a smile, something warm in it, in his eyes. "You already do, Pippa. And your father would be proud of you."

Oh. She looked away, her jaw tight. No crying on Her Majesty's Security Detail.

"Just make sure Imani returns to Lauchtenland in six weeks, alive and well," he said, laughing.

Oh, so funny. But she nodded. "Right-o, sir."

Even if she had to handcuff herself to the reckless princess, Pippa wasn't going to let her out of her sight.

Two

O f course today's adventure had to happen one thousand meters above the ground.

It could be worse, perhaps. Imani could have signed up for the paragliding off the side of a mountain. Instead, she'd opted for the glorious not-at-all-dangerous ride over the seracs and crevasses of the Glacier du Géant to the Pointe Helbronner.

It wasn't enough to just take the cable car to the viewing platform of the Aiguille du Midi, a mere 3,842 meters above sea level. She had to walk out on the viewing box that overlooked Chamonix, with nothing but thin glass between her and a thousand-meter plunge.

Imani spent the full five allotted minutes in the "void"—what she called the viewing platform.

Admittedly, however, despite Pippa wanting to stay safely inside the concrete lair perched on the sheer north face granite peak, the view of Mont Blanc undid her.

Spiring up over 4,800 meters, the tallest peak in Europe, snow had already capped her peak, bright and glistening against a cool blue sky. From the enclosed glass platform, which jutted out five feet into space, it did seem that they were suspended above the glorious valley, enclosed with mountains on all sides.

Up here, too, the air felt thinner, the wind brisker. It had buffeted their car on the way up, sending it swaying. Pippa nearly lost her lunch. Instead, she stood, her face stoic, praying her eggs and toast wouldn't make a reappearance.

And it was cold. She should have packed a hat, gloves because her hands turned to ice.

Pippa couldn't look down, imagining the princess's plummet to the earth.

Why couldn't the girl take a nice hike? Or maybe the train car ride along the valley?

It only got worse, of course, because then, after the viewing box, Imani got in the ticket line for the cable car ride over the Glacier du Géant to Punta Helbronner.

Tourists jammed the station at Aiguille du Midi, a fleet of college-age coeds wearing flannel jackets emblazoned with an International Track and Field emblem on the breast, along with numerous families, probably on fall holiday break from school, filling the restaurants, the café, and viewing platforms.

For once, Pippa thanked Imani for her impulsiveness—no one would expect the princess to be caught in line with a group of rowdy college kids.

Although, in a way, Imani fit right in. She wore a puffy jacket, her dark hair pulled back in a tight ponytail that sprang out into corkscrews, a cotton jumper, and jeans with high-top runners. American to the core.

Imani bought tickets for her and Pippa, then got into the cable car line behind a handful of the coeds.

A man and his wife and their three darling daughters—sounded like loud Americans from their accents—shoved in between her and Imani, and Pippa made an enemy of the parents by scooting up behind Imani.

The coeds were jostling, playing some game in line. One

of the girls nearly spilled her coffee on a man in a red parka, early thirties, maybe, standing in front of them. "Sorry," said the girl, who stepped back and bumped into one of the coeds. He accidentally bumped into Imani, apologized, and Pippa nearly reached for him, but Imani stepped between them.

He seemed a nice enough kid. Dark hair, green eyes, he had a white smile, and he must have made a joke to Imani, because she laughed.

The kid's eyes sparked, and Pippa shook her head.

Imani, breaking hearts on top of the mountain.

Pippa turned to inspect the cable cars—they seemed sturdy enough. For a second, the images flashed through her mind of the terrible cable car crash over a year ago in Stresa, Italy. But then, the emergency brake had been disabled.

Still, the thick cable that spanned the five kilometers over the glacier seemed to sway slightly in the wind.

The line edged forward.

"Maybe this is a bad idea," she said, more to herself.

Imani, however, heard her. "You can stay here. I'll come back."

Pippa gave her a look.

Imani held up her hands in surrender, laughing.

Hardy har har. It wouldn't be so funny for any of them when she landed with a splat in the middle of that glacier.

The cable cars traveled in sets of three, about twelve passengers each, from what she could tell. She edged up behind Imani as the cars came into the station.

"Ellie, come back here!"

The voice rose behind her as a little girl, maybe nine, edged forward, sandwiching herself ahead of Imani.

"I'm sorry. Excuse me." The woman pushed ahead, trying to catch up to her daughter.

It happened so fast, Pippa wasn't sure who to blame. The

little girl got on the gondola ahead of her mother, then Imani stepped inside, and behind her pushed the mother.

The attendant was counting the bodies inside as Pippa reached for the handle to climb in, but the father, his two other daughters in hand, pushed up and handed off one of his daughters to their mother, still inside.

"Excuse me," Pippa said, stepping up.

"Mommy!"

The other little girl shoved in ahead of her, and Pippa stepped back to let her reach her mother.

"That's all," said the attendant.

"I don't think so," Pippa said and started up.

"Ma'am, we don't have room—"

"I'm fine." Imani looked at Pippa, something of pleading in her eyes.

Pippa's mouth tightened.

"Please, ma'am, there is room in the next one."

Right. And really, where was Imani going to go? Besides, her charge wasn't exactly in danger. Except maybe from the good-looking American who happened to get on ahead of her. He held on to a bar overhead, right behind Imani as she stepped up to the window.

Fine. Pippa got on, moved over to the front to keep an eye on Imani. The father got on behind her and waved to his family in the other car. They waved back, grinning.

So maybe she should loosen up a little. Except, that's when people got hurt. People she was charged with saving.

The gondola lurched forward, swinging free of the platform, and suddenly the world dropped out below.

The other passengers went quiet as they traveled over the expanse, their breaths caught just like Pippa's at the view of the mountains rising around them, the beautiful snowscape of runnels and valleys and ledges below them. The wind buffeted the car, but it held sturdy on the massive cable above. Pippa studied it for a long time, just to confirm.

They passed the first station, then dropped into the massive expanse over the glacier field.

To the south, Mont Blanc rose, a lethal, bold wall. Wind whisked snow off the top, hurtled it down the face, lashing the car with its icy breath. The gondola swayed slightly.

"Nothing to fear, guys," said the American, wearing a smile. "These things are made to take the wind."

Blimey.

She turned her gaze back on Imani. Her gloved hands pressed the glass, her forehead against it as she looked down. Her American friend stood behind her, also looking down.

Way too friendly, if anyone asked Pippa.

Behind her, a woman shouted. She turned and followed her gaze to the sight of a giant serac detaching from the mountain-side and tumbling down, catching more snow. In a second, an avalanche rent the sky with a terrible crack, then a roar.

The gondola began to shake.

Screams as people reached for the handhold. Pippa grabbed the railing nearest her and turned to check Imani.

With the swirl of wind, snow, and ice, the gondola twisted on its wire, swinging violently. Inside, passengers were tossed against each other, the walls of the ride, shaken, their screams shrilling the air.

Pippa could only hold on as the snow cloud rose around them, blinding her, rattling their car.

She refused to scream—it wasn't inside her to panic. But she did close her eyes, drill down, and grip the former marine inside.

This was not how she wanted to die. No, her death needed to be glorious, something given in the line of duty.

Just like her father.

Someone fell against her, slamming her head against the glass. She pushed the body away.

"Sorry!"

She pushed him away, cleared her head, her vision.

The first gondola had stopped pitching, the wind dying as the avalanche rolled to a stop some three hundred meters below.

"Imani!"

Of course the woman couldn't hear her, but she pounded on the glass anyway.

She didn't see Imani.

Next to her, the man was pounding on the glass alongside her, calling for his wife.

In a moment, the three daughters appeared, clinging to their mother, crying hard. But alive.

Still no Imani.

If she could, Pippa would climb out of this stupid gondola, go hand over hand to the next car—

There. The girls stepped away, and behind them, Imani was clinging to, of course, the handsome American boy, who had one arm gripped around her, the other viced into an overhead hand bar.

For the first time in five minutes, Pippa let herself breathe.

She was absolutely nixing a return ride.

The cars had continued on their route through the storm, and now, as they passed over the carnage below, started to settle down, the wind lessening.

Imani finally untangled herself from her rescuer and turned to look at Pippa's gondola. Raised a mittened hand. Waved.

Pippa's mouth pinched, but she raised a hand to wave back.

She didn't take her eyes off the girl the rest of the ride. Watched as Imani and the American—she'd dubbed him Track Star, thanks to his jacket—talked and laughed, and oh, she recognized that look of infatuation building on Track Star's face.

And on Imani's. The girl didn't exactly fall in love easily—not after her recent broken heart over a longtime friend from her hometown in Hearts Bend, Tennessee—but she did seem to make friends easily.

By the time they reached the other side and disembarked—and Pippa caught up to Imani in the station—the two were making plans to get together tonight in Geneva.

Of course.

"Your—Imani. Are you okay?" Pippa said, coming into their conversation.

"Yeah. I bumped my head and nearly fell, but Creed caught me."

She just bet he did.

"Creed Marshall," said the young man and held out his hand.

"Pippa Butler," said Pippa. She said nothing more, and not because of Imani's sharp look, but safety, and Imani's preferences, said that she was just a friend. A close, very attentive friend.

And she didn't blame Imani—the minute she mentioned the word *princess* everything changed.

"Cool. I'm only here because of the International Youth Cross-Country run in Geneva last week, but I thought I'd take in Mont Blanc before I had to go back to Minnesota tomorrow."

"So, are you going to ride back?" He nodded to the gondola.

"Sure—"

"No. I'm going to buy us tickets for the train," Pippa said.

Imani turned to her. "We're in Italy. We'll need my passport to take the train back."

Pippa smiled. "Not a problem." She looked at Creed. "Nice to meet you." Turned to Imani.

Who sighed. "Fine. But yes, I'll meet you tonight—where was it?"

"VIP Genève. It's near the river. See you there." He winked, then joined his friends not far away, still reenacting the trauma-slash-high-adventure as they stared out the window to the snow-encrusted peaks.

"No," Pippa said as Imani followed her to the train ticket area.

"You're not the boss of me."

Pippa glanced at her. "I am trying to keep you alive, ma'am."

"It seems to me that isn't up to you." Imani looped her arm through Pippa's. "But I did see how freaked out you were on the gondola, so the train will be just fine. And we'll get to see the village of Chamonix. I know you wanted to visit there."

She hadn't realized she'd let her preferences be known. "Thank you, Your—Imani."

"Listen. I get it. The last thing you need is for me to die on your watch. Scout's honor." Imani held up three fingers. "I will be on my best behavior tonight."

Sure she would.

Pippa forced a smile and pressed a hand against her still roiling stomach.

Five weeks, six days...

He probably had wine embedded in his pores.

Fraser just wanted to put the last forty-eight hours behind him as he drove out of Chester, headed to Minneapolis, and specifically, the suburb of Minnetonka and Hamilton Jones's house on the massive, gorgeous lake.

Overhead, the sky arched impossibly blue, the trees laying down a carpet of bejeweled leaves along the highway. Maple reds, yellow poplars, orange oaks—how he loved Minnesota in the fall. And especially an Indian summer day like today, where he could toss a football around during halftime and remind himself that he was still a member of Jones, Inc.

Hopefully.

Because the sooner he could escape the winery and any more disasters, the better.

He lifted his right hand off the steering wheel and squeezed it. Still, the pins and needles. Still, the slow reaction time.

Maybe what Ham didn't know wouldn't hurt him. Fraser had managed to pull himself together during a mission a month ago down in Florida when Ham had called in the team.

But since then, his grip hadn't improved, evidenced by the disaster in the winery two nights ago. He still couldn't believe he hadn't moved the gear shift into reverse.

Or that he'd destroyed two entire barrels—three hundred bottles each. And his brain just didn't want to face that math. But it equaled thousands of dollars of lost revenue, and he just didn't know what to say to his father.

Even with Neil helping him stack the barrels again after they'd repaired the stanchions, he still hadn't been able to pick up the phone.

Besides, he didn't want to wreck his parents' fortieth wedding anniversary trip to the Loire Valley in France. They'd had so much on them, what with Mom's cancer years ago. And then the tornado.

It didn't help that he'd shown up on their doorstep in July, broken, starved, and angry after being held captive. So, that had to add stress.

He blew out a breath as he passed a massive farmhouse selling pumpkins. Once upon a time, they'd sold pumpkins at the farm, back when his grandfather owned it. Pumpkins, milk, eggs, and fruit.

And then his father had taken over and turned it into a winery, proving that you could change course.

Except Fraser didn't want to change course. He liked his life, liked traveling, liked stepping into the fray. He might not be the tip of the sword anymore, but he could still make a difference. Protect people.

At least, he thought he had, as private security for Jones, Inc.

In the well between the front seats, his phone buzzed, sending the call through the speakers of his F-150. He pressed on the steering wheel to answer, taking a breath before—

"Hey, Dad. I hope you're calling me from France." And not on a sudden flight home thanks to a panicked text from Neil. Who had turned out to be not in high school but college, and working an internship while studying viticulture and enology from the University of Minnesota.

Of course.

Which had made Fraser feel like the hired hand as he mopped up the destroyed wine.

"I am. I'm having dinner with your mother in the shadow of the Amboise Castle, right by the river, having a glass of Vouvray, and I wanted to see how you were."

Fraser drew in a breath. "Um. Good. Everything is good." Sheesh. "Why?"

"I saw the warm spell in my weather app and wanted to make sure you were keeping an eye on the temperature in the barn."

Neil had been over this morning to do just that. "Yep. It's all good."

"I knew it was in safe hands."

Aw. "Dad, um, we had a small mishap with a forklift. The shelving gave way and…" Shoot. "We lost two barrels."

Silence on his father's end.

"Sorry."

"Oh, Fraser, it's okay. There's always some wine that goes bad. In the barrel, out of the barrel—we have insurance, so just make a note of it, and we'll figure it out when I get home."

He blew out a breath. "By the way, I met Neil. I didn't know you had an intern."

His father chuckled. "None of my children seem to want to grow grapes."

Fraser made a face. "Sorry."

"No. You need to follow your own course. God will provide. Sorry—I forgot to mention Neil, what with getting Creed ready for his race."

"How'd he do?"

"Fine. Middle of the pack. He was just excited to be selected to represent America. We left him in Geneva a couple days ago. He's headed home tomorrow. I was hoping you'd pick him up at the airport?"

"No problem. Did you see Iris or Jonas?"

"Iris reffed a game in Klagenfurt a few days earlier, so she drove over to attend the meet with us. Jonas is still off the map somewhere. But Ned caught up with us, with Shae. Apparently, she flew over to see him. He has some leave he's catching up on. They're headed to some fancy hotel in old town Lausanne for a few days. I think he said the Alps Hotel or something. Anyway, he seemed pretty tired. I hope he has some time to rest."

Fraser held in a pang of jealously—Ned, living his best life as an active-duty SEAL, just like Fraser had once upon a time. Maybe he shouldn't have left the teams, but after what had happened to Ham, he just couldn't stick around.

Not when he'd come close to the same fate. Better to separate with an honorable and his benefits than to be forced out.

But he got feeling tired. Sometimes it felt like they were always one step behind the bad guys. "Has he popped the question yet?"

"I didn't see a ring. But maybe that's why she's here."

Maybe. Or perhaps, like Fraser, Ned was contemplating the cost of his life choices on their relationship.

Or rather, Shae was. But then again, Fraser couldn't think of anyone better to marry his live-for-danger brother than a woman who had survived an attack in the wilderness, then returned to take down a murderer.

Yeah, she had the courage and patience to be a SEAL wife.

Hopefully Ned saw that too.

"Your mom is waving me over. Apparently my foie gras has arrived. Thanks, son. I knew we left things in good hands."

"Yep," Fraser said, hating himself, and hung up.

Whatever.

He'd be back on the job as soon as his parents returned home. And until then, he planned on keeping the wine safe if he had to lay out a blanket in the barn and sing the fermenting grapes to sleep.

Twenty minutes later, he pulled into Ham's driveway, nestled back along the lakeshore, and approached an unobtrusive seventies-style house. Over the years, Ham had gutted the interior and remade into a classy masterpiece, with a soaring vaulted wood ceiling and massive picture windows that overlooked the frothy lake.

He rang the doorbell, and when it opened, Ham's daughter— now almost a teen—stood on the mat. Blonde, beautiful, and brave, she'd survived years with her mother in the hands of a terrorist, and now, back in the arms of her father, was thriving under his care. As was Signe, Ham's wife, vibrant and alive after Ham had thought her dead.

So, yes, if anyone could prove that there was life after tragedy, it was these three.

"Hey, Fraser," Signe said from the kitchen as he descended the stairs from the entry. She wore a Minnesota Vikings football jersey, her blonde hair in two pigtails and was stirring a crockpot that smelled deliciously like chili. "Ham's out back with the guys."

He glanced out the sliding door and spotted Ham fading back and throwing long.

It sailed over Jake's head.

"Still putting too much oomph into it, I see," Fraser said.

"It's a way of life." She winked and Fraser headed outside.

Most of the guys—and gals—from Jones, Inc. were huddled up in two groups. Jake Silver and his wife Aria, a pediatric cardiothoracic surgeon, Skeet McKenna, Scarlett, whose fiancé Ford served with Ned on the teams, and of course Orion, a former Para jumper, and his wife Jenny, who stood up and raised a hand to Fraser.

He'd thrown a football with her years ago, back when she was his parents' first foster child. Creed, of course, being the last. And adopted, so now family. But so was Jenny. His father had even walked her down the so-called aisle at her winery-gazebo wedding a year or so ago.

"Hey, Fraser!" Selah Silver had also caught sight of him, and nudged her boyfriend, North Gunderson, who raised his hand. She looked healed, at least on the outside, from their shared captivity, although he tried not to glance away, the old shame lurking.

North had never spoken a word to blame him, however, for not protecting Selah, and in fact had ventured into Nigeria with Ham and Skeet, along with a couple of the Kingston brothers, to rescue them.

Now, Ham also turned from his huddle—North and Selah, Scarlett and Skeet—to jog over to Fraser. "Join up with Jake and Aria, Orion and Jenny. That way Lucas can jump in."

He gestured to Lucas Maguire. Huh, he hadn't expected to see the doc here.

Lucas shot him a look—*calm down*—and Fraser drew in a breath.

Patient-doctor confidentiality, although in this case, the doc was just a good friend who'd referred him to the right orthopedic specialist in Minneapolis.

Still, the man harbored secrets that Fraser preferred to keep under wraps.

"Sure," Fraser said and joined Jake's huddle.

"Hey," Jake said and fist-pumped him. He outlined the next play, pointing with his football to Fraser. "You played wideout in high school, right?"

"Some." Okay, yes, he'd been a bit of a small-town star.

"Perfect. Orion, I'll fake to you. Fraser, you go long."

"What about me?" Jenny said. "Who do you think he learned to catch from?"

"Listen, sis, you—"

"That's 'big sis' to you there, tough guy." She looked at Jake. "I'm officially two months older than this showoff here."

"Let's hope the showoff can catch a pass, because we're one touchdown away from a win."

"And one tackle away from washing dishes," Orion said. "I think you need to throw it to Jenny. Ham'll be on Fraser like white on rice."

Jake nodded. "Okay, Jenny, you go out and sit in the end zone. If Fraser isn't free, I'll throw it to you." He put his hand in. "Break on three."

Fraser lined up, and of course, Ham grinned at him over the line. "You sure you're ready for this?"

"Bring it, big guy."

Aria hiked the ball to Jake, and Fraser slammed hard into Ham, rocking him back.

He hoped.

Then he ran hard for the so-called end-zone, a tree with a handkerchief tied to it to designate goal. Jenny shouted from across from him, Selah after her.

He turned. Put his hand up. Connected his gaze with Jake, who pumped twice toward Jenny, then turned and set the ball sailing.

Weirdly, it felt right. Like he'd found his footing again, just like that, a part of the team, easy and necessary and needed, and he left his feet, his arms up, the ball thrown high over Ham's shoulder.

He followed the throw right into his hands.

Gotcha.

It skimmed Fraser's left hand, and he clamped his right down on it, pulling it in. Landing, falling to the long, soft, leaf-covered grass.

Touchdown.

Except—no, because as he fell, his right hand didn't quite capture it, and the impact jerked the ball out.

Shimmying it free.

Ham picked it up, tucked it under his arm, and ran the other direction.

Fraser sat up just as he crossed into touchdown zone.

"Nope, nope, nope," Jake said, waving his arms as he ran across the field. "That was an incomplete pass."

"Fumble!" Selah's fist pumped the air.

Fraser pushed to his feet. Brushed off the leaves.

"Sorry, bro," Jenny said, and gave him a wry smile. "Almost."

Almost didn't cut it. Not in football.

Not in battle.

Not in life.

"Halftime is over!" Aggie had come outside. "Nachos are ready!"

The others jogged in, good-gaming each other. Ham, however, waited on the patio for Fraser. He handed him the football, then blocked him as the door slid shut.

"You okay?"

Fraser rolled the football in his grip. "Yep."

"Not like you to fumble."

"It's just a game."

"Yep."

Fraser sighed, looked out over the lake. Deep blue, frothy, a little angry under the fading sunlight.

"You let me know when you're ready."

"I'm ready." Fraser glanced at him.

Ham said nothing.

"Fine. But I will be."

Ham again said nothing.

"I'm not quitting."

"No one used that word."

"You didn't have to." Fraser shoved the ball at him.

"But going back out before you're ready could cost lives. And not just yours."

In other words, he was a liability to the team. Ham didn't have to say it for the truth to settle deep in Fraser's soul.

And he might never get better.

Which meant his days at the front of the pack were over.

Ham met Fraser's eyes, Ham's gaze, unflinching and steady on his. "God hasn't forgotten you. There's a plan. You just don't know it yet. But when you're ready to get back into the game, He'll tell you."

Fraser looked away at Ham's house, his beautiful life that he'd waited and worked so hard for. A family he didn't know he had, but had always longed for. A team that he'd built from friends and ex-warriors who had so much more fight in them.

"Fraser, the strength of your faith hinges on your faith that God is still doing good in your life despite all the challenges. It's now that you have to dig deep into your foundation of truth."

Fraser tightened his hand and wished he could feel it. And not just his fingertips, but the faith he'd grown up with.

It seemed that he had nothing beneath his feet these days. "Nachos are ready."

Ham nodded and followed him in.

But Ham's words bumped around inside Fraser for the next two hours as the Vikings managed to turn a half-time lead into a dismal fourth-quarter loss.

Not unlike the turn of Fraser's life, he supposed as he bid the team good night and got into his truck.

Maybe Ham was right. He could barely feel the nuances of the steering wheel.

No way he could grip a gun.

His headlights scored out the night as he turned on the highway.

So then, what?

The stars blinked down from the sky as he passed the Marshall Fields Winery sign and pulled into the gravel driveway. Their massive home—the original farmhouse on one side, a classic colonial addition on the other—sat in darkness.

He got out and walked across the cold patio and simply stood, looking at the field. Spent, dried vines in hibernation.

He closed his eyes.

When you're ready to get back in the game, He'll tell you.

Yeah, well, it seemed lately, he couldn't hear Him. Or maybe he was just out of practice listening.

Inside the house, the landline rang. His parents kept it and an ancient answering machine in the office just for off-hours orders or inquiries.

He went inside and turned on the light, heading for the phone in his father's office. He didn't recognize the number and nearly let the call go to the machine. But that's what he was here for. "Marshall Fields Winery. Can I help you?"

Silence. Probably a telemarketer. He nearly hung up, but a breath, a hiccup of panic in the tone stopped him.

"Hello? Fraser?"

It took a second for the voice to click into his memory. Frankly, he just hadn't spent that much time with the kid.

And they'd had their rough patches. Never really ironed them out, either. Still, "Creed?"

"Fraser. I didn't know what to do—"

"Calm down, kid. Breathe. Where are you?"

"In Geneva, but—listen. We're in trouble. And I need—shh, I know, don't worry."

Fraser had stilled at *we're in trouble*, but the muffled voice on the other end of the phone had his chest tight. "What's going on?"

"I need to get us somewhere safe." Creed's voice shook.

"Who is *us*?"

A pause. "Nobody. Just...a girl. But I don't know what to do."

"Go back to your hotel."

"I would but...okay, okay—"

He was talking to the girl again.

"That won't work."

Fraser ran a hand around his neck, squeezed. "Ned's at a hotel in Lausanne. The Alps Hotel, or something like that. Get there—it's just up the road. I'll call him and tell him you're on the way."

Breathing.

"Creed. It's going to be okay. Just do the next safe thing, okay? Ned will know what to do. And I'll call you in the morning, just to make sure you're okay."

"Yeah. Yeah. Thanks, Fraser." He hung up.

Fraser did too, then pulled out his cell phone and dialed his brother.

And yes, he knew it was after two a.m., so he wasn't completely surprised when the call went to Ned's voice mail. Fraser left a message, then hung up and texted him too.

Then he turned off the office light and went into the family room. Sat down on the sofa.

And quietly, painfully watched as the moonlight painted the barn.

THREE

O h, she had Imani's number.

Pippa stood outside the women's bathroom at the way-too-dark, way-too-chaotic, way-beyond-her-professional-boundaries nightclub, waiting for Imani to emerge. She'd already done a walkaround, made the girl wait until it was empty, then stood at the door to block any other users.

The bathroom didn't have a window, so the only way out was the door. Sorry, Imani, not this time.

"Pardon—"

Pippa held her hand up to a woman trying to enter. "Une minute, s'il vous plaît."

The clubber stepped back, frowning, but joined a line of three other women trying to get in.

Pippa smiled at them but didn't budge.

Down the narrow hallway, dancers filled the dark room lit with neon lights and pulsing with some European hip-hop cacophony. But she wasn't so old that she'd forgotten the appeal of a night on the town, dancing, maybe even the smile of a hot guy fixed on her.

So she'd forgive Imani a little for dragging her out to the club to flirt with the cute guy from the gondola. Besides, Pippa had done her homework on him when they returned to the hotel.

Creed Marshall. Track star in his home state of Minnesota. Ran both cross-country and track. Went to his state championship and netted first place in the sixteen-hundred-meter race. Got a scholarship from the University of Minnesota, where he was studying economics and business.

She dove into his family also. He was adopted by Garrett and Jenny Marshall, who had four other children besides Creed—Fraser, Jonas, Iris, and Ned. Garrett and Jenny seemed like salt-of-the-earth people. Garrett had won an award for his wine years ago.

Benign. Nothing of note except that two of the brothers had gone on to serve in the military, so of course, she couldn't find any photos of them. She guessed they worked in some spec ops capacity. Jonas, however, had a weather blog detailing how he chased storms, although even that was at least a year out of date.

Probably not international terrorists, kidnappers, or murderers, so she could notch it down to Defcon 3. Creed was just a nice guy who'd happened to land on the same gondola as Imani.

And he was scheduled to take a flight back to America in the morning, so nothing could happen past tonight.

Pippa decided to let Imani go, as long as she behaved herself.

So far, so good. They got to the club, and Pippa noted the exits, the layout, and positioned herself at the table, watching Imani interact with Creed and his friends.

Creed didn't even order a drink, which surprised Pippa, as the drinking age in Europe was only eighteen. But he nursed a coke, as did Imani, who had never been a partier, and really, Pippa should calm down.

Imani was responsible. Smart. Had a good head on her

shoulders. And at her age, Pippa wouldn't have liked being babysat either.

The door opened behind her, and Imani came out, glanced at Pippa, and then the small lineup. "Oh." She looked back at Pippa, her eyes wide.

Pippa shrugged, then held the door open for the ladies to enter.

Caught up to Imani, who was headed back to the music.

"I can't believe you followed me to the bathroom," Imani said, glancing over at her.

"Ma'am. It seems to me you'd be used to that by now."

Imani's mouth tightened. "Just...fine." She turned to her, stopped. "Listen. I like this guy. He's nice, and he's going to ask me to dance, and if he does, I'm going to say yes. And if you go out on the dance floor with us, like a sandwich—"

"Your—Imani. I like him too. I did a background check, and he seems safe—"

"You did *what?*"

Pippa met her gaze with her own. "I needed to know what we were walking into."

Imani blew out a breath. Closed her eyes. "Nothing. We were walking into a harmless date with a nice guy."

Pippa almost felt sorry for her. Almost. But this was what happened when you became a *princess*.

"Okay, ma'am. I won't interfere. Not unless I see trouble."

"Thank you."

"But please. Be...aware of your surroundings."

"Me?" Imani's eyes were sparking. "Last time I looked, I wasn't the one who let a murderer into the palace."

Pippa's jaw tightened. "I wasn't the one who vetted him."

"You were on site at the ball. He was one of the servers. And you missed it."

They all had. Only a month ago, while Imani had stopped

over in Lauchtenland for the queen's annual Rose Ball, an assassin had sneaked in and tried to murder one of their guests.

It was a mark on Her Majesty's entire security service.

"Very good, ma'am."

"Please, don't call me ma'am."

"Yes, Your—Imani."

She rolled her eyes and walked over to the table. Creed turned toward her and handed her the drink he'd been guarding. Sweet.

So, yes, Pippa could maybe take a breath. She stepped a few feet away and stood against the wall. Tried not to look too much like a protection agent. She had worn a sequined shirt with her black pants. And black, dressy boots, although they were solid enough to run in.

Faster at least than Imani, who wore a pair of chunky high heels. Mostly, she just needed to be able to catch her, throw her body over her.

She'd let the club security do the rest, should it come to that—

Aw. Loosen up. Nothing was going to happen.

She let out a breath and forced herself not to move when Imani set down her drink and took Creed's hand. But she kept her eye on them as they cut out onto the dance floor and—oh shoot, she couldn't let the woman get that far away.

So yes, she secreted into the crowd, moved appropriately, her gaze on Imani.

Thankfully, the princess didn't spot her. Instead, she had her arms around Creed's neck, dancing, laughing, doing what American coeds did on holiday, apparently.

A man bumped into her, and she resisted the urge to push him back, but he did spin her, and by the time she'd turned, she saw that Imani and Creed had danced away from her.

Imani was nodding as he leaned down and whispered something in her ear. Then she put her arms around him and whis-pered—shouted, probably—into his ear.

He grinned, shrugged, nodded.

Hmm.

They danced longer, the music rising, dancers raising their arms, jumping. The song threatened to turn into a mosh pit, and Pippa fought the urge to grab Imani and pull her off the floor.

Fought and lost.

They were leaving, *now*.

She headed toward the couple, bumping into another couple who were jumping, their drinks sloshing. "Pardon!"

The man turned, frowned at her. "Pardon yourself!"

Oh, an American. She held up her hands as the woman pulled the man back to her. But the music had stirred the masses, and everyone had started jumping, pushing.

Then, a woman fell. Probably toppled off her heels, but she brought down her companion, another woman, who kicked a man, who stumbled and grabbed his partner, and then there were four on the floor, with more shoving, tripping, falling.

Pippa pushed away from the mess, but a man knocked into her. She stumbled back, and just like that, hit the floor, landing on a tangle of legs and arms.

Screams, but Pippa ignored them and bounced to her feet. She pushed like a bull toward the edge of the floor, finding air, breathing hard.

Imani.

She turned, searching, didn't see her.

What if she'd fallen?

Bollocks.

Pippa pushed her way back in, ignoring the various exple-tives, an elbow she got in the back, and found herself on the edge of the mosh. Lights flickered over the bodies—a woman shoved her hand against a bloody lip, another was limping, her boyfriend hugging her around the waist. But others sat on the floor, pumping their arms or climbing to their feet, cheering, even as more dancers fell.

Part of the revelry.

But no Imani. No Creed. They might still be dancing, so Pippa pushed-slash-writhed her way through the crowd, where she'd last seen them.

Gone.

Oh, this was such a bad idea. She freed herself from the floor and marched back to the table. No Creed. No Imani. And now she didn't care that she was outing the princess. "Where's Imani?"

The others in Creed's group shrugged.

"Did you see them leave?"

One of the women spoke up, dark hair, dark skin. Her accent suggested African English. "He left. Just a few minutes ago."

"With Imani?"

"The girl? No. He was alone."

Alone.

Sure he was.

She pushed away from the table. Headed to the door, then shoved her way outside.

Streetlights pushed back the star-strewn night, the air brisk. The club sat just a block off Jardin Anglais, the river shiny in the night. Across the bridge, their hotel sparkled with light.

Imani wouldn't have returned to the hotel, right?

Oh, that girl.

Pippa turned and headed back inside, straight to the security guard. "Do you have CCTV on your entrances?" she asked in French.

He wasn't a big man, wore a suit, his hair groomed, and he considered her a moment.

Fine. She reached under her stupid sequined shirt and pulled out her identification, attached to a lanyard around her neck.

He looked at it, and his eyes widened a little.

"Yes." Pippa stuck her ID back into her neckline. "And tonight, Her Royal Highness Princess Imani of Lauchtenland was here. And now she's not. And we need to find her."

He nodded and pulled a radio from his belt. Stepped away and spoke into it.

Pippa shook her head. How could she have been so—

"This way, ma'am," said the guard and pointed to stairs, secreted behind a black curtain.

She pushed the curtain away and ascended. A man stood at the top of the stairs, a door open.

She walked into an office, a little surprised to see a great window that overlooked the dance floor. Yeah, she'd missed that, too, in the darkness.

"It's one-way," said the man. "The cameras are here."

She walked over to a set of screens, one fixed on the front entrance, another in the hallway to the bathrooms, two more on the dance floor, another facing an alleyway.

"This is a lot of security."

"We have a number of special guests throughout the year. Like your princess. If we'd known she was going to be here, we could have prepared—"

"It was last-minute, and I vetted your place." Although, she'd missed the window, so clearly her information—thank you, Gunner—was out of date. "I just need to see the doors. See if she left in the last ten, maybe fifteen minutes. The princess has a way of...has a mind of her own."

The man—she put him in his mid-forties—smiled. "Crown Prince Fazza is a frequent guest."

Right. But the crown prince of Dubai wasn't a twenty-year-old gap-year student from America, wanting her freedom. And his "mind of his own" probably included buying out the VIP club for the night.

But Pippa simply nodded and stepped up to the monitors, where a technician was rewinding the footage on the front entrance for the last thirty minutes. She stood behind him, arms folded as he fast-forwarded. A few people left, more arrived, and after the twenty minutes elapsed, no princess— "Wait. That's him."

"Who?"

The frame had stopped on Creed, standing outside the entrance. He was alone.

After a second, he headed down the street, toward the boardwalk.

Weird.

"Keep going."

She stepped back and, oh no. "There she is."

Imani emerged from the club. Also alone. Pippa wanted to reach through the screen and strangle her.

Except Imani didn't immediately move away. Instead, she looked back inside, as if waiting...

Oh no. For her security detail. Who was inside, fighting a mosh pit—

"She's texting," said the tech, and Pippa peered closer. Indeed, Imani had pulled out her phone.

Then she slipped it back into her pocket and walked out of the screen.

"Who is she texting?"

Pippa reached inside her pocket and pulled out her phone. Shook her head as she opened the text.

Going for ice cream. I'll be back at the hotel. Don't worry, he's safe. Sorry.

"Me. She was texting me." She looked up at the technician, the security officer. "Sorry. False alarm. Thank you, gentlemen."

"Next time, let us know. We'll put a team on her."

"There won't be a next time, but thank you." Pippa let herself out, then left the club.

Ice cream.

She'd panicked over *ice cream*.

Probably, Imani was right. Creed was a good guy. Safe. And really, it wasn't like an assassin was after her.

The girl was just fine. Safe. Having a nice walk about with a nice, safe guy, eating ice cream.

She should just calm down.

Nope.

Pippa started out into a jog toward the park.

And it was exactly this thinking that got people like MP Aberforth Fickle and his security officer murdered in broad daylight.

Not on her watch.

She broke out into a run.

HE WAS DOWN TO TWO TABLESPOONS OF COFFEE grounds, an egg, a shriveled apple, and leftover nachos Signe had sent home with him.

Which he'd left in the truck.

Fraser took one look at the rain pelleting the window and reached for the coffee.

Really, his stomach was in no shape for food, given the fact that he'd left the fifth unanswered message on Ned's phone and, according to his memory and a Google fact-check, it was after two in the afternoon in Geneva.

Certainly little bro should be up by now. And yes, he might be on leave, but protocol said he kept his phone close by, just in case his leave got unexpectedly, suddenly terminated.

The life of an active-duty SEAL.

Fraser set the water on to boil, added the grounds to his French press, and pulled up his phone. Texted Ned again.

Bro. Not sure where you are, but call me. Asap.

The worst part was that he'd tried to call Creed back, too,

and the call had simply died. And that's when he figured out why Creed had called him on the landline.

Creed's cell phone was dead, and he'd had to pick up a burner phone. And the only number he could remember was the number to the winery.

Fraser should add a few more exclamation points to his text, maybe.

No. What he *should* do was get on a plane.

He reached for the withered apple to throw it away.

"Hey-yoh."

The voice so startled him he whirled and sent the apple zinging at—

Tall man, wearing a raincoat, slightly familiar.

The man ducked as the apple hit the front door. "Whoa!"

"Neil?"

Neil stepped away, looking at the mess, his raincoat dripping on the carpet. He held a grease-stained white bag. "Wow. Pretty grateful for my hockey goalie years right about now."

Fraser grabbed the roll of paper towels and tossed it to him. "You make a practice of entering someone's house unannounced?"

Neil put down the bag on a nearby bench and ripped off a sheet. "Every day. Your dad said I didn't need to knock."

"Knock. It'll save your life."

"Apparently." Neil took off his jacket, stepped out of his rain-boots, then picked up the split apple pieces.

Fraser grabbed the egg carton. "I only have one egg."

"I brought donuts." He grabbed the bag and dropped it on the counter, the Chester Bakery logo toward Fraser. "You dad likes raised glazed, but I got an assortment."

Fraser opened the bag. "Me too. Peace offering?"

Neil threw away the apple pieces. "Could be. If you like donuts."

"I do." He pulled out a shiny raised donut and put it on a

napkin. His water was boiling, so he poured it into the French press.

"The change in humidity can affect the pressure of the casks, so I thought I'd swing by and just take a look at the readings."

See, this was why his dad had picked the wrong babysitter. In fact— "I can't understand why my father didn't task you to babysit the wine."

Neil had retrieved a chocolate cake donut and set it on another paper towel sheet. "Oh, he did. But I didn't think I'd be in town."

Fraser grabbed two mugs from the cupboard. "Oh?"

Neil sat on a stool, pulling his donut toward him. "I was going to go to France for a year of study abroad. Maybe work at one of the wineries in the Loire Valley."

"That's where my parents are."

"One of the places, yes. I think they're doing a whole tour— headed up to Austria, then Germany. Maybe even down to Italy, although they're looking at cold-weather grapes."

See, the guy even knew more about their anniversary trip than he did.

But Fraser just wasn't a guy who could focus on more than one thing at a time. And until now, recently, his life was his work.

And now it was...

He poured coffee into the mugs. "I'd offer you cream, but the cupboard is bare. So, what happened to France?"

Neil smiled. He wasn't a bad looking guy. Tall, over six feet, with dark hair, blue eyes, and an easy smile. He wore jeans and a Minnesota Gophers sweatshirt. "Daisy."

"Daisy? The girl in the barn?"

"Lady. And yes, she was with me in the barn."

"I thought that was..." He made a face. "I thought you brought her here to impress her."

"You're not wrong. But she is studying enology with me at

45

the U and wanted to taste last year's La Crescent Gold. It's a new varietal, but your father has been developing it for years. It has notes of stone fruit and pineapple—which she'd never tasted, so—"

"So you stayed in America for...a girl."

Neil looked at him over his cup of coffee. "She's not just any girl...what?"

"I've just...never..." Fraser lifted a shoulder.

Neil set down his mug. "You've never rearranged your life for a woman?"

Fraser just stared at him.

"Even the right woman?"

"I've never met the right woman."

"That's your problem." He picked up a donut. "You've never been derailed by love."

Fraser rolled his eyes. "And I never will be."

His phone buzzed on the counter. *Finally*. He picked it up and slid the call open. "Ned."

"No. Shae." His brother's girlfriend. "Ned left his phone here when he packed up."

"Packed up?"

"Deployed. Called out. Whatever. Our vacation, nixed."

He winced at the tone in her voice. "Sorry, Shae."

A sigh. "That's okay. Actually, I've decided to take a couple days and do some hiking around here. He might be back—told me to stick around, so, here I am, in beautiful Chamonix, staring at Mont Blanc, without my fiancé."

Fiancé. Hoo-yah. About time. "So, he finally popped the question."

A pause. Then, "Yes. Last night. About two hours before the call to deploy. He left around four this morning."

He didn't know what to say. Except, wait— "You're not in Lausanne?"

"No. I left shortly after he did—I still have jet lag. Why?"

Ned would take him out if he got Shae involved in some international drama. "No reason. It's fine."

"Are you sure? I'm going to be out of touch for a few days, but I saw your message and thought I should call. It sounded urgent."

"It...I don't suppose you kept the hotel room open?"

"We were in separate rooms, but Ned reserved them for the week, so yeah. I'll only be gone a couple days, so I left my suitcase there and just took a backpack. I think Ned did the same."

Perfect. Creed still had a place to go. And he, a place to find the kid. "Can you text me the name of the hotel?"

"Sure."

"And when Ned gets back, ask him to call me." Although, there was no telling where Fraser would be.

Because there was no way he was letting Creed down.

Not after...well, he had a lot of ground to heal between them.

He might not let a woman derail his life, but for family...

"Thanks, Shae. And be careful."

"You sound like Ned." But she laughed as she hung up.

He set the phone on the counter. Looked at Neil. "How do you feel about watching paint dry?"

HE WAS DEFINITELY IN WAY OVER HIS HEAD, FATHOMS deep in trouble and drowning fast.

Creed stared out the window of Ned's hotel room. A tiny room, really, but still fancy, with gold brocade drapes and creamy Italian tile in the bathroom. And the small second-story balcony overlooked a view of some grand cathedral and French Alps to the west. Beautiful, historic, romantic and, for right now...safe.

And the woman sleeping in the bed, curled into the covers, wearing the hotel bathrobe—her wet clothes hanging in the bathroom, her jewelry and Apple watch on a towel to dry—needed that more than she needed history or romance or even, as it turned out, food.

The room-service tray sat on the floor, uneaten french fries and omelet now cold. He'd wolfed his down, however, unable to sleep, still trying to sort out…

What. Happened?

It had been pure luck to run into Ned this morning at four a.m, his brother on his way out to some super-secret SEAL deployment. He'd handed Creed the key and only asked a few questions, satisfied that Fraser would be in touch.

Except Fraser wasn't answering.

His last call had gone to the machine—again—and according to Creed's clock math, it should be in the afternoon in Chester, Minnesota.

He shouldn't get his hopes up. So what Fraser said he'd call? He was busy saving the world, or whatever he did that took him out of the country for months at a time. And no, he simply refused to harbor the hope that Fraser might be, crazily, on a plane. They just didn't have a get-on-a-plane-to-rescue-a-bro relationship.

Instead, Fraser had pushed him off onto Ned, the brother closest to Creed in age and relationship. Ned had been about seventeen when Creed came to live with the Marshalls. Twenty when he was adopted, so yeah, Ned had been around for the dark years. But they got along.

And at least Ned had been willing to help. Except he'd passed Creed back off to Fraser, like a basketball.

Creed shouldn't have been surprised, really, that Fraser had forgotten him. Fraser had never considered him—or wanted him—part of the family. Yeah, big bro had made that ultra-clear.

And frankly, Creed got it. He just wasn't Marshall material.

The biological Marshall brothers were all Big Adventure. They crisscrossed the world like it belonged to them. Even Jonas, the weatherman, was in Croatia on some big storm study. And Iris, the only sister—she fit right in. The woman was one of the only referees in the European League of Football.

So, yeah, overachievers, every one of them.

And then there was Creed. Tall, skinny, and sure, he could run fast, but...

Imani made a sound in her sleep, a shudder, and Creed didn't know whether to wake her up or...

She settled back down, and he sat on a chair, his hands folded.

Yeah, he should probably pray. Because if Imani's story was right, then they were in big trouble.

He scrubbed his hands down his face, too easily back in the water with her, the flashlight of her pursuer scraping the water. He'd stopped feeling lucky and simply gave in to freezing and miserable by the time the man left.

And even then, Imani had made them swim through the boats, through the grimy water to another dock where they'd crawled out and waited another thirty minutes before she gave him the barest of explanations.

"I wanted to wait for Pippa," she'd said, shivering under the moonlight. He sat beside her and pulled her against him, his arms around her. It felt a little forward, but frankly, after spending forty-five minutes in the water or on the dock with her, and before that, dancing and hanging out on the gondola, it felt strangely right.

He also felt weirdly protective.

"Pippa?"

"My...friend. She's...aw, the truth is, she's my bodyguard."

"Bodyguard? Why do you need a *bodyguard?*"

That's when she looked up at him, those hazel eyes almost golden in the moonlight, her dark hair wild around her head, so terribly waterlogged and beautiful he couldn't breathe, and delivered the news that left him paralyzed.

"I'm a...a princess."

A princess.

Thank his mother's manners he didn't burst out laughing. Instead, he just stared at her, trying to sort that out.

"Ever heard of Lauchtenland?"

Um. "Maybe? Sort of?"

"It's a kingdom the size of your thumb in the North Sea, off the coast of England. My mother sort of married the prince, which makes me—"

"A princess."

"With a security detail."

"Pippa."

"Phillipa Butler, decorated former marine, and daughter of legendary, or maybe infamous, if you believe the rumors, Sir Phillip Butler, killed in the line of duty."

He had nothing. But that accounted for a lot, didn't it? Especially the way her security detail had looked at him when they got off the gondola. Freaked him out a little.

Pippa could dismantle a person with those ice-cold blue-gray eyes.

"She hates it when I go places without her, so I thought... you know, that I'd tell her I was going to get ice cream. But she didn't follow me out, so I texted her and left."

"I should have walked with you."

She sat up, shivering hard.

"We need to get you to back to your hotel—"

"No! No." She was breathing hard. "Sorry. I..." She swallowed now and met his eyes.

Wow, she was scared, a sort of drawn expression crossing her face.

"Imani. What's going on?"

Her breath shuddered out. "I was walking through the

park—I thought, you know, brightly lit, no problem—and that's when I spotted a couple men talking. They were in the shadows, not far from the fountain, and I know they didn't hear me, because they were arguing."

"What about?"

"I don't know. It was in French. And then one of them just— he just punched the other one. I couldn't believe it, and I just stopped, stunned. The guy fell, and the other guy pulled out a knife and..." Her hands shook as she brought them to her mouth.

"I got you," he said, taking her hands. "You're okay."

She met his eyes, nodding. "Where did you come from?"

"I thought you stood me up, so I was walking back and I heard you scream."

Her eyes widened. "He stabbed him. In the neck. I...yeah, I screamed. And then I ran. And then you—" She gripped his lapel. "You saved me."

"You were the one who pulled me into the lake."

She closed her eyes. "I didn't know what to do. I just..."

"Shh." And what could he do but pull her close, put his arms around her again. "It's okay. We'll find Pippa and tell her—"

"No." She looked up. Pushed away. "No, we can't."

"Why not? She's your security—"

"Because she works for him."

He stilled. "What?"

"The murderer is head of the queen's guards."

He just blinked at that, searching her eyes. But she nodded.

"You're sure."

"He was at the hotel yesterday when we arrived. I saw him talking to her."

"It was dark, Imani. Are you sure?"

Her breath shuddered out. "Before I ran, while I was still screaming, he got up and turned and looked at me. Right at me. I recognized him. He was even wearing the coat—the Lauchtenland uniform, with the gold sleeves. It was Gunner Ferguson, head of the Royal Guard, I'm sure of it."

He ran his hands down her arms. "Okay, we can go back to my place—"

"No, we can't go there either. Because she vetted you. She saw you...and what if..." Her eyes widened. "What if she's involved somehow?"

"Involved...in what?"

"I don't know. I don't...wait. About a month ago, I was home for the queen's birthday. Queen Catherine. She had a ball, and during that ball, there was an assassination attempt on some ambassador. I don't know—but it was bad. And...maybe this had something to do with it."

"So, maybe he was protecting you—"

"Then why would he chase me?"

He had nothing at that. Except. "Okay. We can't go back to my hotel—or your hotel—until we know you're safe." He stood up and reached for her. "We'll call my brother. He'll know what to do."

He'd been searching his pocket and came out with a dead phone. "I need to get something that works."

She also pulled out her phone. "Yep."

"I saw an all-night market not far from here. Maybe they have disposable phones."

He slid his hand into hers.

She didn't let go for hours. Not really. Not when he found a phone and called home—the only number he could remember. Not when he discovered that Lausanne wasn't just up the road, thank you, Fraser. Not when he hired an Uber to take them the thirty-eight miles to Lausanne and drive around town until he found the Alps Hotel.

Not even when he went into the lobby to find Ned, only to practically run his brother down, a backpack over his shoulder.

Clearly on his way to his own brand of trouble.

Ned didn't ask questions. Just handed over his key card to Creed, told him to wait for Fraser to call him, and to lay low.

Which meant getting Imani into the room, securing the locks, letting her take a hot bath while he waited for the sun to rise. Ordering breakfast. And then, as she bundled up and fell asleep, trying to figure out what to do next.

The absolutely wrong thing had been to turn on the television and scroll through the channels until he came to an English-speaking station.

Not local, but as he sat in the armchair, his legs up on the ottoman, his head back, trying to get some shut-eye that didn't include Imani's scream ripping through his brain or the memory of that icy white light scanning the dark waters, he'd heard the report.

Snapped his head up and scrambled to turn up the volume as the reporter continued her story about a man found stabbed in the English Garden in Geneva.

A face flashed on the screen, and Creed tried to memorize the name. Some nuclear physicist.

But that wasn't the part he remembered the most. No, a couple of eyewitnesses had seen two people fleeing the scene. A woman and a man. Both young, holding hands and running hard.

They dove into Lake Geneva and got away.

Gulp.

The police were asking for anyone with any other information...

He'd glanced at Imani, still sleeping, and then went into the bathroom and lost his breakfast.

Because he clearly wasn't cut out for this kind of adventure.

And three hours later, as Imani still slept, he wasn't feeling any better.

But apparently, he'd been abandoned.

And it was up to him to keep the princess alive.

No problem. No problem at all.

Outside, the sun had begun to fall, glimmering over the tops of the buildings, the red tiled roofs, bleeding through the tall steeple of the Cathedral of Notre Dame of Lausanne.

Behind him, Imani stirred. Stretched. Rolled over.

She was really pretty. She had put her hair up in a towel, and indeed, she appeared like some sort of foreign, magical princess. His throat thickened.

Of course she was a princess. Wow, was he in trouble.

Imani opened her eyes. "Hey."

"Hey. You hungry? You didn't eat much."

She sat up, pulling the covers with her. "Yeah. Famished."

"How about if I go out and get us something to eat?"

"I'd give my kingdom for a pizza."

He stared at her.

"That was a royal joke. Loosen up, James."

"James?"

"Bond? Hello? Sheesh." She threw the pillow at him. "If you're going to be my new bodyguard, you're going to have to keep up with my humor."

He grinned, but then his smile fell. "Should I address you as Your Highness or something?"

"No! What— No. Please. Just Imani."

Hmm. But he didn't want to argue with her. Not until he could untangle their mess.

"Okay, Just Imani." He threw the pillow back at her. "I hope you like pineapple."

"Hey!"

But he'd already scooped up his now-dry wallet and passport and headed for the door.

The hallway was quiet. The place was only three stories, and he took the stairs down to the lobby and headed outside.

Pizza.

How he wished he had his phone.

But the smell of mozzarella and tangy red sauce filtered down the street, and it was like God cared, because he could practically follow his nose. He walked down the block and spotted a placard on the sidewalk.

Look at that. He walked inside and found a menu. Did some pointing and nodding and thought he'd ordered a pizza with ham and pineapple.

He waited outside at a table with an umbrella. So maybe this wasn't going to be a disaster. They'd lay low a few days until he could get ahold of Fraser, who would then get in touch with many of the military contacts he had that he wouldn't talk about.

A guy didn't get kidnapped by the Boko Haram in Nigeria without being involved in something...global. Which meant that Fraser could fix this. Hopefully.

A waiter came out with his pizza in a box, and the smell could do him in. He might not make it back to the hotel.

Creed picked up his pace as he walked back, the sun now sliding below the skyline, the shadows on the street darkening. Autumn hinted the air, a few leaves scattered on the sidewalk.

He shouldn't be thinking about romance when he was sharing a hotel room with a princess. Hello. That was a big hands-off, wasn't it?

Nodding to the concierge in the lobby, he took the stairs up to the second story and down the hall with the golden rug and...

Something crashed inside his room.

What?

He grabbed his card and buzzed himself in—

A man stood opposite the bed, his forehead bleeding. On the floor, a lamp sparked, then died.

"Creed—look out!"

The man turned—he wore a leather jacket, and the only clear shot of him was a cut across his forehead and the knife that he slashed toward Creed.

He got the pizza box, the knife stuck into the medium-sized, thick-crust ham and pineapple, extra cheese.

Then Creed kicked him, and the man pedaled back and hit the nightstand.

Creed rushed for Imani.

Grabbed her and pulled her out onto the balcony.

Then he shut the door and pushed a chair under it.

"Who is that?"

"I don't know!" Imani was fully dressed in her jeans and a beaded black top, her hair back. "He knocked, and I thought it was you—how stupid can I be—what are you doing?"

He'd gone to look over the edge of the balcony. Turned back to her. "He's coming through there in about one minute. We need to get out of here."

Already, the door rattled as the attacker fought with the chair.

Imani leaned over the edge. "Are you kidding me?"

"Look. There's an awning right next to us. Get on that, then lower yourself down."

"Are you *kidding* me?"

He looked at the door, back at her. "As your newly appointed personal security, not for a bloomin' second. I'll go first, and I'll catch you."

"You'll catch me?"

But he ignored her and stepped over the iron railing. It wasn't so far he couldn't lower himself and jump. He landed, maybe a bit hard, but looked up. "Don't let me down, Princess."

Her mouth tightened. Then she threw her leg over the edge and climbed out onto the edge.

She wasn't wearing shoes. But she had added socks, so that was good.

"Now what?"

"Climb onto the awning and—"

The door opened, and her attacker burst through.

Imani screamed and let go.

She landed hard, on top of him, and she wasn't as skinny as she looked. But he scrambled to his feet and pulled her up.

A knife landed in the planter beside them.

"Run!" He grabbed her hand and didn't look back.

FOUR

I t wasn't exactly the worst day of her life, but it felt close.

Pippa stood in Imani's room, looking over the disarray of clothing—most of it on her bed as she'd clearly struggled to find exactly what to wear to the VIP club.

She should have been dressing for her little scamper across the country.

A princess of Lauchtenland, on the run, in connection to a murder.

Pippa picked up her backpack and searched for Imani's passport. She'd handed it to her when they crossed out of Italy and back onto Swiss soil and forgotten to take it back.

Nothing. Which meant maybe Her Royal High Troublemaker had it with her.

Yeah, she should be on her knees worshipping the loo right now, except she hadn't been able to eat all day, so there wasn't anything else to surrender.

Pippa went to the window, looking out over the falling darkness. Already, lights splashed the water, and with all her heart, Pippa wished her princess had gone out for ice cream.

Wished she was simply out, having an epic heyday with her American hero.

But no. And Pippa should have known something wasn't right when she passed by the park, searching for Imani, and spotted the police lights, the commotion. She didn't know why, but deep in her gut, she knew.

Imani was at the center of that trouble.

And not for a second did she believe that the girl had stabbed someone. But yep, the description of the two who ran from the scene of the crime matched her princess and her current knight in shining armor.

Oh, she'd like to get her hands on Mr. Track Star, wring him out a little. Figure out how and why and what they had to do with the murder of renowned nuclear physicist Gerwig Buchen.

But to do so, she had to find her. Them.

And that meant telling Gunner Ferguson she needed his help.

Yep, Pippa should be hugging a loo.

Instead, she walked across the room, opened the door, and crossed the hall. Knocked on her boss's door.

Braced herself.

It opened, and Gunner in all his handsomeness stood there, real concern in his eyes. "Pippa. Everything okay?"

Behind him, she heard voices, and she peeked in to see his cadre of Her Majesty's Security Detail commandos hovering over a table covered in what she guessed were blueprints and schedules.

"Yes. Sir. I um..." She drew in a breath. "Can I talk to you? Outside?"

He glanced at his team, then back to her, frowned.

"Please?"

He gestured with his head to the hall, and she stepped back while he followed her. He drew the door partially closed behind him. "What's this about?"

"Uh. Sir. It's...the princess." Wow, this was harder than she thought. And how selfish was that, because Her Royal Highness Princess Imani might be in Real Trouble.

Bollocks!

"The princess went missing last night, sir. She slipped out of a night club on my watch, and...she's not returned."

He stared at her, and she wanted to wince at the fury forming in his eyes. "Are you sure?"

"That she's missing?" Gulp. "Yes. She's not here, and I don't know where she is—"

"Have you tried calling her?"

He must think her daft. "Yes, sir. Numerous times. The phone goes to voice mail. And I've texted."

"Have you pinged her phone?"

"It's not...it's possibly destroyed, sir."

"Destroyed?"

See, there was this eyewitness who saw them jump in the lake. "I have reason to believe she might have...gone swimming." *Oh, Pippa!* "She was sort of, maybe...involved in a—" She swallowed. "Maybe she saw a murder."

His mouth opened, and to his credit, he simply ran his hand down his face. Took a breath.

"What do you mean?"

"There was a stabbing last night in the park, and an eyewitness saw two people—one of whom may look like Imani—flee the scene."

He simply blinked at her.

"I tracked down the other person. Her—friend. A friend. A male friend who she met on a gondola ride we took earlier in the day, and he invited her out and he seemed nice. I vetted him—"

"Get to the point, Pippa. Did you find him?"

"No." She cleared her throat. "I went to his hotel and interviewed his roommate, a man from New Guinea, but he hadn't seen Creed since he left the club, and he hasn't returned either. I'm so sorry, sir, I—"

He held up his hand. Blew out a breath. "Okay. So, is she in danger?"

The word turned a screw inside. "I don't know. They could just be scared. Or...maybe I'm just assuming they saw something."

"You've said before that Imani has a propensity for sneaking out."

"Yes, sir. Often. She is not a fan of personal protection."

"I understand that, Pippa, but it's your job to keep her safe, despite herself."

"I know, sir."

"Okay. Let's see." He glanced into the room. "I'm understaffed right now, but I suppose I could pull someone—"

"No. Sir. I can find her. I don't need help. Really. I've spent a year with her. I know her."

He met her gaze, and she held it.

"Okay. We still need to find her, but maybe we don't alert Prince John and Princess Gemma quite yet."

"No?"

"They're on their yacht in Portofino, and there's nothing they can do. No need to worry them. Not yet." He raised an eyebrow. "Is she wearing her necklace?"

"Yes. And that's what I wanted to ask you—could I have permission to activate her GPS."

"By all means, Pippa, and keep me looped in." He reached into his pocket and pulled out a key card. A scan of it on her phone or computer would unlock the GPS system for all the royals.

"Very good, sir. And again, I'm—"

"Just find her. And pray she's not hurt." He stepped inside and closed the door.

She closed her eyes. See, that hadn't been so...

Aw, who was she kidding? She'd be lucky if she stayed on princess detail after this. She might be relegated to watching one of the royal corgis.

Back in her room, she opened her computer, then her phone, and scanned the code on the card. All the royals' jewelry had tracking devices, but Imani wore a ruby necklace that she loved and conceded to wear daily. The GPS system was waterproof and, barring an EMP attack, could be tracked anywhere in the world.

By satellite. Which was why Pippa had to get permission to access it.

The phone's NFD tracking opened the program, and in a moment, Imani's code pinged.

Lausanne? She zoomed in.

A *hotel* in Lausanne.

She got up and headed to the bathroom.

An hour later, she stood outside a quaint hotel, just a block off the shores of Lake Geneva. Three stories, with red awnings over the ground floor windows, and scrolled wrought-iron balconies laden with hanging flowers. Ground lights lit up the place and the small garden café next to it, and diners at tables enjoyed dinner.

None of them was her mischievous princess and the Track Star.

Oh, if she burst in on them doing something, um, irresponsible...

She took a breath, not sure how she'd gone from Imani in Trouble to Imani in a Tryst, but apparently, she ran headfirst into imagining the worst.

Either way, this little adventure was o-*ver*.

She headed inside.

A boutique hotel, but posh, with travertine tile on the floors, gold accents in the lobby. No lift. She took the stairs, following the tracker on her phone, and came to the second floor.

The GPS wouldn't tell her what level the room was on, but she'd start here, work her way up. She followed it down the hall...

Stopped in front of a door, her heart thumping hard.

It was open. Partially, at least. She hadn't brought her handy little Glock 26, thinking that she probably wouldn't shoot Creed, despite what she found.

But she did have a taser, and this she pulled out, flicked off the safety.

Eased open the door.

The man stood with his back to her, wearing a jean jacket, a pair of cargo pants, boots. Short hair, although not quite military short, and just from the wide set of his shoulders, his lean torso, the stance of his legs, he looked like he could handle himself.

Clearly not the boy from the bar.

He must have heard the door opening, because he turned, hard. Stared at her.

Blue eyes. Painfully, impossibly blue—so blue they stopped her cold.

And then she spotted what dangled from his hand.

Imani's necklace. The *tracker*.

"Who are you?" She raised the taser.

She had the sense of a tiger, his eyes darkening, crouching, ready to pounce.

"Who are *you*?" he said, his voice quiet.

She pointed to the necklace. "That doesn't belong to you."

"Who does it belong to?" He lifted it, and it dangled from his fingers.

Only then did the disarray of the room sink in—a lamp shattered on the floor, the bed mussed, pillows on the floor, and was that a bloody hand on the doorframe to the balcony?

"Where is she?"

Pippa wanted to check the bathroom, but she wasn't about

to let him leave her sight. Not when he might be the only link to Imani.

Who was clearly in trouble, even if she'd snuck away for a romantic rendezvous with Track Star.

"Where is who?" he said.

Pippa drew in a breath. "What happened here?"

He stared at her. "Rugby match?"

She blinked, just for a second. Was that a joke? "Excuse me?"

"Dumb question. Dumb answer." His eyes sparked. "Listen. I don't know who you are, but clearly, you're looking for the same people I am—" He shoved the necklace into his pocket.

"I'll take that."

"I don't think so."

She took a step toward him. "Then think again." He had an American accent, and that clicked, deep inside.

"Put down the taser."

"Give me the necklace."

His lips made a thin line, and he shook his head. "I'm not sure what happened here, but this is the only link to—"

She pulled the trigger.

The taser probes shot out like bullets, and one of them hit his arm, the other his chest. His entire body tensed, and he grunted as he yanked out the probe.

His knees buckled and he fell, hands on the floor. "Seriously?" He ground out his words through clenched teeth.

But with the probs out, his muscles would soon stop retracting. She reached for his pocket.

He lunged forward and grabbed her ankle. Yanked.

She went down, slamming onto the carpet.

Oh, tough guy wanted to fight.

And maybe it was the fact he'd so casually stolen the necklace. Or even the unresolved boil in her gut from her meeting with Gunner. Or probably the frustration of the past ten months, trying to keep track of a princess who, against all advice, rebelled at every hint of protection.

But really, it was the bump on her hip, the flare of pain in her shoulder that made her roll and scrabble for the taser, inconveniently bumped from her grip.

She spotted it, there, nearly under the bed, and reached for it.

His hand clamped on hers. "Oh no you don't."

"You started it—" She fought his grip, prying away his fingers with her other hand. "I just...want...the *necklace!*"

She ripped the taser from his grip and scrambled to her feet.

He grabbed a pillow off the floor, held it in front of him. "You're empty."

"This thing can still hurt you." She lunged at him, and he deflected with the pillow, although sloppily. She smiled. "I can do this all day. Give me the necklace."

He reached into his pocket, held it up. "Not until you tell me what this has to do with my missing brother."

Brother?

She lowered the taser. "You're...a Marshall?"

"Yes. Why?"

She raised the taser again. "Then maybe you can tell me what your brother did with Her Royal Highness Princess Imani of Lauchtenland."

HE JUST COULDN'T WIN, ON EITHER SIDE OF THE ocean.

Fraser lay on the floor, staring up at Black Widow, or whoever this overly tough woman thought she was, his entire body burning, and rued his impulsiveness.

Not a usual move on his part—to simply jump on a plane for

Switzerland in a semi-state of panic. He wasn't a panicker and usually gave life-altering moments a smidgen more thought. But the winery was in more-than-capable hands, and...

And okay, he'd lunged at the thought of doing something...useful.

That something didn't include him thrown to the floor, fifty thousand volts of electricity still zinging through his veins.

Every muscle still spasmed, and he would have emptied his gut, except he had nothing but a biscotti in it—gone hours ago. But he kept his voice steady, the pain locked inside as he stared at the woman, digesting her words.

A *princess*?

His face must have betrayed him, because she frowned. "Yes. A princess. Your brother Creed met Imani yesterday, and clearly, they've hit it off."

Creed, you dog. But given the fact they were standing in the middle of a hotel room, the bed mussed—clearly slept in—a pair of high heel boots on the floor...

Maybe Creed needed another talk. You know, the one given by his dad that asked him what kind of man he wanted to be. The standard *you're sixteen now, and here's how you handle all those hormones and yourself.*

Except, what if Creed hadn't gotten one of those?

Or maybe the kid just didn't care.

But that wasn't the most important issue at the moment because, um, *princess.*

Fraser didn't know where to start except, "And you are?"

She considered him a moment, her eyes—a shade of blue-gray—narrowing. She wore her dark brown hair back in a tight ponytail, a white shirt under a leather jacket, dark pants, and even before she answered his question, he knew.

"I'm her—"

"Security."

—protection detail."

Nailed it. She had a sort of Black Widow vibe, all challenge and huff in her demeanor, as if she'd spent way too long in a man's world and hadn't yet realized that women didn't need to be *men* to be equal to, or even better than, men.

At least, in his book. Maybe in her world…

Although, given the current situation, he might have a little chin-up defensiveness too. "And you lost her."

That made her mad. Her lips pursed, and she cocked her head. "I think that has a lot to do with your brother and his list of crimes."

"Crimes?" He pushed himself up, his body still shaking a little, keeping the pillow between his chest and her little black taser that, yes, could still hurt him if it touched his skin. Wow, he hated those things. But they'd been deployed on him too many times in training, so he'd learned how to shake it off, get back on his feet. Now he kept his voice cool and even, unaffected by his currently racing heartbeat. "What crimes?"

"Kidnapping?"

"That's not the read I got on his call. Creed was scared, and your little princess was in his ear, telling him what to do, so I hardly think this is a *kidnapping*, honey."

He stilled, just a little, at his own word. But it had just sorta slipped out.

His own version of a taser.

It seemed to work because her eyes widened. "Did you just *honey* me?"

He smiled. He didn't know why—he had worked with dozens of women in the military and very much respected their skills and what they brought to the game. To his recollection, he'd never *honey*ed any of them. "Or would you prefer *sweetheart*?"

Her mouth clamped shut, her gray-blue eyes sparking. "Clearly you don't have the same charm as your brother."

He didn't know why that irked him, but he lost his smile.

"I'm plenty charming, to women who aren't trying to electro-cute me."

A beat.

She sighed. "I just want the necklace. And maybe some answers."

"Like, why does the room look like there was a scuffle? And that someone got hurt?" He pointed to the blood on the sill. "Me too, Natasha."

She blinked at the name but paused. "You didn't do this?"

"I was going to call the front desk and complain about housekeeping, but I was here about two minutes before you, and the room was empty."

"Where did you find the necklace?"

"It was in the bathroom on a towel, along with an Apple watch and some earrings." He gestured to the floor. "Oh, and they must have left in a hurry, because those look like some seriously expensive shoes."

She glanced down at the pair of leather boots.

And just like that, he took the taser from her. One quick grab—left handed, because his right had given out on him in the tussle for the weapon under the bed—and suddenly she was the one holding the pillow. She backed away, holding it up.

"Calm down. I'm a do-unto-others kind of guy. And I'm in no mind to be tased again." He flicked on the safety. And then he held up the necklace. "Tell me why this is so important."

She considered him, then lowered the pillow onto the bed. "It isn't anymore."

"Now you're just playing hard to get."

"Fine. Maybe your brother didn't kidnap her, but did you know he was involved in a murder?"

His smile fell. "Murder?" A terrible knot formed in his gut.

"Yeah. Your boy was involved, somehow, in a murder last night, and there's a BOLO out on him and my princess. It's not with Interpol yet, but it will be."

He shook his head. "Creed wouldn't...isn't...No." But in truth, it nudged a tiny, secreted, purposely forgotten fear that sat deep in Fraser's gut. Had been there for nearly a decade, really, waiting to be rooted out.

Realized.

No. He shook his head again. "He's a good kid."

She held up her hands. "I'm not the only one who wants him, and the sooner I find him, the sooner I can help untangle him from this mess."

"Kidnapping and murder. Your words, your charges. I don't think so."

She opened her mouth, looked away, then back at him. "Fine. Bottom line—if he keeps the princess safe, then I'll walk away, no harm, no foul. No accusations. No indictments."

Hmm.

He tucked the taser into his belt, in back. Held up his hands. "Listen, I don't know where your princess is. Or my brother. But given the state of this room, I think probably they're in trouble."

Her mouth pursed and she crossed her arms.

Silence pulsed between them.

"Okay, Captain America, where did they go?"

He bit back a smile. He didn't know why, but the fact she got his Marvel reference...

And something about the way her eyes glittered with a sort of challenge...

"I don't know. But I'm going to find out." He raised an eyebrow. "Does the Royal Protection Service of Lauchtenland want to join forces? A sort of diplomatic agreement that doesn't include tasers or—"

"Or stealing from the Crown?" She held out her hand.

Right. He dropped the necklace into it.

"That's a start." She pocketed the necklace. Sighed. "Where would your brother go?"

"What about your princess? Who says Creed is calling the shots here?"

That took her aback, and she blinked at him.

Bingo. He'd landed on something, without even aiming. "Is this something that happens...a lot with your princess?"

A muscle pulled in her jaw. Finally, "Imani is a bit of a wild card." She walked to the door and studied the handprint. "I've spent the last year with her, traveling the world. Gap year."

"Sounds fun."

She glanced at him. "If you like sleeping in yurts and youth hostels and trying to vet every situation as you walk into it."

Oh, right.

"What can I say? She's American and wasn't born into royalty, so I get it. But she is still a person of value to the Crown, and should anything happen to her..." She held up the necklace. "The necklace has a GPS tracker built into it. That's how I found them. Which begs the question—how did you know they were here?"

"This is my brother Ned's hotel room. Like I said, Creed called me last night, panicked, and I told him to come here. I didn't know he was involved in a murder."

"Where's your brother Ned? Did he do this?"

"What—no. He's a SEAL, on vacation with his fiancée, except he got spun up this morning, early."

"And where is said fiancée?"

"Hiking the Matterhorn, I think. I dunno. She's her own person."

"Where were you?"

"Minnesota."

"And you got on a plane?"

Okay, yes, that did seem, from a distance, a little like overkill. "I was worried." He had walked over to the broken lamp. Glass littered the floor, and he picked up a ceramic shard, dried blood on the edge. "I'm still worried."

"Right. Very good. So, we'll go back to my hotel, and Gunner and his team will sort out everything you know about Creed and where he could be—"

"I don't think so, sweetheart." Fraser stood up.

"We're back to that?"

"I'm not going to sit around answering questions when—"

"When there's blood on the door frame?" She folded her arms, took a breath. "Okay, Captain, what's your brilliant plan?"

He ran a hand across his mouth. His body still burned, his muscles convulsing, and really what he needed was a hamburger, some fries. Maybe a European beer, although that would just make him sleepy, and given he'd had about ten minutes of shut-eye on the plane, thanks to the ten-year-old in the economy seat next to him, probably a bad idea.

Still. Think, Fraser.

"You're bleeding." She frowned, stepped close to him.

He looked down. Somehow, he'd caught the sharp edge of the ceramic on his palm. He dropped the shard.

She tossed him a towel lying on the bed.

He pressed it into the wound—not deep, just a scratch, but stupid.

And he hadn't even felt it.

"I don't think the blood is hers, first of all. This lamp was used as a defense, a panic move. Maybe by Creed, but could be by your princess. My guess it that she got her attacker good, and he wiped the blood off with his hand."

She was listening, and now turned to the door. "This isn't just a handprint. It's smudged, as if he gripped this same place a few times. As he was trying to—"

"Kick out the door." Fraser had walked over and now pointed to the broken jamb. "They escaped over the balcony."

Pippa stepped out into the space, and he followed, looked out over the edge.

"Creed could jump this."

"Probably, Imani could too."

He stared out into the night, the darkness that hovered over the city pushed back only by the glitter of the streetlights.

In the distance, the Alps rose in dark shadow.

Wait.

"My sister lives in Como, Italy. It's just over the border—"

"I know where Como is." She went back inside and picked up the boots. "You think he went there?"

"I don't know."

"So it's a wild guess."

"Yes. But...I think that's what I would do."

"And Creed is your twin?"

He gave a laugh-non-laugh and shook his head. "Not even a little. But in a panic, I'd reach out to family. Or at least my team. And his team is our family. I think. I hope." But even as he said it, the words burned a little.

He hadn't done a super job of reaching out to anyone lately. "Listen. My sister Iris's place is the best I got. So I'm headed there. And if you and your royal protection want to join me, you're welcome." He threw the towel away onto the bed and grabbed a tissue, crunched it over the wound, which had stopped bleeding. "But you have to give me your best scout's honor that you won't taser me again. Ever."

She smiled. Then held up three fingers. "Let's go."

For a second, he really wished he believed her.

FIVE

The last thing she wanted was some tag-along American slowing her down.

"Nice digs."

Pippa didn't know why his voice, deep and just a little gravelly—probably from fatigue—got under her skin, buzzed, and lit through her entire body like a bloody allergy. But the man's very presence simply...

He'd called her *honey*. And *sweetheart*. And on the Uber ride back to Four Seasons in Geneva, Pippi Longstocking.

She should have never asked his name. Frankly, Captain America seemed just fine. But she was being polite. And perhaps functional. "I didn't catch your name," she said as they got in the back seat.

"That's because my throat closed after you leveled me with your toy gun."

"Not a toy. Real. And you seemed to rebound just fine."

"Some people have a heart attack. You could have killed me."

"And miss all this? What a cryin' shame that would have been."

"Fraser. Marshall." He held out his hand across the seat in the tiny Fiat Panda.

"Like Jamie."

He raised an eyebrow.

"Outlander?"

"Not a clue."

"Sad." She took his hand. "You can call me Phillipa. Or Pippa."

"Pippi? Like Pippi Longstocking?"

"Pip-*pa*. Ah. Like...um, *ahhh*—"

"How is that again?"

She closed her mouth.

He grinned at her, added a little chuckle.

And that's when it first started. His voice, the annoying chuckle. Maybe calling him Captain American was right—she'd always thought the Marvel character a little too smug, too Dudley Do-Right, too...

Perfectly irritating. She couldn't decide if him getting on a plane to fly across the ocean was sweet or simply...swagger. The hero swooping in to save the day.

She didn't need heroes. Didn't want heroes.

Heroes got hurt. Heroes broke your heart.

Heroes died.

No, thank you, she didn't need a hero, and most of all, she didn't need Captain Marshall following her to her suite to make commentary on her life.

Still, there he stood, in the living room of the suite, his backpack propped on the floor to hold open the door, watching her in the adjoining room, arms folded, and she couldn't seem to ignore him.

"Yes. The contingency from Lauchtenland has the entire top two floors."

"And the view." He walked over to the window, staring out at Lake Geneva. "Gorgeous."

"Yes." She slipped into the bedroom and threw a change of clothes, a small toiletry bag, her charger, and some headache meds into a backpack. She deliberated on her conceal-and-carry Glock 26, then decided to leave it behind. It would only alert metal detectors and slow them down.

But she did reload and repack her taser.

She'd be back in twenty-four hours max. If it took longer than that to find Imani, she'd throw herself off a bridge, save Gunner the trouble.

Speaking of, his voice thundered through the room. "Pippa?"

Perfect. "Sir?" She emerged from the room, her backpack over her shoulder. She set it on the royal-blue plush velvet sofa.

"Please tell me that you've located our princess."

She glanced at Fraser, back to her boss. "Working on it, sir. I discovered where she spent the night, and we're on her trail." Oh—she hadn't meant to include Fraser!

Gunner raised a dark, perfect eyebrow. "And who is *we?*" He gestured to Fraser, who'd turned.

Fraser held out his hand and headed toward Gunner. "Fraser Marshall."

Gunner took it, considering him. "Any relation to Winchester Marshall, the actor?"

"He's a cousin, actually. Distant. Why?"

"We met. But how are you involved..." He glanced at Pippa, back to Fraser. "What's happening here?"

"Fraser is the older brother of Creed, the boy that Imani is with."

"Man. He's twenty, mates," Fraser said. "But yes, they're together."

She looked at him. *Ix-nay on the alking-tay!* The last thing she needed was more questions about Creed and what he and Imani had maybe—hopefully not—been up to.

Although, her boss needed to know about the bloody tussle in the hotel room.

But he was more interested in Fraser. "Really. And you're here because..."

Pippa stepped in. "Because he...he thought Creed...he was—"

"I was in the area, and Creed and I were supposed to connect." He lifted a shoulder, like no big deal. "I think he might have gone to my sister's place. We're headed there."

"She lives in town?"

"Not far." Something about his easy shrug, his demeanor, deflated all the tension in the room. As if these two were simply out seeing the town, had forgotten to call home.

And then Fraser smiled, and Pippa felt the world tilt, the look of it completely disarming.

Who was this guy? Because apparently, he could lie like a bloody rug.

"Good." Gunner looked at Pippa. "You're still following the GPS on the necklace?"

"Keeping a close tab on it." She swallowed. "Sir, I should probably tell you that there were signs of an altercation at the hotel." She swallowed. "Blood."

He stilled. "The princess's blood?"

"Probably not, but we're not sure."

He ran a hand around the back of his neck. "I'll have my team check the hospitals in the area." His jaw tightened. "I am at full capacity trying to prepare for the arrival of the Lauchten-land entourage, but if you believe the princess to be in danger—"

"My brother is with her. And we're very close behind," Fraser said.

Her boss nodded, and a long silence pulsed between them. "Okay. I'll give you twelve hours. If you haven't found her by tomorrow morning—"

"I'll find her, sir."

Gunner nodded, then turned back to Fraser. "You look a little like him. The actor. Although he might be taller. He's in all those Jack Powers movies."

"Yeah. He might be taller. But I'm faster."

Gunner cracked a rare smile. "Right. What do you do?"

"I...currently, um, help run a winery."

Gunner gave a nod. Pointed at Pippa. "Twelve hours. Bring her home. And keep me looped."

"Yes, sir."

Gunner stepped out of the room and continued down the hall.

"Let's go." She picked up her backpack and headed for the door.

He followed her. "What's going on here that everyone is descending?"

"It's the annual North Sea Summit. We're not officially members, but the North Sea Coalition has been trying to get Lauchtenland to join, and Hamish Fickle, our representative, is a proponent."

"Why?"

She opened the door, held it for him.

"Because if we join, then we'd have the protection of the North Sea countries. And that's not a big deal, really, but a couple of those countries are also in NATO, so..." She lifted a shoulder.

"So if Lauchtenland gets in trouble, and any of the North Sea allies come to her aid, then potentially, you have a global contingency at your disposal."

"Potentially. I think that's what Hamish is shooting for. Protection from the big dogs. Like the US and the Brits."

"Pippa."

The voice made her still, and she turned around to see Fredrik walking from the lift, his key card in his hand, a backpack over his shoulder, trolleying a carry-on bag behind him.

He still looked...capable. Dashing. Terribly perfect. He wore a suit, dark pants, matching jacket in the style of the guard without the gold cuffs. Tailored for his physique.

An old streak of warmth went through her, but she shook it away. That was another time, another place, and probably never again, really.

After all, she shouldn't date the brother of her boss.

"Fredrik. I thought you'd be around here somewhere."

"Just got here. I had some things to tie up in Lauchtenland." He walked up smiling, his short, dark hair perfect, recently shaved—a rule in the queen's service—and looked down at her. "What's going on?" His gaze went to Fraser, the unkempt American beside her.

She didn't mean to compare—it wasn't a contest, really— but Fraser was an inch taller, broader in the shoulders, maybe also in the torso. However, he seemed frayed, his dark hair ruffled, his shirt collar rumpled, and he wore faded jeans, worn boots.

Not a hint of culture in his Yankee getup.

He held on to his backpack and looked at her with those magnetic—nope, too intrusive eyes.

"Nothing. Just heading out," she said. "When does the royal entourage get here?"

"The prince and princess? Not for a couple more days."

Phew. That gave her time to get to Como, scoop up the princess and get back, and Bob's your uncle.

"Hamish and his team arrive in about an hour. The summit begins tomorrow afternoon." He glanced again at Fraser. "Going somewhere?"

"Como, Italy," Fraser said, and smiled.

Funny, this one seemed a bit chillier. Mostly teeth.

"Who are you?" Fredrik said, no smile.

"Just...a tagalong." She didn't know why she'd said that. But Fraser cocked his head at her. It was sorta true...

Fredrik's mouth closed into a tight line.

Fraser looked back at him. "Heading in the same direction." He lifted a shoulder.

"Why Lake Como?" Fredrik directed his question at Pippa. Then he frowned. "Where's the princess?"

"Imani...is..."

"Waiting for us," Fraser said. "Let's go, Pippi."

Ah. Pip-*pa.*

Fredrik raised an eyebrow.

Oh, she didn't want to explain. "Cheers," she said to Fredrik, and followed Fraser down the hall to the lift. Fraser was holding the door open.

She scooted in, and he let the doors close.

"You've got a little something for that guy, huh?"

"Me? What? No. We...we served together."

"And he's related to your boss."

She looked at him. "How did you know that?"

"They look similar."

"No, they don't. Fredrik is...for lack of a better word, prettier. More European. Thinner nose. Leaner."

"They carry themselves the same way."

That, she got. "Yes. Like they're in charge of the entire world. That's very Ferguson."

"Something like that. But this guy feels less...I don't know, something in my gut—"

"He's a decorated soldier. And not just anyone gets appointed to Her Majesty's Security Detail."

Fraser held up a hand. "Got it, Pip."

"Pip—"

"*Ah,*" he said as they got out. "Right. So, planes, trains, or automobiles?"

Oh, how was she going to spend the next four hours with him? Four or...wait. "What do you mean, planes, trains, or automobiles?" He walked across the travertine lobby.

She caught up, glad she'd changed shoes into practical boots.

"I did some recon. The last bus left forty minutes ago. Creed and Imani had a good head start on us, so they probably took that, or maybe even the last flight out. There's a flight out tomorrow morning, takes two hours. Or we can grab the train. It leaves in two hours, but we'll be in Como by morning."

"A train."

"We could charter a plane."

She drew in a breath. "Do you drive?"

"I'm American. We drive everywhere. But it's a question of renting a car at this hour."

"Blimey. Train it is." She headed outside and asked the bellman for a cab. "But I'm not riding in the general seating."

"Don't want an old woman with a chicken sitting on your lap?"

She just stared at him. "What are you going on about?"

He laughed as the cab pulled up.

Somehow he squeezed his massive body into a Fiat 500c. She climbed in next to him, her backpack on her lap.

He put his arm around the back of the seat to hold himself up. "I feel like I should put my feet down and yell *yabba dabba doo!*"

She shook her head and leaned up to the driver, speaking French. "Train station," she said. "And please ignore the loud American."

"You really didn't get that?" Fraser said, also in French.

Perfect.

But she was terribly, painfully aware of his body thrown against hers as they maneuvered their way to the train station.

"I feel like I'm in a Black Hawk, flying through the Hindu Kush range. Sheesh."

"Or on a camel in Ethiopia."

He glanced at her. "See, that was funny. You don't have to take life so seriously."

She looked away. "You don't have a princess missing, your entire career dying before your eyes."

A beat. She glanced at him, but he was looking out the window, his jaw oddly tight. "No," he said finally, quietly. "I don't."

He didn't speak again the entire ride.

They arrived at the train station, he untangled himself and they went in, and he bought them two tickets to Como, via Montreux and down through Brig and the southern Alps, up to Andermatt, then finally down to Lugano and over to Como, Italy.

They'd change trains twice.

He handed her a ticket. "Only first class for the...what's the female equivalent of a knight in shining armor?"

"A woman," she said, and headed down to the platform. The train was boarding, and she showed her passport, then climbed aboard and found their compartment.

Okay, so this wasn't terrible. Comfy couches, a table, pull-down bunks, and a door that latched. She did need a decent night's sleep, fatigue tugging at her.

And dinner.

He set down his backpack. "I hear ya."

She glanced up. "What?"

"That stomach of yours says I'd better feed you or it might be dangerous to spend the night in here, locked in, just you and me and a dinner fork." Then he smiled.

Oh bother. There it went again, his voice under her skin, deep and thick and rumbly and...

Maybe not quite so annoying.

"I'll get some grub. Don't go anywhere without me."

She lay back, her feet up on her couch, the backpack behind her head. Closed her eyes.

Then she held up three fingers. And for right now, meant it.

SHE SLEPT LIKE SHE MIGHT BE ROYALTY.

Peacefully, deep. No pea to disturb her.

No, she slept like a warrior.

Which was why he hated to wake her.

"Pippa?"

He refused to let the Pippi slip again. He hadn't exactly meant it the last time, but the tight bud of her lips suggested that he should step back.

But inside that icy exterior, there might be a living, breathing, maybe even tender soul, because as she slept, she hummed.

Like she might be dreaming. Maybe something happy.

Which, after the wretched twenty-four hours she'd experienced, he sort of hoped so.

So, yeah, her words in the taxi had bit into him, gnawed away. *"You don't have a princess missing, your entire career dying before your eyes."*

Yep, he got that. More than she'd ever know.

So, after he'd returned from the platform vending machine with his dinner loot, getting back on just in time for the doors to shut, when he'd found her sacked out, he'd opened his prepackaged ham-and-cheese-on-French-bread sandwich, devoured it, and gulped down a Fanta in silence.

Then he'd stayed awake so that they wouldn't miss their change of trains an hour later in Montreux.

But now, they were here. "Pippa, it's time to change trains."

She drew in a breath, then opened her eyes.

"Montreux?"

"Yeah."

"That was fast."

"Yeah."

She woke, blinked to life, silently got up and grabbed her backpack, and followed him without a word to the next train.

He set down the sandwich in front of her as they settled into their new digs—not unlike the other, but this one came with pillows and a blanket in tidy, sanitized plastic.

She ate her sandwich, staring out the window, drank her Fanta.

"You all right?" he said softly.

"Thanks for dinner."

"This is just the first course. I got you a good old-fashioned Snickers bar for dessert."

He barely got a smile.

"We'll find them."

"Oh, I hope so." She looked at him, sighed. "Sorry, it's just... it's been a year, you know?"

"Yeah?" He opened a bag of chips and handed her one.

"When Gunner asked me to watch over Imani, I thought... sure. How hard can it be to keep a watch on a twenty-year-old girl?" She wore her blanket over her shoulders, her hair a little undone from its ponytail.

Sheesh, the woman suddenly looked *real*. He blinked away the image of her tasing him.

"The problem is, Imani didn't grow up with the rules and expectations of the House of Blue, so she has no idea what is expected of her."

"House of Blue?"

"It's the royal dynasty of Lauchtenland. Prince Gustaf and Prince John, Queen Catherine, and now Princess Daffy and Princess Gemma. And my family has served in Her Majesty's Security Detail for generations." She picked up the bag of chips and opened it. "My father actually died protecting the PM, but still, under the service of the queen."

"PM?"

She looked at him, eyebrows up. "Prime Minister?"

"We don't have one of those."

"It's like your president. In a way. Not quite. But we're a small country, so the PM and even the MPs—members of parliament—work very closely with the monarchy."

"And get royal protection."

"Yes. Especially when they're on royal grounds, which Aberforth Fickle was when he was assassinated. My dad took round two as he threw himself in front of the king consort."

He put down his chip bag. "Wait. Your dad was assassinated?"

She dug around in her chip bag. "Sorry. I'm tired. I tend to say things out of course when I'm tired." She had found the winning chip and pulled it out. "I thought Imani might be my ticket to Princess Gemma's direct service." She ate the chip, then folded up the bag. "I thought, hey, this will be easy. We'll travel the world. I might have to steer her clear of a few handsy guys, maybe some bad street food. No problem."

"The hard work of a royal bodyguard."

"Right? Except, about a month ago, we came home for the queen's ball, and right under our noses, an assassin got into the palace and nearly killed an American ambassador. A complete fiasco of Lauchtenland's security team." She leaned back, pulling the blanket around her. "I'll probably need to resign after this little adventure."

"We'll find her. She's fine—I'm sure of it. Creed is streetsmart, if anything."

She reached for her Fanta, gave him a look.

"Creed spent the first ten years of his life in inner city Minneapolis, dodging drug dealers and drive-by shootings."

She capped her drink. "You make it sound like *West Side Story*. Certainly—"

"His little sister was killed in a drive-by, and his brother dealt drugs. He regularly watched his father beat his mother, until she died and his father disappeared, and through all that, he took care of his kid brother, finding them food, learning how to steal and survive and..." He ran two hands over his face. "He's a good guy. Really. He came to us pretty broken, but my dad...he's got this way with foster kids. Creed wasn't his first—we have a slew of kids, adults now, who consider my parents their parents. Only difference is that my folks adopted Creed."

She had leaned back, still holding her bottle of Fanta. "Blimey. That's a story."

"He's come a long way. But he probably still has some of those instincts. Once it's drilled into you, it doesn't leave. He'll protect Imani, I know it in my bones."

He made it sound convincing. And probably, it was all true.

He just wasn't sure exactly what laws Creed might break doing it.

She made a face, nodding. "Okay then. I'm going to take you at your word." She leaned forward. "But let's get back to that 'once it's drilled into you, it doesn't leave.' You're military, aren't you?"

He drew in a breath. "Was. Navy. I was on the teams."

She met his eyes.

"SEALs."

"I know what the teams are. We had some crossover training in the Marines with some of your guys."

"You were a marine."

"For Lauchtenland. It's...perhaps it's different than your Marines." She capped her bottle. "It was the only path to royal service. But yes. I was a sure-shot. You call them snipers."

"So today—"

"I could have taken off your face but, you know, it's so pretty." She winked.

And he had nothing, his mouth opening.

"Good night, Captain." She tucked the backpack under her head and pulled the blanket over her.

And then, almost instantly, like a combat veteran, she slept.

He, however, lay on his bunk, listening to the rhythm of the train, one thump after another, trying to unravel that wink.

Sleep swept over him without an answer, and for a while, he was dreaming. Underwater, swimming, easy, the hiss of his regulator in his mouth, moving without pain.

No Boko Haram screaming in the background. No fire. No hunger—

The jerk of the train yanked him awake.

He blinked. Something, a shudder, a ripple of metal—

The wheels started screaming.

"Fraser?"

He sat up in the darkness. "Hold on to something."

Because even as he said it, the train began to—tip?

No, they couldn't be—

The train jerked on its side, and he hit the compartment door, Pippa on top of him. Metal screeched, sparks shooting past the window.

"Hold on!" He wrapped his arm around her, and with the other, his left, grabbed the rail. Then he braced his foot against the seat.

She was doing the same opposite him, holding with both hands to his door railing, an embrace around his neck.

The train jerked and bumped, and metal rent. Their car sheered off, spun.

The window shattered.

The train squealed, moaned, the cars jerking, howling.

Screams filled the air.

Then, with a sickening crunch, the car stopped.

Sparks still flew, firelight in the night.

Pippa breathed hard against him, holding on. "Are you...okay?"

He had twisted his knee, but it wasn't bad. And she'd protected him from any shattered glass. "I'm fine—but are you hurt?"

"No. I think. Maybe—yeah, some glass." She eased away and looked over her shoulder.

He could barely make it out, but what he spotted turned his gut. A shard of window had embedded into her shoulder, in the meat below her neck. Any farther north and—

"I see it. You'll be fine. I just need a light."

Screams rose from around them, from other compartments, but he couldn't help them, trapped inside his own. Outside, he thought he heard water rushing. In the flashing lights, dying quickly, he spotted his backpack. He reached for it and pulled it to himself.

It nearly fell out of his stupid useless grip, but he managed to catch it on his legs. He unzipped the front pouch and found his mini Maglite.

Handed it to Pippa. She twisted it on. "Blimey. We nearly ate it."

A massive pine branch had taken out their window, shaggy and dark and stabbing the top bunk. Her backpack was caught in the limbs. She raised her hand to reach for it, then pulled back, wincing.

"Give me the light."

She handed it over.

"Turn around."

She maneuvered in the space, and he got a good look at the glass. Although the piece seemed large, it didn't seem that much had embedded in her shoulder.

"I'm going to take this out, but you're going to bleed. My guess is that you'll need stitches."

"I don't have time for stitches."

"I have some duct tape in my pack."

"All right. That'll do."

He rustled around in his bag and pulled out the tape, then a small ankle sock. Rolled it up into a tight ball, then ripped off a piece of tape. "This will probably hurt."

"Just do it."

He pulled back her collar, and she grunted.

"Do. Not. Move."

"Mm-hmm—"

He eased it out, her noise low and long, but she didn't cry out. Blood gushed from the wound, maybe an inch wide, another inch deep. It could probably use two layers of stitching.

Shoving the sock onto the wound, he held it there and handed her the glass. "Souvenir."

"I think the scar is enough." She set it away from them. "Just finish."

Her breathing came shorter, but she wasn't crying. Tough girl. *Tough woman.*

He put the tape over the sock, then added another piece. "I think you're good. For now. We'll need to get it looked at when we get...wherever we are."

"We just passed Brig, so maybe...somewhere in the Alps?" She reached for her backpack, groaned but found her phone and pulled it out. Powered it up.

"How do you know that? Weren't you sleeping?"

"Mm-hmm. Okay, GPS has us about three miles out of Brig." She clicked to satellite view. "We're between two mountain passes."

He was shining the light on the tree. Although it seemed lethal, especially at the velocity it had skewered the train, it wasn't that big. The train lay at an angle, and he braced himself on the seat and the door and tore off some smaller branches. "I think if I push this down, you can climb out."

"And what about you?" She braced herself, like him, and followed the shine of his light outside. He spotted people running, maybe passengers trying to escape too.

More sparks in the night, like fireworks.

"My weight will push it down."

"Okay." She reached for her backpack.

He grabbed the strap. "I'll hand it out to you."

She nodded and then climbed up on the tree, straddling it. He pulled it down, putting his weight on it, and the tree cracked, bent.

"Shimmy out. But watch for broken glass."

She ducked her head as she slid through the opening, slowly, out into the night. Then she dropped into darkness.

"Pippa?"

"Throw out the backpacks!"

He tossed hers out.

"Next one!"

His went next.

"Now you. There's emergency people here if you want to wait—"

"I'm coming out." All those sparks had formed a fist inside. He climbed on the tree.

The cracking warned him a second before the limb broke, dropping him back into the compartment.

He didn't mean to let out a sound, but heat burned through his leg as he landed on the door, which jabbed his kidney.

Oof.

"Are you okay?"

He'd cut his leg on a piece of metal, poking out from beneath the seat. "I'm fine!" But he'd need his duct tape. And maybe a tetanus shot.

But worse was that he'd lost his leverage out of the train car. The end of the tree, the part still poking through the window, jutted above his head, and he'd have to jump, do a pull-up, and mount it to get out.

He pumped his right hand. *C'mon, don't fail me now.* Then he climbed up on the seat. He could barely reach it with his right hand, let alone feel it. But if he launched himself, he could get his right hand, then his left on the trunk...

Ready or not.

He leaped up, grabbed the branch, and with everything inside him, held on.

His grip slipped just as his left hand caught the branch. He grunted, repositioned his right hand, and fought to pull himself up.

"Fraser! Help is here. They have chainsaws!"

His body burned, but he'd pulled himself up to his waist. But without the rest of the tree limb for leverage, the branch wouldn't move.

He didn't have the space to get through the window.

"Fraser!"

A fireball shook the air, turned the sky to day, and sent a shock wave through the entire train.

Fraser fell, slamming into the door, grunting as the handle put a fist into his back. Again.

"You gotta get out of there!" Pippa was at the window, tugging at the tree. "C'mon!"

He got up. The world behind her bloomed with firelight. "Pippa, run!"

"No! C'mon. Get out of there! Now! Move it, Navy!"

He ran his hand over his face, then launched himself at the branch. Hung there, kicking, fighting to pull himself up.

His grip was slipping—

Behind Pippa, people scrambled away from the flames.

"Pippa—go!"

The branch cracked. Then, with his weight on it, fell, broken off.

It cleared the window. And it made a sort of ladder.

He scaled it, reached the window, and practically dove through.

Pippa caught him, bringing him right down to the broken earth. Around them, the fireball of the train gutted the darkness.

He breathed in terrible gulps, even as he scrambled to his feet.

Then Pippa's hand was in his, pulling him. "Run!"

He scrambled with her across a shallow river and up the bank on the other side, to a road.

Passengers gathered there, some hysterical, others in stunned silence.

Fraser simply sank down, right there on the road, staring at the carnage of a passenger train derailed. Flames crawled up the train, and in moments, his carriage roared.

Pippa sank down next to him.

Looked over at him in the glowing light.

"Thanks," he said.

"Yeah, well, that's what we royal bodyguards do."

Six

In Pippa's worst nightmares, Imani was on that train.

That horrific possibility only came to her as she watched the fire trucks douse the train.

The fire lit the sky, illuminating the tall mountains that rose around them. A few questions to the fire captain revealed that an avalanche had covered the track, snow, boulders, and rocks.

It took an hour or more and a flash of her identification to get a list of passengers. She finally confirmed that no, Imani—at least anyone going by that name—wasn't on the train.

Only then did she start breathing. Start letting the reality of their accident sink in.

She let an emergency medical worker clean her wound and close it with a couple butterfly bandages. Answered the questions of a local investigator. And then noticed that Fraser had gotten hurt—a wicked scrape down his leg that he used superglue from his pack to repair.

She guessed there might be a lot of glue on his body, because after the fire department doused the train, after the emergency personnel airlifted victims, after the police finished taking statements, Fraser got up, took her hand, flagged down a ride from a passerby, got them back to Brig, and found a hotel.

One room—the quaint boutique lodging was full.

He dragged her upstairs to the small room, and without a word, built a pillow wall on the queen bed. Then he pulled off his shirt, toed off his shoes, grabbed his edge of the covers, and collapsed on the bed.

In seconds, he'd fallen into a hard sleep.

But in those few moments between waking and dead sleep, she'd seen scars. On his back, on his torso, on his arm. The ones on his arm seemed fresh.

She lay there, listening to his breathing, staring at the ceiling as the night loosened, as gray spilled into the room, and tried to figure out how her life had derailed so quickly that she was spending the night in a tiny hotel room with a stranger.

Who had saved her life just as much as she'd saved his.

She rolled over, watched him sleep.

He really wasn't a bad-looking man. Sure, he might be a little rough around the edges, his whiskers a couple days thick, but he had long, whispery lashes, and when he slept, he looked downright sweet.

A massive difference from the man who'd clawed his way out of the train. Or even defended himself in Creed's hotel room.

It seemed Fraser Marshall had a few different sides.

And maybe he *was* a little charming. After all, he'd tracked down some dinner. And Fanta. And a Snickers bar, which suddenly, she very much wanted.

Most of all, he'd gotten her out of a train car that, without him, she might have burned to death inside. So there was that.

So maybe having a temporary partner wasn't terrible.

Unfortunately, she was still thousands of kilometers from finding Imani. She rolled over and stared at the slanted wood ceiling.

And probably because she was tired and unguarded, her

father slipped into her head. *"Stay focused. Distractions are what get people killed."*

Yes. Right. Of course.

She put her back to Fraser, and then, finally, she slept.

She woke to the sound of the shower through the closed bathroom door. The sun streamed through the small window, filtered through gauzy drapes, and she got up. She'd changed clothes last night before dropping into sleep—yoga pants and a T-shirt—and now finger-combed her hair, braided it, and curled it into a tight bun at the nape of her neck.

She'd give her life savings for a cup of tea but didn't see any such amenities in the room.

Instead, she went to the window.

Gorgeous. Brig seemed to be nestled into an alpine valley. On either side, snow-covered peaks rose into the blue sky. The hotel overlooked the cobblestoned town square, surrounded on three sides by quaint shops, a café that spilled out into the square, and at the end, a beautiful old palace with Italian-style towers and round cupolas.

Reminded her of the old town square in Port Fressa.

Imani, where are you? Please be safe.

She pressed her hand against her hollow stomach. A glance at the bathroom, and the sound of the shower still running suggested he'd be in there for some time.

And maybe she didn't want to be here when he emerged, smelling clean and manly and...

Stop. She had no room for anything beyond finding Imani and getting her safely back to Lauchtenland. Maybe locking her in the north tower or something.

She'd stopped hoping that she'd hang on to her job.

Grabbing her jacket, she slid it on, then pulled on her boots and headed downstairs to sleuth out some jam and tea.

She found it on the first floor. A long rough-hewn dining room table filled the length of a room, with serve-yourself tea, hot water, fresh breads, and jam. She made herself a cup of tea, then, on a guess, stirred up a cup of instant coffee.

Then she slathered two pieces of bread with jam, balanced it all on the teacups, and headed back upstairs.

She'd forgotten her key. Or maybe she'd never gotten one, so she used her boot to knock on the door. "Fraser?"

In a second, it opened.

Yep, just as she thought. Fresh out of the shower, emanating a soapy, masculine, annoyingly intoxicating smell, his dark hair tousled, still wet, and wearing, thankfully, a clean pair of jeans and a black T-shirt that seemed a little too small for those shoulders, frankly. A towel hung around his neck.

He hadn't shaved, though. So American. That helped keep the down-girl inside her alive and working.

"Thought you'd ditched me." He held open the door with one strong capable arm and stepped aside.

Down. Girl.

"I just went out for breakfast." She headed inside and set the food down on a small table.

"And you even got me coffee." He closed the door, and suddenly the room seemed terribly small, terribly intimate. "What, are we friends now?" He grinned at her, his blue eyes sparkling, and she picked up her tea and went to the window, hoping for air.

"Let's say...people with similar goals." She sipped her tea. Oh, it found her bones, and she just might live.

"Right. Focus. Well, my morning report is that I called my sister while you were out."

She shot him a look. He was holding that tiny teacup of coffee in his massive hand. Yeah, it looked silly. "And?"

"It went to her voice mail."

She made a face.

"So, what's our next move, Pippa with an *ah*?"

She wouldn't smile—fine. Oh botheration!

He smiled back.

All right, this was going to be a long day.

"My guess is that the train is out, so we'll need to hire a car," she said.

"If we get to our next stop, Andermatt, we can take a train from there."

"Through the Alps?" She made a face.

"The other choice is to let the American drive." He winked. "Pick your poison."

Her jaw tightened. Not that she hadn't learned to drive—she'd even taken a protection driving course. But it had been nearly two years since she'd been behind the wheel… "Promise not to drive us off the road?"

He held up three fingers.

"Let's do the train."

He laughed. "I see how it is."

"Fine. Let's rent a car."

He finished his coffee. "On it." Then he picked up the bread and jam, his backpack, and headed to the door. "Meet you downstairs."

The door closed behind him. And it occurred to her that he might be giving her some privacy.

Apparently chivalry hadn't died across the pond.

She locked the door, however, then showered and cleaned up, and thirty minutes later, her hair still wet but braided and reknotted into a tight bun, she felt more like herself and less like a college coed who'd ended up in the wrong place for the night. Even if it had been innocent.

In fact, she realized that she'd slept the night through without waking to voices, memories, or even the hard thump of her heart that usually led to her pacing, breathing, and warding off one of her rare panic attacks.

So, wow, that was good.

He was in the lobby, nursing another cup of coffee when she came down carrying her backpack.

"I found us a ride to Andermatt. From there we can rent a car. Or whatever." He gestured to an elderly man who stood on the front steps of the hotel, leaning against an ancient Škoda hatchback, smoking a cigarette.

"Who's that?"

"Petr Kasper. He owns the hotel."

A regular entrepreneur.

But Baron Kasper, as he introduced himself, seemed accommodating. He offered her the front seat, but she elected for the back so she could text Gunner, and maybe check her email, in case Imani had reached out.

As it turned out, she had no reception, so that was a bust. Meanwhile, Fraser crammed himself into the front seat and, to her surprise, spoke German to the baron as they drove west an hour.

She picked up most of it, of course. Even the part where the baron asked Fraser if they were enjoying their honeymoon.

What—

She looked at Fraser, but he seemed nonplussed by the question, and she knew that was the story he'd fed to the man.

He even looked back at her, smiling and winking, when he told the man about their beautiful hotel in Geneva—ahem, *her* beautiful hotel.

Nice digs. His words found her, rumbled through her.

All right, that was enough.

The baron asked about the accident, especially as they slowed along the highway where the train had crashed. Cleanup machinery jammed the riverbed, trying to remove the burned rubble from the track.

She turned away, back to her text to Gunner. *Still looking. Train troubles. Will check in today.*

She pushed Send so the app would send it when she got service.

Then she checked her email, which she'd opened back at the hotel when she'd had internet.

Nothing from Imani, but it did look like she'd received something from...seriously? Stone Brubaker, from *The Morning Show*, Lauchtenland. She clicked on the email.

Stilled.

She must have gasped, because Fraser turned in his seat, frowning. "Everything okay? Did you hear from Imani?"

"No. Nothing like that." She glanced at him. Oh, why not? "The twentieth anniversary of my father's death—and the death of PM Fickle—is next month, and Stone Brubaker wants my take on Hamish Fickle's RECO party."

He just blinked at her.

"The RECO party is antimonarchy. Hamish's uncle, however, Aberforth Fickle, was a sovereign monarchist, and on the day he died, he was giving a speech on the importance of the monarchy, actually putting forth a writ that the queen should appoint the minister of state, or prime minister, like Monaco, instead of simply being a figurehead. His argument was that democracy leads to anarchy and that the sovereign has the responsibility to lead the country, so we should give her the power to appoint the leader of government.

"My father was a monarchist by tradition, but since he was on the platform guarding Fickle and the king consort that day, there were rumors that he let the assassination occur." She deleted the email. "He was cleared, at least with the queen, formally. But in public opinion..." Her throat had thickened.

No, he hadn't let it occur, but he had been distracted. She closed her eyes.

"Pippa?"

"It's fine." She drew in a breath, opened her eyes. "It's old news. I'm deleting it."

He rented a car from the Eurocar desk at the train station. A cute Fiat Panda that had his knees up nearly to his chest but that he handled like a Grand Prix racer as they rounded sharp bends, rising and falling with the mountain roads.

They'd gobbled some lunch at a kiosk—a rosti, aka hash browns stuffed with cheese, onion, and surprisingly, apple, topped with bacon and a fried egg.

A thousand times better than her usual protein shake and coffee. But then again, she seemed to be living life outside the lines.

She didn't hate it. At least, for this blink of time. Forever, she'd lose her mind. But for now, she leaned her head back against the rest and took in the beauty.

The road south led them directly through the northern Italian Alps, and mountains rose around them, jagged, white-capped, lethal.

"I looked into the avalanche—we were at Mont Blanc a couple days ago, and they had an avalanche after a terrible wind gust. It looks like the same storm front moved through the valley and took out the train."

"I'll keep an eye on the road. I promise not to drive us into a snowdrift." He glanced over at her.

"I can't help it. My job is to look for contingencies, worry about the future, the what-ifs."

"I get that. When I was on the teams, we ran every scenario we could think of, just in case."

A deep sigh came after his words, however, and it had her looking at him. He drove with a relaxed confidence, one hand on his knee, the left holding the wheel, his elbow on the window armrest.

But a muscle pulled in his jaw, and he sighed again.

"Something on your mind there, Captain?"

She didn't know why she continued with the nickname. He

just seemed so...larger than life. And right now, she just wasn't herself either.

"It's nothing. Just, memories." He glanced at her, offered a wry smile. "But as my buddy Ham says, there are no regrets, just lessons."

"Oh, I think there are regrets. But yes, learn from them. Make sure they never happen again."

She noticed, as he spoke, he squeezed his right hand, flexing, squeezing. She'd seen him do that on the train too. And those scars...

"Did you hurt your hand?"

He glanced at her, then down to his hand. Back to the road. "On the train? No. I was...it has some nerve damage from a recent op. I broke my wrist, and it took a while to get to medical help. It'll be okay." He ended with a nod, as if he might be convincing himself.

Hmm. But he clearly didn't want to talk about it.

So, "Tell me about your sister. Why is she living in Como?"

"Why not Como? It's gorgeous, and she travels all the time for work. She did a year abroad years ago and got involved reffing a club football team in Milan. Loved it so much she stuck around, got her creds, and started reffing at junior, then pro games."

"Football. You mean futbol." She corrected his pronunciation.

"No. I mean football. American football, although here it's called the European League of Football."

"There are European football teams playing American football?"

"Many. The Vienna Vikings, the Berlin Thunder, the Hamburg Sea Devils, and others. It's growing. The NFL even plays a game at a European venue every year to help support the sport."

"And your sister is a ref. That's...cool."

"Yeah. She's all right." But he smiled, a warmth to his voice.

"Your family seems pretty close."

"I guess. We like each other—I blame my parents for that. They made us cheer each other on. Go to each other's games, root for each other. I missed out on a lot of that because I left for the military right out of high school, but yeah, they're a good bunch."

"How old were you when Creed joined your family?"

"I had left for the Navy by then. So I didn't know him well. Don't actually know him at all. We don't...there's some history."

"Yeah?"

He sighed. "I sort of accused him of stealing from my parents, in the early days. Mom had moved him into my room, and I got home for leave and I might have been a little hot about it. I didn't want him going through my things...I know. Very middle school. And instead of saying anything, I saw this money clip on the dresser. It was my dad's and had a wad of cash in it, and I sorta...I think I scared him a little. Turns out that my dad had given him the clip. Which sorta sat in my craw too, because it was a family heirloom of sorts."

"You felt replaced. Or betrayed."

He looked at her. Raised a shoulder. "Whatever. I left shortly thereafter and haven't been around much since then. Creed got his own room when Iris moved out. Jonas and Ned bounce back now and again, so Mom kept their digs. And mine."

"And yet you jumped on a plane for him."

Another shrug. "He's still family. And you don't let your family down, right?"

She gave a small shrug. "I don't know. I'm an only child. And after my dad died, my mom sorta dove into her work. She's a barrister and focused on her firm. She remarried—my father's partner, actually—but not until I had moved out. She lives her life, and I'm focused on Imani."

"And royal service."

"Yes."

"Because?"

She had nothing. Just looked at him. "Um, because it's...it's all I've ever wanted to do. It's who I am."

They were following a river, the hillsides green, dotted with quaint chalets, pine trees, and the occasional run of sheep.

A regular fairyland.

Focus. "That's why this year, and these past two days, have been such a nightmare. I lose Imani and I've not only lost my job but I've...I've destroyed our family name."

"Because of the accusations."

"It's a small country with a long history. People remember. Regrets don't die in Lauchtenland."

"I get that. Mistakes on the teams tend to stay with you."

"Why did you become a SEAL?"

"Same as you. It's what I wanted for as long as I can remember." He looked at her. "Except I'm not a SEAL anymore."

"You mentioned that. Why not?"

"Long story. It involved an off-the-grid op to rescue some Army Rangers in captivity. Approved, unofficially, but it was working its way up the disciplinary chain, and I decided to get out before I met with a less-than-honorable discharge. I now work private security for my buddy, Ham, as part of his Jones, Inc. group."

"And that's how you hurt your arm?"

"Mm-hmm."

And that's where the conversation ended. Two strikes, and she decided not to probe anymore. He wasn't the only one who wanted to keep his secrets and let the past die.

They were nearing the town of Lugano, tiny houses scattered on the hillside.

"We're about an hour from Milan," he said. "And hopefully, Imani and Creed will be there, and this nightmare will be over."

"Yes. Hopefully."

But sitting here with Fraser, winding their way through the most beautiful country she'd ever seen, it didn't feel so much like a nightmare, did it?

It wasn't a five-star hotel, or even Ned's posh place, but at least they were safe and warm and Imani had stopped freaking out.

And the youth hostel served instant coffee in the lobby. That was a win.

Creed stood on the balcony of his room. From here, through the mansard roofs of the nearby buildings, some of them five-star hotels, he could make out the deep blue of Lake Geneva, and farther, the Alps of Italy.

Maybe they should have gotten on a train or a bus, like his first impulse. His sister Iris—a sister he barely knew, really—lived somewhere in Italy. But that would be bringing Imani even farther from safety.

At least in Geneva she might be able to contact her security officer, Pippa. That was his second impulse after he caught her off the balcony last night and ran.

He'd taken them through neighborhoods and roads and then back out to the main street and hopped on the first bus he saw.

It took them to a central station, and there he found a bus to Geneva.

It was nearly midnight when they arrived at the youth hostel. He'd suggested going to her hotel, but the look in her eyes gave him the answer.

Again, she wouldn't let go of his hand, and that made him feel both like a superhero...

And terrified to his bones.

Someone had tried to kill—or at least hurt, maybe kidnap her. And that someone was still out there.

"Did you recognize him?" He kept his voice low, the conversations on the bus to Geneva muted. "The guy—"

"I know. And no. He was...bigger. Balding. I was in the bathroom getting dressed, and I thought it was you, so I came out and—he was just right there. I panicked and grabbed the lamp and..." She closed her eyes then, and he put his arms around her.

"Maybe you were wrong about the guy in the park. Maybe you didn't recognize him," he said after a moment.

"No." She lifted her head. "I did. I think maybe he told the other guy to..." She swallowed, her eyes wide. "I need to find Pippa."

This, he agreed on.

After they found a safe place to land.

Probably she was right, however, because they'd had to walk past the hotel on their way to the hostel, and even as her hand had tightened in his, he'd spotted the media, the lineup of limos.

Something was going down at the hotel. Something she didn't want to get caught up in.

So, they'd shown up at the youth hostel, and the only private room with a bath and WC he could get was a double.

Two single beds. Which he then took and pushed to opposite sides of the fairly bare room. Because he was dog-tired, his adrenaline dropping, and he practically melted into bed.

Now he stood, freshly showered, debating going back to his hotel to get his backpack, thankful he had his cash, staring out at a world that had sort of lost its luster.

His parents were going to kill him when they heard about his off-the-grid adventure. Not that he had to report to them, really, but...

But with everything inside him, he wanted Garrett Marshall

to think of him as his son. And the Marshall children didn't do crazy things...

Okay, that wasn't true. Fraser was the definition of a person who lived on the edge. And Jonas—he chased *storms* for a living. And Iris was a football ref in Italy. And who knew what trouble Ned was in, so what*ever*.

But they didn't break the law. They weren't criminals.

And they'd never had an international BOLO put out on them. He needed to get Imani back to safety, clear this up, and get home before someone—ahem, him—got arrested.

Sometimes, if he let himself, he could still be the guy who'd wanted to run when Fraser accused him of stealing all those years ago.

"Creed? What's going on?"

He turned, and Imani came out, dressed, but with the sheet from her twin bed wrapped around her. It was a little chilly out, the smell of autumn, drying leaves, a hint of chill from the Alps in the air.

"You're in your bare feet."

"I took a shower."

"I see that." She nodded to his wet hair. He probably needed a cut.

"Want coffee?" He held out his cup.

"With every bone in my body." She took a sip. "Mmm. Ever since moving to Lauchtenland, it's been only tea. I'm not a fan."

She was so pretty; she probably didn't even know it. Or the effect she had on him, the way she laughed—it felt like a song, the kind you want to keep humming. He drew in a breath.

Princess. He needed to keep that word in his head. Because she might look like the all-American girl, but she now lived in a whole different world.

"We need to find Pippa," he said as she handed him back the coffee. "And I need to get back to America. I already missed my flight—"

"I'm sorry. Oh, wow, I didn't even think—"

"Hey. Hey—" He turned to her. "It's no big deal. Really."

"When did it leave?"

He checked his watch, still working after the dunk in the river, thankfully. "About twelve hours ago."

"You should have told me."

She had the most amazing hazel eyes. They darkened when she worried, like now. He touched her arm. "Imani. I'd rather make sure you're safe."

And although she'd been holding his hand for the better part of two days, suddenly, something shifted between them. A silence. A beat.

An awareness that felt vastly different from the fun they'd had at the VIP bar or even in the gondola. And he'd been very careful to keep his distance at the hotel, and last night, so...

He pulled his hand away. Swallowed.

She bit her lip and looked out over the rooftops.

Yeah. And in that moment, he very much wanted to set down his coffee and pull her into his arms.

Very much wanted to tip up her chin and meet her eyes and then softly, perfectly kiss her. At least, he could try to keep it soft and perfect and tame the terrible urge that roiled through him.

And it was that urge that made him turn away from her and hold on to his coffee with both hands. "I think you should go back to your hotel."

She made a soft noise. Not quite acquiescence, but maybe not argument either. More of a resigned grim agreement, like a person getting their wisdom teeth out. Then, "How?"

Her expression looked dubious. "The hotel will be filled with ambassadors and diplomatic envoys and, especially, Lauchtenland guards."

"So, that's good, right?"

"Or is it? I mean, if Gunner Ferguson is at the center of this, how many other guards are involved?" She shook her head. "Why didn't I memorize Pippa's number? How stupid was that?"

"The only reason I know my parents' number is because they refused to let me have a phone until I turned sixteen. I had to call home for rides from practice."

"Did you get ahold of your brother?"

"I called him twice—last night and today. Nothing. Just the machine. It's weird."

"Then it's up to us." She took a breath. "But you're right, I need to get into the hotel. Let Pippa know I'm okay."

"What if she's out looking for you?"

"Where?"

Right. "Okay. How?"

She pulled the sheet across her face, revealing only her eyes.

"A niqab? Isn't that sort of...sacred?"

She let it go. "Probably. But isn't trying to stay alive sort of sacred?"

"Right. But it's banned all over Europe."

"But not at a diplomatic event."

"Right. Okay. A face scarf it is. Brilliant."

She smiled, her eyes warm.

He practically fled the balcony.

"Wait, where are you going?"

"To buy you a disguise?" He turned. She followed him and now stood there, swallowed, and nodded.

Right. The last time he'd left her, she'd been attacked. He pulled out his phone and handed it over. "If anyone comes in who isn't me, call...whatever passes for 911 here."

She took it. "Bring back breakfast?"

"One pineapple pizza coming right up."

But he got a smile from her. It fueled him all the way down the stairs and onto the busy street.

He fell in with the crowd, vowing to buy a baseball hat too.

He made his way to the boulevard along the river, the smells of fish and brine stirring into the air. A kiosk selling souvenirs caught his eye, and he bought a baseball cap with the Geneva Seahawks embroidered on the crown. Pulled it down over his hair.

Then he walked down the boardwalk until he spotted a woman's store and went inside. Not a niqab to be found. He did, however, find some long scarves.

He bought two, both teal.

The smells of baking bread, cookies, and even something savory filled the air. He found a bakery and bought two cheese croissants and a tart.

When he emerged, he stood exactly across from his hotel, the park where this entire nightmare started. It wouldn't take him long to get to his hotel, get his backpack, his bag.

Which meant a change of clothes. And a toothbrush, although he'd purchased a couple toiletries kits today at the hostel, which included a disposable brush in each.

It wouldn't take that long, and he'd be back before she was out of the shower.

And then, regardless of what happened, he'd have his gear.

His silly trophy, but there it was, something he'd gotten because he'd participated.

Still, it was more than his brother—his real brother—ever had. And probably more than his mother had ever dreamed for him, and...

Shoot, he wasn't nine years old and bringing home a spelling bee trophy for his mother to admire. He swallowed a burn in his throat.

Besides, what if the hotel was being guarded? They hadn't identified them—not yet. But maybe...

A horn trilled and he moved out of the way of a bicyclist. "Sorry!"

He needed to get back.

Turning, he retraced his steps, sorting out a plan in his head. He'd wait for Imani outside the hotel—no, that wouldn't work. What if she saw Gunner—or he saw her? He'd need to get inside.

He could sneak in the back, via the loading dock, like they did in the movies. But then what? Security would never let him on the upper floors.

Maybe she didn't need him. Once she got into her hotel room, Pippa would be there.

And Pippa would sort it out. Hopefully. She'd seemed a little stern but not unreasonable.

But what if Imani needed him—and now what, he was her guardian angel?

Maybe. Or maybe he just wanted to be.

He took the stairs up, all six flights. Knocked, then used his key to get in when she didn't answer.

Maybe she was in the shower.

Nope.

He let the door close. "Imani?"

She sat in the middle of the bed, her legs folded, one hand over her mouth, staring at a picture on his phone.

"What's going on?"

He walked over, sat on the bed beside her.

"I hooked up to the internet here. Just wanted to...I don't know why." She handed him the phone. "There was a train derailment last night, about three hours from here." Her hand shook a little as she pointed to the picture.

Shots of the train wreck. A fiery ball that lit the night. Carnage. "I don't understand."

"They had a picture of some of the people in the wreck." She swiped the pictures until she came to a picture of a woman standing in the wreckage, staring out as if shocked.

"Pippa?"

"It looks like her, right?"

Orange-backdropped her, but yes, it very much looked like the woman he'd met.

"Why was she on that train?"

"I don't know." He lowered the phone.

She folded her up her legs, wrapped her arms around them. Took a breath. "If she's there, she's not at the hotel."

He did that math too. "You should try to call her."

"I will. But I think it's time I went home."

"To Lauchtenland?"

"To my mom. She and Prince John are on a yacht in Italy, enjoying a holiday. I was supposed to meet them here in a few days, but...I don't want to wait. I don't think I can wait." She gave him a pointed look.

"What?"

"You're in trouble too, and you can't babysit me forever."

He suddenly didn't know why not.

"But I do have a favor to ask..."

"Anything."

She smiled, something sad in her expression. "Would you go with me to Portofino?"

He took her hand. Wove his fingers through hers. "Princess, I'll go with you anywhere."

"Isn't this illegal?"

They stood in the patio entry of his sister's two-story townhome, made from some ancient winery or something, overlooking the glorious Lake Como. Fraser held the tire iron he'd found in the back of the car.

"I'm not breaking a window. And it's my sister's place."

"But she's not here. And she doesn't know we're here, so that's breaking in, right?"

Fraser knelt before the lock on the door. "Again, it's my sister's place."

"This would be illegal in Lauchtenland."

He stood up. "We're not in Lauchtenland. We're in Italy. Tired and crabby and hungry in Italy. And I'm going inside my sister's place, because I know she won't mind if I use my father's old trick of getting into the house, go inside, rummage through her refrigerator, and then, please, for the love, go to bed and get a decent night's sleep. So just, put a sock in it, Miss Law and Order, okay?"

Pippa stepped back, her hands up, and shoot, he didn't mean his tone.

In fact, up until now, he'd sort of not exactly hated their ride.

Beautiful. Easy. And talking to her felt...well, she was a lot like him, maybe. Focused. Determined. And she didn't complain, even though her neck wound had to be hurting her.

Moreover, if Iris wasn't here, then Imani and Creed weren't here.

And they were back to nothing.

"Sorry," he said.

"You're right. How do you do this breaking-in thing?"

"It's easy. And really, only works on sliding glass doors, and only if someone forgets to put down the rod that keeps them from opening."

He crouched and wiggled the flat end of the crowbar into the bottom channel of the door. "I'm going to lift up, and when I do, you pull on the door handle."

"So now I'm an accessory?"

"I go down, you go down."

She offered a scant smile, then leaned over him. "Ready when you are."

"Now." He hiked up on the door and she jerked.

It slid open with a pop. "Wow. That's completely terrifying."

"Which is why you never get a ground-level hotel room with a sliding door." He stepped inside the kitchen.

He'd only been here once, about a year ago when he'd been between jobs. Her home was one of four in the building, renovated, the original stonework in place both outside and in. Around the back of the garage, a private courtyard with bougainvillea and potted geraniums seemed the perfect getaway, complete with a table and chairs and a terracotta chiminea.

Inside, more plants, and a great room that she'd renovated to include a small kitchen. The floor was the original stone, however, covered with thick rugs and a comfy section that faced a flatscreen. Stainless steel appliances, a massive stone farmhouse sink, and a dark granite island. A faux bouquet sat in the middle of the table.

"This is nice."

"My sister has great taste. My parents are renovators—they redid our entire farmhouse. I think she got the bug from them. She did most of the work." He closed the sliding door behind Pippa.

A clean, new, smooth white-pine staircase led to the second floor, and he carried his backpack upstairs to one of the two bedrooms. "My sister's is the big one, but take the other. There's a loft upstairs that overlooks the lake. I'll suffer up there."

She smiled at him, so maybe he was forgiven.

Two single beds were shoved against opposite walls in the slanted-roofed attic. A grand picture window, floor to dormer ceiling, jutted out and showcased the beauty of Lake Como. Nestled in the valley of dramatic mountains that fell straight down to the water, why not live in Como?

He stood in the window for a bit, the deep azure blue almost hypnotizing. For some reason, Ham picked then to tiptoe into his mind. *God hasn't forgotten you. There's a plan. You just don't know it yet. But when you're ready to get back in the game, He'll tell you.*

Yeah, but until then, the wait was a rock inside him. But with views like this, maybe it wasn't torture.

"Fraser?"

He turned away from the window. Pippa stood at the door. "How about if I make dinner."

"You cook?"

"I have more than one trick up my sleeve." She winked.

What was it with her winking? It left him completely nonplussed.

Like the stupid train, derailing.

She turned away and headed downstairs.

Calm down. She had a job, and he had...well, not a job guarding a princess.

He heard dishes rattling downstairs.

"We're going to have to go shopping," she said when he arrived in the kitchen. She'd found a grocery bag. "I can go alone if you want to stay here and get some shut-eye."

"Nope," he heard himself saying. "I'll go with you."

"All right, then." She headed back out through the sliding door, and he did a quick search for the keys. Found them hanging on a hook by the door.

Like mother, like daughter.

They found a patisserie not far from the house, on a perfectly cobbled street with stores on either side, still open for business in the late afternoon. The sun hung over the mountains, pressing heat into the day, and a few leaves tumbled down the street as they walked.

"This reminds me of the main street in my home village of Wython. It's in the northern part of the country and one of the oldest. In the summer, wild roses bloom in the boulevards, and the air smells of the greensward on the mountains. Pop always stopped by the bakery on the corner for a bit of fresh meringue on his trips home from the palace."

"He didn't come home every night?"

"Oh no, he lived there. Mostly. He came home on the week-ends, sometimes, and for weeks in the summer, on holidays. And whenever he could. We only lived there until I was eleven. My exams got me into Hove Grammar, which was about an hour from Wython, so we moved to Dalholm, near Hadsby Castle, and he transferred there. Then he was home more often. It was always a grand moment when I came home from grammar to find Pop sitting at the kitchen table with fresh scones and jam."

He liked how she talked, her accent. It made her both myste-rious and yet sweet. He could see her as a child, braids down, in uniform, sitting up to the table to eat her scones and jam, sipping her tea.

"He sounds like a good man."

"Very much so. He was a marine also. Decorated. And he loved serving the House of Blue. I know in my heart he consid-ered it his greatest honor to give his life for the Crown." Her mouth had pinched tight, however.

"Pippa?"

"It killed my mother when the accusations were made. She fought for his honor, and of course, Queen Catherine decreed honors on him, but the rumors lingered." She glanced at him. "I hope you like pasta, because this was my father's favorite recipe."

"I'll love it." He'd probably gobble down a plate of grubs if she set it in front of him, but as it turned out, she was right.

Pasta with oil, fresh parsley, mushrooms. She'd thrown in prawns and squeezed on lemon juice. He'd found a bottle of Marshall Fields Winery, a La Crescent Gold, in his sister's pantry and cracked it open for them. She served dinner with a flaky baguette, greens salad with oil and vinegar, and he'd pull the moon from the sky if the woman asked.

"You make sounds when you eat," she said, leaning over the plate as the night fell around them in the courtyard. A candle flickered in the center of the table, a curlicue of smoke lifting into the darkness. His sister had strung tiny twinkle lights around the grotto-like area, and if he didn't know better, he'd suspect fate—or God, because he didn't really believe in fate—of bringing him here for romance. Which was odd, because that had never, not once in ten years, been on his agenda.

"How else will the cook know I love her food?"

Oh. And how was she supposed to ignore that? She leaned back in her chair, holding the wine. "I know I should be worried. And I am—really, I am. But...I dunno. Something in me says she's okay."

Imani. Right.

"She is. I'm sure of it."

"But..." She put the wine down. "I think I need to face the facts. I need help. I have no idea where to go from here. Except Portofino."

"Italy?"

"The prince and princess are on a yacht docked in the harbor there. Hopefully. And I think this is news best given in person. I already texted Gunner, however, so he'll make that call. He might be mobilizing the troops right now. Without me."

"Pippa."

"No. It is what it is. I should have taken better care of her. I was so...angry with her. But she's out there, by herself—"

"With Creed."

She raised an eyebrow.

"Aw. He's a good kid. Grew up with Marshall values."

"Man."

"Right. Man." He smiled at her.

She ran her fingers down the stem of her wine glass. "I did try and teach her some self-defense moves."

"Like what?"

"Ever see *Miss Congeniality*?"

"S.I.N.G? Seriously?"

"Solar plexus, instep, nose, and groin. She saw the movie

and wanted to know if it would work. It's not perfect, but it'll slow someone down enough to get away."

He laughed. "Remind me not to get in your way. Oh, wait…"

She laughed with him, and maybe he didn't mind getting tased if it earned him that smile.

She took another sip of wine. "This is good."

"Thanks."

"You don't want to take over your dad's business?"

"No. I have a job."

He saw her eyes go to his arm. He hadn't realized he'd been flexing and tightening his hand. And yes, he'd dodged her twice today when she'd asked, but…

Well, regrets. And frankly, he didn't want to crack them open on such a beautiful night. Still. Maybe it felt right. Safe. "On my last assignment, I was captured by the Boko Haram."

Her mouth opened. Closed. "I'm sorry."

"It's okay. I'm working through it." He looked away from her at the flicker of the flame. "I sometimes dream that the big guy, Abu Hassiff, shows up at the winery."

And suddenly, he was sitting there, naked, under the starlight. He made a face. "Not sure—"

"I get it."

He looked at her. She sighed and picked up her wine glass. Met his gaze over the top. Her eyes looked wet. "I talked to my father for a very long time after he died. Dreamed that he was in the room. Dreamed that he wanted to say something to me… but nothing would come out." She looked back at him, wiped a hand across her cheek. "I was there the day he died. Watched him take the bullet for PM Fickle."

"Pip."

"My grammar was having a day out, a special tour of the castle, and the PM was on the grounds, and I thought…I'll just sneak away and watch my father. Except I wasn't supposed to be there, and my dad saw me. Just out of the corner of his eye, but

I saw him frown. And just like that, Fickle was shot." She finished off her wine. "I can't help but think if I…" She paused.

Wait, did she think… "Pippa, it's not your fault."

She looked away.

"Things happen. People get the drop on you, even on the best of days."

She nodded, shook her head, then made a face, and he was right there with her, nodding, shaking his head, making a face because, again, regrets.

And he couldn't let her be the only one. "Abu Hassiff got the drop on me too. I was in a small village, in the back of a burning church, looking for survivors, and the truck drove up behind me. By the time I came back to the front, the terrorists were already there, shooting. If I hadn't gone around…"

"Regrets."

"Yeah. It doesn't matter how many ways you excuse yourself; it doesn't make them easier." He, too, finished off his wine. "Even if you learn from them."

She met his eyes across the table, hers so beautifully blue-gray. "You're not such a bad tagalong, Captain."

He smiled. "And you're a pretty good cook, Natasha."

"You're making breakfast." She picked up the plates. He gathered the glasses.

Overhead, the stars blinked down at them, and for a moment, in the wind, he thought he heard the soft whisper of a voice.

He just couldn't make out what it said.

SEVEN

"**Y**ou're not such a bad tagalong, Captain."

What. On *earth?* She had practically flirted with the man.

Worse, she'd meant it. She liked having him around. Liked his bad jokes.

Liked his fierce focus.

Liked the man who wasn't afraid to tell her the hard things.

Pippa sat in the darkness of Iris's guest bedroom, the moon shining in along the wooden floor, dressed in her yoga pants and a T-shirt, staring at her phone.

Gunner still hadn't texted back after her update. She'd finally sent him another text, telling him she was going to Portofino. It made sense, really.

If Creed hadn't brought Imani to his family, maybe she'd bring him to hers.

Imani, where are you?

Pippa's entire body longed for sleep, but her brain simply wouldn't shut off. And it didn't help that Fraser kept invading her brain. Fraser, helping her wash dishes, the simple task of wiping them dry and putting them away feeling so...easy. Fraser, sitting at the table, nursing his glass of wine, his arms folded across that too-amazing chest, looking at her with those pensive blue eyes as she told him about her father. *"Pip."*

He'd said her name so softly it felt like a whisper in her soul, and the look in his eyes, compassionate—she'd felt it right to her bones. And then his words, spoken from a place where, honestly, he *understood*, given his own story. *"Things happen. People get the drop on you, even on the best of days."*

Yes, they did. But she lived her life anticipating the what-ifs. Fearing them.

And now she was living inside it. But tonight, weirdly, she'd stopped panicking. Stopped, really, thinking.

Just enjoyed dinner and the moonlight and a conversation with someone who didn't look at her through the lens of judgment. *"You're not such a bad tagalong, Captain."*

She lay back on the bed, dropping the phone, putting her hands over her face. What was she thinking? *Focus!*

It was then that she heard it. Deep growls, the kind that emanated from inside someone's soul. Or deep in their dreams.

She sat up, then moved off the bed to the door.

A shout, garbled—so not a word, but probably something important, trapped inside Fraser's nightmare.

Hopefully a nightmare and not him taking down an intruder, someone who had followed them from Geneva.

Which seemed farfetched, but not impossible, because who knew what Imani was caught up in.

She ascended the stairs, and the growling persisted along with another shout, and by the time she got to the open door of the room, she knew.

He was fighting his memories.

"Fraser."

He lay on his back, twisted in the covers, his shoulders moving, his body tensing, and the sound persisted, deep and feral inside him.

"Fraser." She stepped closer, not wanting to wake him too fast.

He stopped moving.

She took another step.

"I'm okay."

He pressed his hands to his face, sighed, then sat up. The covers fell to his waist. He was shirtless. Oh.

"The Boko Haram?" she said quietly.

His breathing came fast. "Yeah."

"Shake it off. C'mon. Get up. I'll make you some tea."

He nodded, then turned, put his feet on the floor, and reached for his pants on a nearby chair.

She turned away while he put them on. "I'll go—"

"I dreamed that Abu was here. That he took you."

The floor creaked, and she turned back.

He was standing there in the moonlight, draped in shadow, and she got a glimpse of a toned midsection, the jeans low on his hips.

"Me?"

He made a wry face.

"Probably residue of the train crash." She turned again.

"Don't go." The soft voice froze her, and she turned back. He still stood in shadow, but the starlight illuminated his face, his gaze on her. "Did Gunner text you back?"

Gunner? Gunner—who? No, she got it, but frankly, right now…somehow, she managed to shake her head.

He took another step closer. "We're going to find her. I promise."

She nodded, found his gaze. "I know."

His hand slid down to hers, something in his eyes.

She felt his gaze shiver through her entire body.

Oh, no, no— "What are you doing?" she said softly.

"I'm not sure. I just…um…"

She couldn't—no. Bad, bad idea. "It's just the last thirty-six hours of crazy, right?"

He nodded slowly. "Right."

"Right."

But she'd taken a step toward him too.

He lifted his hand and pushed her hair back, behind her ear. "I like it down. It's pretty."

His touch turned her skin electric, and her breath caught.

"Pippa." He drew in a breath. "Okay, yeah, maybe we need some tea." He pulled his hand away.

Tea? No, she didn't want tea.

In fact, right now, the only thing she wanted was—

"What's that?" He grabbed her arms, holding her away. "Shh."

She stilled and heard it too.

Someone was breaking in. As in, jimmying the sliding glass door, just like they had, given the scrape and popping sounds.

She sucked in a breath. "Someone's inside."

"And if it was Iris, she'd use her key." He moved her aside. "Stay here."

He was kidding, right?

He tiptoed to the door, then held out his hand to her, another *stay here.*

Which she refused to heed. *Hello.* He wasn't the only one trained to confront trouble.

He scooted down the stairs like a deer, noiselessly, and then along the landing of the second floor. It overlooked the ground level, and indeed, someone had come into the house. A man, given the shape and size.

Fraser skulked along the landing, then headed for the stairs.

She ducked into her room, went to her backpack, and retrieved the stun gun.

A shout sounded, then a thump and another shout—she ran

out, spied two men grappling. Hard to tell them apart in the darkness, but Fraser was shirtless, so that helped.

He was on top of the other man, who then decked him, a fist to the face.

Fraser fell off, and she pointed the taser at the attacker. This model had a fifteen-foot range, and she could put him down with just the…right…shot—

The attacker got up, towering over Fraser. "What's the—"

Fraser hooked his feet around the man's ankles—

She fired.

No, oh no—

The man fell, and Fraser jumped on him.

The prongs landed in Fraser's back, and his entire body stiffened. He let out a shout, then fell back, his body convulsing.

"Fraser!" She threw down the gun and ran down the stairs.

"Fraser?" The other man stood up, staring down at poor Fraser.

Through gritted teeth, Fraser clawed at the prongs in his back, fighting the electricity that surged through him.

Then suddenly, his attacker turned him over and yanked them out.

Fraser let out a shout, but collapsed back, breathing hard, his entire body shaking.

"Fraser!" She hit the landing, not sure—

The man stood over him, kneeling, one hand on his chest. "Just breathe, bro. Just breathe."

Bro?

Fraser reached up, grabbed his wrist. He still shook, although it had diminished.

"You'll be okay. Give yourself a minute."

He leaned up. "Jonas. What…are…you doing…here?"

"What am I doing here? What are *you* doing here?"

Jonas? As in his storm-chasing brother?

That seemed right, though. Similar build, same angular jawline, short hair.

"It's a long story," she said when Fraser simply lay back, breathing. She knelt next to him. "I'm so sorry."

He looked at her. "We had...a deal."

"I know. But you moved..." She looked over at Jonas. "Sorry."

"No, I get it. Strange guy, breaking in. Great shot, by the way."

"She was...aiming for you."

"Was she though?" Jonas grinned, looked at Pippa and winked. "I think she put the right man down."

"Get off me." Fraser pushed Jonas away. Sat up, shaking his head. Looked at her.

So, gone was the heat she'd felt earlier. Or maybe replaced with a different kind of heat. "Seriously? I thought you were a sniper."

"You're a sniper?"

"Was." She turned back to Fraser. "And you *moved*."

"I didn't know you were shooting at me! I told you to stay put."

She blinked at him. "Right." Shaking her head, she stood up. "That does help, mate. I forgot for a second who you were."

He frowned, his mouth tight.

"Who is he?" Jonas said. "And who are you?"

"I'm Phillipa Butler, private security for the House of Blue. And he..." She stepped away as Fraser found his feet. "He's Captain America."

Jonas raised an eyebrow. "You're not wrong."

Fraser glared at him. Back to her. She held up a hand and headed to the kitchen. Turned on the light and grabbed a kettle and filled it with water.

"But what is the House of Blue?"

"It's the royal family of Lauchtenland," Fraser said. "She's Princess Imani's bodyguard."

"Who?"

"Just...a girl. An important girl. That Creed has apparently run off with."

Jonas let out a low whistle, and she turned on the water on the stove.

The two men stood there. Fraser still bare-chested—she blinked away the memory of them moments before, upstairs. Yeah, that was a close call.

Jonas wore a jean jacket, cargo pants, boots. But she was right—the two looked very similar, except for Jonas's lighter hair. Fierce, bold, and painfully handsome.

Maybe she had gotten her aim right, because there wasn't a hope of Fraser again looking at her the way he had upstairs.

Which was good. Very good. Because that guy was trouble. Distracting. Downright dangerous.

She turned to Jonas. "Her Royal Highness—and your little brother—are in big trouble. They're implicated in a murder in Geneva and have been on the run since. And the longer they're gone, the longer..." She drew in a breath. "We need to find them, and pronto."

"Which brings you here?" Jonas said. He'd dropped a satchel inside the sliding door and now set it on the sofa.

"We thought maybe he'd come here. Which begs the question—why are you here?" Fraser pulled out a chair at the table and sat down. He bore a red mark on his jaw that he seemed to be oblivious to.

"I've been working in a town about an hour east of here, Brescia, but I'm headed out to Slovenia in a couple days, and I've been camping out here between projects."

"And this is a thing—breaking in?" Fraser said.

Pippa couldn't help but smile.

"I left my key here last time, so I thought I'd do dad's trick." He lifted a shoulder. "And it's not really breaking in."

Fraser looked at Pippa. She rolled her eyes and turned back to the kettle, now shrieking.

She took it off, grabbed three cups, and searched for tea. She found a tin of bags as well as instant coffee and set that on the counter.

Jonas walked over and grabbed the coffee, ladling in a heaped tablespoon. "So, Creed did what?"

She set the kettle on a hot pad. "He and Imani hit it off on a gondola ride near Mont Blanc. They went out to a club, and I'm not sure what happened. I think there was mention of getting ice cream—"

"Ice cream."

"Imani has to have gelato wherever we go, so my guess is that it was her idea. But along the way, they got caught up in a murder—"

"A murder."

"A nuclear physicist," Fraser said, grabbing another cup. He, too, added coffee.

Americans.

Jonas took his cup to the table. "Creed isn't the type to murder anyone." He pulled out his phone and typed in something.

"What I said." Fraser also joined him. She noticed the red marks on his back. "But he was seen running from the scene with her. And now there's a BOLO out on him."

"There's more than that." Jonas showed his screen. "Apparently your House of Blue has listed him as a possible kidnapper of Her Royal Highness Princess Imani." The picture showed a formal shot of Creed in his track uniform, probably pulled from a college roster page. He turned back and flipped the screen. "Yeah, she's cute."

He turned the phone back around.

Imani. A paparazzi shot, taken in Athens. If he looked hard, he'd probably see Pippa standing not far away, trying to shoo away the photographers.

Imani didn't have a huge following, but her fame was growing.

Pippa closed her eyes, pressed her hands to her face. *Gunner, what are you doing?*

"We'll find her," Fraser said softly, a hint of the man from upstairs.

Pippa nodded. Raised her head. "We'd better. Before the royal guards do. Because even if your brother is innocent, Gunner and his team won't ask questions before they use lethal force to get her back."

Jonas stilled, as did Fraser. He got up, walked over to the sink, and poured out his coffee. Then turned to her. "We leave at 0400 for Portofino. Get some sleep."

Then he headed upstairs.

"Now, that guy I recognize," Jonas said. "May the force be with you."

Americans. So obsessed with their cinema. But yeah, that guy, the shirtless guy who didn't back down from a fight...that guy she needed.

Exhaustion, the release of the adrenaline after being tased—again—shut down Fraser's brain for a good three hours.

He slept like a stone, no more nightmares of Pippa being shot, her beautiful blue-gray eyes widening as he stood, unable to move, tied up and helpless as Abu held a gun to her head.

Yeah, no wonder he'd lost his common sense there when he woke to her standing there in the semidarkness. But she'd been the one to run into his room with her brown hair down, all wild-eyed and caring and—

He scrubbed his hands over his face and sat up. The dawn had just started seeping over the far mountains, cascading onto the surface of the lake like molten fire. Ringing the lake, the mountains had turned purple, the place serene, an enclave.

No wonder Iris had settled here. In her busy, challenging life, she needed a place for a time-out.

Maybe that's what the last twelve hours had been. A time-out. But now he needed to find Creed and get him to safety. And it did not include wrapping Pippa into his arms—and especially his life.

"You taking off?"

He turned, and Jonas was sitting up in a chair at the foot of his twin bed, reading on his phone.

"Don't you sleep?"

"Most of my work is done in the middle of the night, so...no. I usually grab some shut-eye after breakfast, get up around three. You still snore."

"No, I don't."

Jonas lifted a hand. "Sixteen years of sleeping next door to you. Trust me on this."

Fraser scooped up a pillow and threw it at him.

Jonas batted it to the floor with a smile. "How are you, man? Dad gave me the 411 in Geneva. Said you came home pretty wrecked."

"One day at a time." He flexed his hand. No change. "Just trying to get back in the game, you know?"

"Because?"

He had reached for his jeans and now looked at Jonas. "Because it's what I do. What I've always done. Who I am."

"But maybe it doesn't have to be."

He said nothing as he buttoned his jeans, reached for his shirt.

"Dude, you were *taken captive*. By *terrorists*."

"It's the job." Fraser tucked in his shirt, grabbed his socks.

"It *was* the job. But...maybe it's time to switch gears."

He'd sat down on a nearby chair and now looked up. "And do what? Make wine?"

Jonas shrugged. "Dad was acting sort of weird in Geneva."

This stopped him. "What?"

"We had dinner with them, after Creed's race. A couple times it looked like Dad wanted to say something, but Mom stopped him."

"Really." He sat back.

"Do you think he wants to sell the winery?"

No, that didn't make sense. "He has this guy, Neil, working for him. He's been working on new recipes for the La Crescent Gold, and the Marquette Crimson. Says they might be award-winning. I don't think...no. It's not that."

Jonas nodded. "You're probably right. It was just...something didn't feel right."

Fraser reached for his boots. "I'll talk to Dad about it next time I see him."

"By the way, does he know you're over here in Europe, chasing after Creed? I mean—does he even know what Creed is in to?"

"Nope and nope, I think. Creed called me on a burner phone, so I don't even know how to get ahold of him. And my guess is that he doesn't have my number. Our call got cut off—I told him to find Ned. I think he did, but Ned's off-the-grid, so..."

"You need help?"

"No. Pippa's pretty capable."

"Yeah, she is." He laughed.

"Funny. Again, she was aiming for you."

"Mm-hmm."

Fraser got up, grabbed his backpack.

"What's going on between you two?"

"Nothing."

"Yeah. Right. I'm trained to look for weather patterns. Anomalies. To forecast storms and especially lightning strikes. From where I'm sitting, that strike has come and gone, and you've got some sort of storm raging inside."

"No storm."

"It's Camy Simpson all over again."

Fraser stilled. Looked at him. "I was fifteen."

"And she had you all messed up in your head, if I remember right. You wrote her name on your notebook. Let her wear your jersey. Asked her out to homecoming."

"Whatever." He'd loaded in his gear, checked it, and now closed the bag.

"What happened there? One minute you're leaving for the dance, the next I see you leave in the middle of it."

He grabbed his toiletry bag. "Yep. But she went home with somebody else, so that's what you get for giving your heart away. Lesson learned. Thanks, bro, for that stroll down memory lane." He headed for the small adjoining bathroom.

He turned on the water, stared at himself in the mirror. Ran a hand over his beard. He needed a shave.

Jonas got up and came to the door. "Hey, thirty-three. I didn't mean it that way. Just...you like her. I see that."

He loaded up his toothbrush. "And what do you want me to do about it? She's part of the royal guard of Lauchtenland. It's not an easy position to get. And..." He looked at his brother through the mirror. "Frankly, I don't know what's next. Hopefully, I'll get feeling back in my hand, but Ham's right—I go back too early and people get killed. So...I got a big fat nothing on my horizon. Except, of course, going back to watch paint dry."

"You've been painting?"

Fraser brushed his teeth, spit. "I don't know, okay? I just know that I have to find Creed and get him out of trouble. Get

129

him home. And then...then I'll figure out how to...what to..."
He grabbed a towel.

"Oh, I get it. You're irked that you even like this girl."

"I barely know her."

"She impresses you."

He sighed. "Yes. A little."

"And she understands you too."

He looked away. *"I get it."* "Maybe. She knows what it means to give your life to something."

"But suddenly, you don't know what that is. And maybe, if you're honest, you want more."

He looked at Jonas and he put his toothbrush away. "Are we still talking about me?"

Jonas drew in a breath. "Maybe. Maybe not. But I know you. You never quit something without having something else waiting. You get injured in football, you start working out for hockey. You fail out of the first year of college, and you join the Navy."

"I never should have taken that scholarship for hockey. I always wanted to be a SEAL."

"And then you quit the SEALs and became private security. Sort of SEAL-lite, with fewer rules."

"Your point?"

"Seems to me that the trouble is that you want answers, right now. A place to put your focus. But sometimes it doesn't work that way. You have to live with the storm of indecision inside."

Fraser lifted a shoulder, then pushed back out of the bathroom.

Jonas followed him. "The problem isn't the storm. It's the idea that it won't work out the way you want. And you just can't take that."

Closing his backpack, he looked at Jonas. "You get a philosophy degree out there?"

"Lots of time to think while you're waiting for lightning to strike. More darkness than light." He paused. "The hardest part of waiting is the worry that it won't work out like you want. But, bro, that thought right there is the danger."

"What do you mean?"

"Because the more we wait, the more we're panicked. The more we're tempted to jump in, do something about it."

Fraser put the backpack over his shoulder. "I don't do well with sitting. I like to be doing something. It gives me purpose."

"I know. But what if you've turned your purpose into an idol?"

Fraser just blinked at him.

"Idolatry, at its core, is believing that something can give you what only a relationship with Jesus can. Maybe this time-out God has given you is His way of showing you that you need Him more than you need a grand purpose."

Fraser stood at the door. "I don't need a grand purpose."

"You've always needed a grand purpose. Even in grade school, when you wanted to own the hill."

Fine. He allowed himself a grin. "Who are you, and what did you do with my impulsive, storm-chasing brother?"

"He grew up a little. And storm chasing taught me to adapt and wait for the full picture to develop. And that includes Pippa."

"Again. There's nothing between us."

A beat, and in it, Fraser saw himself reaching out, capturing her hair between his fingers, longing for the taste of her lips on his.

Oh, wow, his heart banged hard against his chest.

"Sure there isn't," Jonas said. He stepped up to him, his hand out. "Be safe, bro."

Fraser grabbed his hand, then stepped in for a hug, slapped him on the back. "Don't get struck by lightning."

Jonas laughed.

"You sticking around long?"

"I'm taking off tomorrow. But I hope Iris gets back. When I texted her, she said she'd be here."

"You know how she is. Free spirit."

"Yeah. She's probably fine."

Something hung in his brother's eyes, though. "Something you're not telling me?"

Jonas shrugged. "Just a feeling that she's...I dunno. Maybe dating someone? She won't tell me. But this isn't the first time I've shown up expecting her, only to have her gone, without a word."

"That is weird."

"It's probably nothing. Listen, go find Creed."

Fraser clamped his brother on his shoulder, then headed out the door into the hall. The smell of coffee drifted upstairs.

Pippa was waiting in the kitchen, sipping tea in a cup. She looked up when he came down.

Natasha was back. She was dressed back in the black pants, boots, black shirt, her hair pulled back, all business.

Focus.

Except she handed him the cup and gave him a smile. "I made you coffee."

"You might have just saved my life."

She laughed. And everything inside him sort of exploded— the tight fist he had over the impulses from last night, the look of horror in her eyes last night when she had tased him.

And especially the sense that, suddenly, she wanted him along.

And worse, for a moment, she looked at him with something warm and determined and focused in her eyes, and he just wanted to step up to her, wrap his hand around her neck and kiss her.

He took a sip.

"That smells good." The voice came from Jonas as he came down the stairs.

Just like that, Jonas's words were in his head. *And maybe, if you're honest, you want more."*

He headed for the door. "I'll get the car." He'd parked down the street. He glanced at Jonas, who just grinned at him. "See you 'round." Then he walked past him out the door.

But as he stepped outside into the awakening morning, he thought he heard the whisper again from last night.

And this time it might have said...*Pippa.*

EIGHT

"We're almost there. Do you have a plan?"

Fraser's quiet words beside her jolted Pippa out of the conversation she'd been replaying in her head. The one where Jonas asked her, of all people, how his brother was doing.

From her vantage point, pretty bloody well. He still sported that dark beard, the one with tiny flecks of red, and he'd changed into a clean shirt, a pair of jeans, and bore a look that told her that today, they'd find Imani.

And Creed.

So yeah, he seemed pretty put together, and she said as much to Jonas as Fraser stepped out of the sliding door, walked across the patio, and then onto the street to get the car, which they'd ended up parking a few blocks away.

"Hmm," Jonas said.

"Why?" She probably hadn't needed to ask that. She didn't have time, really, but the way Jonas looked at his brother, then turned back to her, what looked like concern in his expression had her pausing. Asking.

He drew in a breath.

"He told me about Nigeria, if that's what you're worried

about." Maybe she wouldn't mention the nightmares, though. Seemed like if he wanted his brother to know, he would have told him.

Jonas filled a cup of coffee. "When I was twelve, there was this kid at our school—foster kid. But he especially didn't like me and used to throw around words on the playground. Fraser told me to ignore it, and usually, when he was around, they backed off. So I did. Then one day, he stayed after school and was waiting for me. Dante jumped me, and we got into a brawl. I might have been able to take him, but he had a couple kids with him, and when Fraser came out, I was down. Fraser freaked out and lit into the guys. They took off, but it dug into Fraser. He felt like he'd failed me."

"He's the oldest."

"And a team guy. And I'm not just talking about the SEALs. He's the guy who kicks the door down and goes in first. This injury, and the capture in Nigeria, has really done a number on him. One of the guys he was with was killed. And the doc he was protecting got shot. I think he feels like he has something to prove. To himself. Maybe to God."

She'd finished her tea by then, but Jonas's words sank in. "And Creed. He told me about the fight with Creed."

"Right. Yeah, that was bad. Back then, he was probably thinking about the kid I tussled with. But Creed is a Marshall now."

"And Marshalls have each other's backs?"

"Always. And I think he looks at you as a partner, so I'm hoping you have his back too."

His words hung in her head as she nodded, then washed her cup and headed out to find Fraser. He was waiting in the Panda, getting a GPS route to Portofino.

"Ready, Natasha?" he'd asked as she got in, that familiar, easy spark to his blue eyes. But she knew the truth.

She knew what he was hiding.

Because she hid it too.

The fear that, at the end of the day, people would die. And it would be all her fault.

"Ready, Captain."

They stopped for breakfast enroute at an autostrada just south of Milan. She bought a hot panini and a coffee and decided that she didn't mind road-tripping with Fraser. He told her stories of the winery, how his father had taken the legacy dairy farm and turned it into a vineyard, the different varietals of wine they produced. She told him about growing up in Lauchtenland, the House of Blue, and the story of Prince John losing his first wife to a horse accident, meeting and marrying Princess Gemma, and some of Imani's past year's travels.

"You really rode a camel?"

"And an elephant. And took a canoe up the Amazon. This girl—" She shook her head. "I can't wait to wake up every day to a schedule and not having to worry if the person I'm supposed to protect will suddenly try and ditch me for deep-fried squid on a stick."

He looked at her.

"Taiwan. Night market."

"She does seem like a handful."

For some reason, his words sparked something inside her. "No, she's just really inquisitive. And an American. You Yanks like to do things your own way."

He laughed then. Glanced at her. "Yeah, we do."

They were just outside the city of Santa Margherita, east of Portofino. They descended out of the grip of the mountains, the terrain surrendering to the sea. The route drove them through the city until they came out to a harbor, yachts and motorboats lined up at the long docks.

The town could be a postcard, with its tangerine or lemon painted homes that climbed the hillside, their terraces over-looking the blue-gray of the Mediterranean Sea. Palm trees grew from manicured planters along the boardwalk, and as they drove along the coast, passing scooters and bicycles, the smell of the sea filtered through Fraser's open window.

Ahead, another harbor, this one more enclosed, hosted sailboats, their tall masts dissecting the cloudless blue sky.

"What's the yacht called?" Fraser said.

"The *Serenity*. They docked off Portofino for the week. A sort of holiday before the summit in Geneva. But they can't get into the Portofino port, so they have a rented slip, here, for the tender that goes from ship to shore."

"How do we get to it?"

She'd been humming over that problem since leaving Como. That, and Jonas's words. *I'm hoping you have his back too.*

She didn't know what to do with that. "I could call the ship, but I'm not sure how to get ahold of it. And I'd really like to get to Imani and Creed before Gunner."

"Because of the shoot first, ask questions later thing? Yeah, me too."

"Maybe we rent Jet Skis?" She pointed to a building overlooking the harbor that rented skis and scooters.

"Brilliant." He pulled into a nearby spot across from the harbor. He left his backpack, so she did too, and then he pocketed the keys and they headed across the street.

A younger man greeted them in Italian as they entered, and somehow between Pippa's broken Italian and Fraser's basic grasp, they managed to rent the last two-seater available.

"I'm driving," Pippa said, and to her surprise, Fraser nodded.

But he returned to the car and came back with a monocular.

The Jet Ski was beached on the far side of the harbor, in the sand, and she'd already familiarized herself with the controls. Fraser helped her move the machine into the water, floating there. She noticed he kept his boots on as he walked into the water.

She'd taken hers off and stuck them in the seat compartment, then donned a life jacket.

He slipped one on too.

Now she boarded the Jet Ski, leaning forward so he could climb on in back.

The sense of him behind her, his strong legs on either side of her hips, his fingers looped into her life jacket felt...

Maybe Jonas was right. Partners.

"Let's search the harbor," he said.

They motored around the harbor, searching the yachts. She'd never seen the *Serenity*, so she didn't know what, exactly, it looked like. But nothing in the harbor seemed fit for the House of Blue.

"There's plenty of boats on the horizon," Fraser said, scanning with his monocular.

"We'll head toward Portofino," she said and gunned them out to sea.

The water sprayed out behind them, droplets landing on her skin, her hair. Fraser seemed to move with her on the Jet Ski. The sea had turned choppy as the sun rose, as the wind rolled in from northern horizons.

They traveled up the coast toward the tiny port city of Portofino, the coastline rising, turning rocky. Estates sat on top of the hills, amongst tall cedars, and the sea turned a deep aquamarine. She'd never been to Portofino but had seen it in pictures. Houses built right against the coastline, only the boardwalk between the front door and the sea.

As they traveled, Fraser began scanning the boats at anchor, spilling out from the tiny inlet that led into the harbor.

"Get out farther—there's a boat about a mile out that's deep blue." He'd leaned down to shout into her ear.

She followed his point and spotted the yacht. Four stories, rising from the sea, with a deep-royal-blue hull. The Lauchtenland flag flew from the tall communications mast.

"That's the one." She turned and headed out across the waves. Spray hit her face as they plowed forward, fighting.

Fraser's hand tightened on her waist.

As they drew closer, she spotted a couple boats tied up to the back deck. She slowed just as Fraser moved to her ear. "Take a look."

Then he leaned around her and took control of the steering, the throttle.

She let go, he handed her the monocular and grabbed the other side.

Felt a little close to be tucked into his embrace like this, but it was better than stopping and being sent back to shore in the chop.

He did slow, however, even as he kept them moving forward.

"What do you want to do?"

It took a moment to find the boat, then to spot what Fraser saw.

But the moment her gaze landed on the group of men standing on the back deck, she stilled.

"They look armed to me."

He wasn't wrong. She made out Fredrik and a handful of other officers, she imagined torn from their job protecting the Lauchtenland contingency in Geneva to apprehend a runaway princess and her cohort. Although, if said princess was returning to her parents' yacht, how runaway could she be? How kidnapped?

"Why are they here?"

"I don't know," she said.

"It looks like you said—shoot first, ask questions later. We need to get there before Creed does. Get behind me." He let go with his left hand and leaned away.

She turned to look at him. "What? I can drive."

But something about his expression had changed, and she saw a fierceness that very much reminded her of her father.

Then, "Please, Pippa." He didn't have to say it—she saw it in those blue eyes. Former Navy SEAL.

A warrior who made his living on the water.

She stood up, and as he leaned to the right, she turned around and climbed behind him.

Settled in.

"Hold on to the handles by your seat, and whatever happens, don't let go."

She leaned back, found the handles, and tightened her grip. "I'm good!"

And with that, he opened up the throttle on the Jet Ski.

They took the first wave on the nose, plowing through it, the spray saturating her. And then they planed out and suddenly, she was flying. He stood up, negotiating the waves as they jetted off the crests, landing in the valleys then climbing and launching again. Water wet her face, but she found the rhythm as they rode the waves. He finally sat down, cutting the engine and motoring them toward the yacht.

Impressive, with not only four decks, but the bottom deck had a space for Jet Skis and other watercraft, the sizable motor craft that ferried them to shore stored behind in a garage that could lift the motor craft up and store it inside the yacht.

At the prow, a helipad accommodated the land-to-sea needs, as well as any dignitaries or family that joined them at sea. Above that, two more decks hosted a hot tub, a dining area, and twelve staterooms, along with living quarters for the staff and captain. The eagle's nest was armed with state-of-the-art radar, communications, and even weaponry, should the ship come under attack.

She'd read the specs shortly after the superyacht joined the fleet of royal transportation, just in case she ever landed duty aboard the House of Blue yacht.

Apparently, today was that day.

Gunner had moved his men out around the yacht, all of them in uniform, a serious bunch armed to the teeth.

Creed was apparently the number one threat to the Crown, enemy numero uno.

"What is going on?" She voiced her thought aloud as they came up to the boat, stopping about twenty feet away.

"Stop!" A young man—she didn't recognize him, so he must be in the newest fleet of recruits—pointed his sidearm in their direction.

"Whoa, hang on there, Captain Lauchtenland." Fraser turned off the motor and lifted his hands. "We're the good guys. I've got Her Royal Bodyguard Pippa Butler here—"

"Where is Gunner Ferguson?" Pippa asked over Fraser and his bumbling of protocol. "Radio to him. Tell him that Pippa Butler is here."

"That's what I said." Frasier dropped his hand to the throttle.

"Stop!"

Fraser lifted his hand again. "You weren't kidding."

Nope, not in the least. Not when it came to the royal family. They bobbed in the water, the sun hot, and she took a moment to scan the ship.

Didn't seem as if Creed was aboard yet so maybe—

"Pippa?" Fredrik came running down the sideboard of the ship. "Hold," he shouted to the recruit, who lowered his sidearm. He waved them in.

Fraser turned on the machine and gently throttled it toward the boat.

"What's going on here?" Pippa said.

"We're waiting for kidnapping demands," Fredrik said, reaching out to help her aboard the yacht.

"Kidnapping—" Fraser followed her out, tying off the front line of the Jet Ski to the stern. "You guys have got this way wrong."

"Really." Fredrik turned to him, then back to Pippa. "We intercepted a call from Imani to you yesterday morning."

She stared at him. "What? Why didn't I get it?"

"I don't know. She said, however, that the only way she's coming back is if conditions are met. When Gunner asked what those were, she wouldn't speak to anyone but you or her mother."

That made sense. Princess Gemma might be the only one Pippa trusted right now too.

Okay, not the only one. Fraser stood beside her, his jaw tight. *I think he looks at you as a partner...*

"Creed didn't kidnap her."

"Sure looks like he did." Fredrik pulled out his phone. "We pulled this off the CCTV in the park. They got it to us shortly after you left for Lake Como."

She looked at the footage he pulled up on his phone. A grainy picture of what looked like a park where, under the lights—yes, Imani, running down the sidewalk.

And behind her, a man—yes, she recognized Creed as he came into the light.

Then the picture turned hazy, but she could still make out the man grabbing Imani around the waist, his hand around her mouth, pulling her into the woods.

"That looks like a woman running from a murderer to me," Fredrik said. He tucked the phone back into his pocket.

"Why are you here?"

"Because we were able to grab the phone's MAC address and trace the call. They were in Geneva, but before we got to them, they'd left."

"Geneva," Pippa said. Glanced at Fraser. His mouth had tightened.

"We picked up the signal a few hours ago, however, in Milan."

"Milan?"

"We did a search—they might have taken a night train from Geneva to Milan, hopped on a day train to Santa Margherita. Less conspicuous."

"But why come here if she's been kidnapped?"

Fredrik gave her a thin lipped shake of his head. "Konrad Vogel."

She stilled. "Wait—"

"Yes, the son the Bernd Vogel."

A beat. "No."

"Who is Bernd Vogel?" Fraser asked.

She turned to him, her chest thickening. "The man who killed my father."

Fraser, appropriately, just stared at her.

"And, more appropriately, the man who killed PM Fickle."

She turned back to Fredrik.

"What does this have to do with Imani and Creed?"

Fredrik pulled out his phone again. "Look familiar?"

It was the man in the red jacket from the gondola. Talking with Creed at the top of the mountain, on the Italian side. After she and Pippa had left to buy tickets back. "That's Konrad, talking with your boy there."

He pressed the video—also grabbed from CCTV, given the quality—and saw the two chatting. And then Creed handed him something.

"What is that?"

"We zoomed in. Looked like a brochure, but who knows what was on it," Fredrik said. "We're not taking any chances. If this guy has Imani, then who knows what he wants."

"Nothing," Fraser said. "He wants nothing. I don't know how he got mixed up in all this, but I can promise you, he's innocent."

Fredrik pocketed the phone. "We'll see after we apprehend him."

A man came running down the gangway. She recognized

him—Lanny Bickel. "Sir Gunner, Imani just tried to call her mother."

Pippa looked at him. "The prince and princess are on board?"

"No. They aren't here—they're touring Cinque Terre for the day. By the time they get back, this will be all over."

"They don't *know*?"

Fredrik held up his hand. He turned to Bickel. "And?"

"The call went to voice mail, but Imani told her mother they were coming out to the boat. They're on their way, and we're ready."

Pippa couldn't ignore the way Fraser's jaw tightened. She turned to him. "I promise. I won't let anything happen to him."

He turned to her. Drew in a breath. "I'll hold you to that."

"I don't know about this, Imani." Creed sat in the back of their water taxi, the wind in his face, his hand clasped in hers—this time his move, because something just didn't feel right in his gut.

Despite the beauty of the day, the bright sun arching overhead, the multi-colored buildings that surrounded the harbor, the fishing boats, the squawking seagulls swooping in for lunch...

Innocent, but still...

"Are you okay?" Imani glanced at him. She had her hair tied up and back with one of the teal scarves he'd purchased. Somehow, on the night train, he'd managed not to touch her hand, managed not to make a move, despite the way she laughed and looked at him like he might be a hero. He'd bought them a pizza at a kiosk—that was cool. And Fanta, and some cookies. And they'd played *gin rummy* and *war* and a game called *kings in the corner*, and she'd told him about her life in Hearts Bend, Tennessee, where she grew up before moving to Lauchtenland.

At the least, they were friends.

Maybe that was it. In less than ten minutes, he'd deliver her to her parents, and then...then she'd return to her palace, and he would go back to Minnesota.

He could make out the big blue yacht in the distance. This all felt like a weird fairy tale. And now, after all their running, this felt too easy.

"Creed. Seriously. What's going on?"

He ran a hand around the back of his neck. "I dunno. It's just...a feeling. Like the day my little sister was shot."

"Your sister was shot?"

"Drive-by shooting. She was eight. We were playing in the yard. My mom had found this cool sandbox at a yard sale—it was shaped like a turtle—and I had this set of hot wheels. I would make roads and tunnels and...anyway, I heard a car back-fire, and I stood up. We were in our yard—there was a chain link fence around it, and my mom always kept it nice, you know? With flowers and a swing set. Safe.

Janelle was playing on the front walk, her Barbies set up. She had this little car she like to drive."

He didn't realize his voice had thickened until Imani squeezed his hand.

"Sorry. I don't know. I just always see her there, playing with her Barbies. We had a cat, and I remember it looking at me a second before it mewed, then jumped away. Because right behind it came the car. An old caravan. It was driving too fast, and just before it got to us, the door slid open."

He drew in a breath. "I think I shouted, I don't know, but I... I just stood there, paralyzed, watching. It was my sister who grabbed me. She pulled me down, and we hid behind the sand-box. Only, one of the bullets ricocheted and..." He looked at Imani. "She was shot."

"Oh, Creed."

"Yeah. They never caught the guys. My brother was in a gang, and it was a sort of gang initiation for a different gang—they were supposed to get him. But...anyway, ever since then, every once in a while, I get that feeling inside, that a drive-by is about to happen."

"And you feel this right now?"

He stared out at the beautiful azure-blue water, holding on to the side as it got choppy. He wore a lifejacket, because he wasn't the greatest of swimmers. "Stupid. We're fine."

"We are. I just need to talk to my mom. She'll clear this all up."

The Italian that helmed their small fishing boat—he'd hired the man for an hour to take them out to the yacht—began to gesture to the boat.

And a big boat it was. Shiny blue hull, four stories, a flag at the top whipping in the wind. And a slew of boats tied up to the back. Maybe it even had a pool.

"Any idea what he's saying?"

Imani shook her head. But she smiled and nodded to the man, pointing to the boat. "Yes, that's the *Serenity*."

"Nice boat."

"It's new. I've never been on it."

Cool. But what he really wanted was a way to tell her that... maybe she'd changed his life a little. Made him realize that he might be a little more Marshall than he thought.

That he, too, could be a hero.

They drew closer and he cupped his hands over his eyes. Stilled. "Imani. They have guns."

She, too, shaded her eyes, searching the boat. Her hand tightened in his. "He's here."

"Who's here?"

She looked at him. "The guy from the park. The shooter."

"Which one?" No, wait, it didn't matter. He turned to the driver. "Turn around."

The man couldn't understand him, so Creed stood up and gestured with his arm. "Turn. Around!"

The driver frowned at them under his Italian fisherman's hat. Creed reached over and pulled the throttled back.

The boat stilled in the water, the momentum driving it forward. "Go back!"

Shouts from the boat, and now the driver stood up in his seat. Said something to them in Italian—gesturing wildly.

Yeah, whatever, whatever—

Imani stood up and took his hand. "Why is he here?"

"I don't know—"

And that's when the Italian gunned it. He cranked the wheel and put the throttle down and spun the boat so hard that Imani went flying. She stumbled right over the edge of the boat—

And Creed went with her. He managed to catch himself on the edge, and Imani's grip tore from his.

"Imani!"

But the boat was speeding away, and Creed couldn't even see her in the mess of foam and spray.

Aw— He leaped up on the seat and jumped in.

The chill of the water shocked him, and he kicked to the surface.

The boat churned up the wake, and for a second, the wash caught him, stirring him. But he kicked and held on to his life jacket. "Imani!"

"Here!" She raised her hand, also bobbing in the water. "Creed!"

He kicked toward her, fighting the waves, wishing he'd learned how to swim better back in grade school. Water filled his mouth, and he spit it out, still kicking toward her.

A motor revved not far from him, but he kept his gaze on Imani, still waving her hands.

"Imani!" He caught her grip and pulled her in, holding on to her life jacket. "I got ya. I got ya!"

She held his wrists, her big hazel eyes in his, breathing hard. "What are we going to do?"

"Creed!"

The voice lifted over the waves.

What—

He searched, listening as the voice called again.

It couldn't be.

Then he saw him. Skimming over the water in a Jet Ski, the one guy, the very last guy that Creed expected. Or maybe the only guy that Creed could really expect, because that's who he was...

The oldest Marshall brother, swooping in to save the day. Sunlight burnished his dark-blond hair, and he looked every bit as rugged and fierce as Creed remembered him.

Always scared him a little, honestly.

Not today. "Fraser?"

He stretched his hand out even as he slowed the Jet Ski. Creed grabbed it.

"I got you, bro."

Bro. But he didn't stop to let the word find his bones. Instead, he pushed Imani toward Fraser. "You can trust him. He's my brother!"

Imani's mouth opened, but she nodded.

Fraser pulled her up onto the ski. Looked at Creed. "Can you tread water?"

"Yeah." Not entirely true, but he had the life jacket.

As Fraser gunned it, the foam and waves the Jet Ski churned up left Creed spitting, blinking, wiping seawater from his eyes.

Fraser. What was his brother *doing* here?

Moments later, Fraser appeared again, this time alone, and pulled Creed from the water, counterbalancing as he levered himself up on the seat and then Creed climbed behind him.

"Hold on," Fraser said, then smiled at him. "Good to see you, kid."

And Creed had absolutely nothing as Fraser drove them to the yacht.

Imani stood on the deck, a towel wrapped around her, dripping, waiting for him. And next to her stood Pippa. He couldn't read her face. Worry? Relief?

But for a moment, as they slowed, gliding in to the deck of the massive yacht, the drive-by feeling filled his gut.

Something...

"Jump off, kid," Fraser said as he held the Jet Ski.

Creed climbed off, onto the deck, and approached Imani. "You okay?"

She smiled at him, glanced at Pippa. "Yeah—"

That's all she got out before guards emerged from the salon and deck beyond her, their guns drawn, shouting. "Get down! On your face!"

What—

He put up his hands. Met Imani's eyes. She was shaking her head, shouting, "Leave him alone!"

And then Fraser was there, right beside him, hands out. "Stand back. Stay where you are!"

It was Pippa who gave the order. He saw it in the slight nod of her head, the way her lips tightened.

Then Creed's body was hit with volts, a charge that sent him to his knees, knocked out his breath, and caught the scream in his throat.

Fraser caught him as he went down, his own body convulsing.

He couldn't move. Couldn't breathe as the guards rolled him over, then cuffed him. They finally removed the barbs.

Next to him, Fraser was also cuffed, face down, a man standing over him. They hadn't removed Fraser's barbs. "Stay down and no one gets hurt."

Fraser turned his head, looking at Creed, meeting his eyes. "Sorry, kid."

And he didn't want to say *I knew it*—but, yeah, he knew it.

He wasn't a hero. Never had been. Never would be.

Then someone picked up Creed by his shoulders, shoved a hood over his head, and led him, stumbling, away.

"MY BROTHER IS NOT AN ASSASSIN!"

Fraser rounded on Pippa the moment the door closed to the quarters where they'd confined him. Staff quarters, because there wasn't a window in the room. Just a very small bunk and, thankfully, a toilet, because the sea had kicked up, and with it, a weird and frustrating bout of seasickness.

Or maybe that was just his frustration roiling over.

Could be his body rejecting a third jolt of electricity in three days. Hello.

"Keep your voice down. The prince and princess are due on board in a minute, and we don't need you shouting."

Pippa had changed, wore a fresh Lauchtenland uniform. Blue, with a blue suit-jacket and gold cuffs, her hair primly back.

And she smelled good too. While he felt like something that had been dragged from the depths of the sea. Salt in his hair, on his skin.

"Where's Creed?"

"Being interrogated."

"He'd better have all his fingernails when you guys are finished."

"We're not those kind of interrogators. Wow, it's small in here." She touched her head where she'd bumped it on the bunk.

He just looked at her. She stood about three feet away, taking up all his pacing space. Okay, maybe he didn't have to shout.

Just wanted to. Still, he schooled his voice. "What is wrong with you people! You don't just tase someone. Sheesh."

"It could have been worse."

"How?"

"We could have shot him."

He just stared at her for a long moment. "Shot him. For what? He was surrendering."

"He was approaching the princess—"

"Probably to ask her for help. Maybe she'd also promised him that nothing would happen to him."

Pippa's eyes briefly narrowed, then she cleared her throat. "We didn't know that."

"He spent three days with her!" Yeah, he was shouting again, but he didn't care if the entire country heard him. "If he wanted to hurt her, he would have done it already. He clearly cares for her. You saw him dive in the sea to grab her. He doesn't swim well, by the way."

She swallowed. "He was in a stressful situation—people are unpredictable in a stressful situation."

"I was *right there*. I wasn't going to let him do anything."

"And if you couldn't stop him? We couldn't take that chance."

"So you had to tase me too?"

Her mouth tightened.

He stared at her. "Did you learn nothing about me when we were together?"

She sighed. "I'm sorry it had to end this way."

"Yeah, me too, Natasha. Just stay away from me."

She turned toward the door.

"No, come back here."

She sighed and turned around. "What?"

"What's next?"

She wore a grim look. "He'll be returned to Lauchtenland for further investigation. Trial. Sentencing."

He just stared at her. "You're serious?"

"Yes. She's a royal princess. What did you think would happen?"

"Um, that you'd listen to her, to him. Find out what really went on."

"He was seen with a known assassin, Fraser. We need to sort that out."

He ran his hands over his face. Lowered his voice. "Let me talk to him."

"That's not a great idea."

He just stared at her. She looked away.

"Pippa. He's scared. He's alone. And you and I both know that there's something else going on here. He'll tell you everything he knows—I'm sure of it. But let me figure out what he doesn't know."

She started to shake her head.

"I was a SEAL. I was trained to not only interrogate people but to hear what they weren't saying. Let me talk to him."

"You'll only try to help him escape."

He blinked.

"Promise me you won't."

"Won't—"

She met his eyes. "Help him escape."

He couldn't make that promise. So he held up three fingers. "Scout's honor."

She gave him a look, then finally nodded. "Okay. When they're done talking to him, I'll come and get you. And then, Fraser, you're leaving this boat."

He blinked at her. "What?"

"Your journey with Her Majesty's Security Detail is concluded. I need to get the princess back to safety. There will be a boat waiting to help you leave."

She met his eyes, and for a second, he thought that hers glistened. "Thank you, Captain, for everything you did."

Another beat, as if...as if she might be waiting for him to say something. Do something.

And for all the rage inside him, for a second, he saw himself reaching up to take down that silky dark hair. Saw himself touching her cheek with his hand, then winding his hand around the back of her neck and gently, sweetly, easing away the grim slash of her mouth.

Because in truth, he just couldn't believe that she'd betrayed him.

Then she turned and let herself out of the room.

The door locked behind her.

He sat on the bunk.

What just happened?

She didn't just...tell him how to escape the ship?

No, he was reading into that. But he had a Jet Ski. He didn't need help getting himself and Creed off the boat, unless...

Unless the princess—and Pippa—were going to escape with him?

Because there was no way that Pippa Butler would betray her country.

He lay back in the bunk and tried to think of the horizon.

Maybe he'd slept a little, because he woke to footsteps outside his door. It opened, and he sat up, blinking into the sudden light.

Fredrik stood in the frame. "Pippa asked me to fetch you. Said you wanted a few words with your boy before you were escorted off the boat."

He got up, stretched. Fredrik held open the door as he came out.

"Sorry about the take down, old boy. Just following protocol." Fredrik slapped him on the shoulder.

Fraser ignored him. "I'd better find my brother in one piece."

"Oh, we haven't succumbed to waterboarding yet, Yank. We're still civilized over on our side of the pond."

The sun had set, simmering over the ocean, rays of deep orange casting over the platinum-gray sea.

Fredrik led him up the stairs to the second floor and down the gangway to a small salon. From the look of the room, it seemed it might be the captain's office.

Creed sat in a chair, his hands still tied behind his back, his eyes closed, head down, hair around his face.

"Has he had anything to eat?" Fraser said, closing the door behind him.

Fredrik looked at him. Fraser met his gaze, raised an eyebrow.

"As you wish." He nodded to a man by the door, then left.

Fraser sat in a chair opposite Creed. "You okay?"

He raised his head. Open his eyes. Fraser hated the despair in them.

"I feel like I was kicked by an elephant."

"You'll be okay." He looked at the guard by the door. "Undo his hands. He needs a drink."

"No," the guard said, and Fraser worked very hard at shoving his hands into his pockets.

"Fine." He got up, poured a glass of water from a pitcher on a table, then held it to Creed's mouth. The kid leaned his head back and drank.

"Thanks."

Fraser sat back down. "Listen. I know there's a long story behind all this, but give me the short of it."

Creed leaned back. "I didn't kidnap her."

"Not for a second did I think that," Fraser said.

Creed lifted an eyebrow.

"You're a Marshall. And because of that, I'm here. And I choose to believe you, okay?"

Something sparked in his brother's eyes, and he nodded. "Okay."

Fraser leaned forward. "Now, tell me the story."

Fredrik came in somewhere after the great escape from the hotel room in Lausanne. Fraser got him to agree to cut Creed's zip ties while he scarfed down a piece of cold chicken. It looked good, but Fraser's gut still didn't want food.

He continued with their trip back to Geneva, seeing the train accident, and then their overnight train to Portofino.

"Why didn't you just come back to the hotel?"

Creed wiped his mouth with a napkin. "Imani..." He glanced at Fredrik, back to Fraser. "Imani only trusts Pippa. And her mom."

He was lying...but Fraser nodded and leaned back.

"Okay, kid, back to the cuffs."

"Seriously?" Fraser stood up.

"Orders," Fredrik said. "Until we can confirm he's not involved in an assassination attempt."

"I'm not!" Creed punched to his feet.

Fraser caught his shoulders. "We know that."

"He doesn't!" Creed looked at Fredrik, back to Fraser. "He just sees me and has me pegged as a criminal."

Yes, Fraser could see how Creed might feel that way. "What were you doing, talking to a guy in red parka?"

Creed just stared at him, nothing of guile in his brown eyes. "I don't know. I keep telling them that. I don't know this guy. I didn't even remember him until they showed me a picture. I gave him my brochure of Old Town Geneva. He said he was headed there—that's all I know. All I did. Until I found Imani running." His eyes had glazed a little.

"I believe you."

"Time's up, American."

Creed's breathing hiccupped. "You're leaving?"

No. "Sorry, kid."

"But—I thought you said—"

"There's nothing more I can do." *Yes, Creed. I've got your back. Just trust a little.*

"No. I'm not staying here. I didn't do anything! I was just trying to help Imani!" He kicked the chair, fighting his restraints.

The royal guard by the door stepped toward them.

Fraser wrapped his arms around Creed. "Shh. Stop struggling. Or they're going to tase you."

Creed was shaking, and he hated that for him. That he couldn't tell him to hold tight.

That Fraser was coming right back around to take him off this ship and out of the clutches of the Lauchtenland Royal Guard.

Because he wasn't leaving without his brother. That was a promise.

"Nil Desperandum," he said quietly in his ear. Then met Creed's eyes, nodded, and walked away.

Fredrik led him down the gangway to his Jet Ski.

Fraser climbed on. Looked at Fredrik. "He's a good man."

"He's a man in trouble. But if he's innocent, we'll honor that." Fredrik held out his hand.

Fraser debated, then shook it.

He pulled away from the boat, firing up the ski, heading back across the waves, the wan light enough to see shore. He knew Fredrik watched him, so he kept moving until the boat became a distant light.

Then he stopped the Jet Ski and waited for the sun to set.

Nil Desperandum. *Don't despair, Creed.*

NINE

E ither way, if Imani's story was right or wrong, someone
was committing treason. And Pippa dearly hoped it
wasn't her.

But maybe treason was the only way to get to the truth. And
the longer Pippa sat and listened to Imani's story, the more she
felt it in her gut.

Imani still wasn't safe.

They couldn't stay.

"Are you absolutely sure about what you saw?"

She'd secured them in Imani's cabin, located on the second
level, just down the hall from where Creed sat in lockup.

"Yes," Imani said. She'd showered, changed into a pair of
jeans and a T-shirt, her hair combed back into a tight bun. And
she'd gone from terrified and shivering, wrung out from the
dunk in the sea, to angry and pacing. "I'm sure it was Gunner
Ferguson who shot the man."

Gunner. Pippa was trying hard to wrap her brain around
Gunner Ferguson murdering someone. But what if Konrad was
up to his father's tricks—taking down people loyal to the
Crown?

Seemed like Gunner might be protecting the realm.

But it also gave reason to why he might be chasing Imani. To explain?

No, it didn't feel right, any of it, starting with arresting Creed.

She'd had to drag a hysterical Imani to her room, wrap her in a towel, and tell her to calm down.

Even she'd been gutted to see Creed tased. But he had made a lunge toward Imani, and the guards had protocol.

"He didn't do anything! He took care of me—I begged him to bring me here, and he did. And you tased him?"

"Calm down, Your Highness," she'd finally said and made her sit in the bed of her stateroom. "We'll get to the bottom of this, but we need to remember who you are—"

"I'm nobody!"

"That, Princess, is not true. And it's that lie that keeps getting us in this mess."

Imani stared at her then, as if hearing the words for the first time. She finally wiped her face.

"Now, tell me what happened."

Imani told her the entire story, from the moment she'd left the VIP club.

"And Creed was the perfect gentleman the entire time. He saved me from the man who broke into the hotel," Imani had said during her telling of their adventure. "He had a knife, and he looked like he wanted to kill me."

She had to give Imani kudos for cracking the lamp over the man's head. And Creed for thinking fast to get them over the balcony.

But the only conclusion was that the man who had chased Imani and Creed in the park was in league with the man who'd come after them in the hotel.

And that's when she decided.

They were leaving the yacht. Tonight.

With Fraser.

Then she left to communicate that to him after leaving Imani, before Fraser got kicked off the *Serenity*.

She'd seen Fraser walked by her door, being escorted off the boat, and dearly hoped he'd gotten her hint.

Please.

Pippa now sat in a nearby overstuffed chair. The sun had set, the moon rising, a trail of luminous light tracing the dark water. They needed to move, and fast, because if she knew Fraser, he'd be back for Creed anytime.

And if she was leaving, it would be with Captain America.

She put her hands over her face. What was she thinking? She should just tell Prince John what she knew—

And then what? Even if Gunner was arrested or detained, who was this other man?

"Pippa?"

"Just thinking, Your Highness."

"You believe me, right?"

She looked up. Imani had been all fire and spit an hour ago. Now she looked at Pippa with such hope, something moved inside her.

For all Imani's independence and rebellion, it wasn't easy to be alone. To be the one who didn't fit in. The one who people looked at as different.

No wonder she'd wanted to leave Lauchtenland. Spent the year trying to find a place to fit in. Pippa got that too.

She took Imani's hands. "Yes. I do. And I'm going to keep you safe. But first, we need to talk to your mother."

"Why?"

And here came the crazy part. "Because I don't think it's safe to go back to Lauchtenland."

Imani drew in a breath, her hazel eyes wide. "Because you think they won't believe me about Gunner?"

"He's a decorated soldier. And the captain of the guard. But I believe you, Imani, and I don't want you near him until we can figure this out."

She'd never seen Imani look at her the way she did then.

It was all she needed to request an audience with Princess Gemma. Of course, it helped that Imani went first into her mother's room and then invited Pippa in.

And it helped that Princess Gemma, too, was American. That she understood her daughter's independent spirit. There was that moment when Imani told her mother that Creed had been tased, and Pippa thought maybe she'd be discharged then and there. But no, and to Princess Gemma's credit, she simply pursed her lips and nodded.

But fear hung in her expression.

And then she asked Pippa for her opinion of the situation.

Her. Opinion.

"Permission to speak freely, ma'am?" Pippa asked, and Princess Gemma, with all her regal beauty, simply pulled out a chair and patted it.

"Please sit down, Pippa. You've earned it after the crazy year with my daughter."

No comment there, of course, but Pippa couldn't believe she was sitting across from Princess Gemma, having a conversation.

"And yes, please. Say what you need to say."

Pippa paused, then, "I know that's a lot to take in. And that probably, you just want to send Imani back to Lauchtenland. But I have an idea."

Princess Gemma's mouth tightened, and she glanced at Imani, back to Pippa. "I'm listening."

"Thank you, ma'am. The man I was with—Creed's brother— he's a former Navy SEAL and works private security. I'd like to hire him to keep watch over Imani with me, just until we figure out what is going on. If Gunner is...if he has committed murder, then we need to know why. And we need to find this man who attacked Imani. But most of all, I need to keep Imani safe. And I believe he will help me. Us. Lauchtenland. Because he is—"

"Not from Lauchtenland."

"Correct, ma'am. And we can trust him."

Princess Gemma looked at Imani, then back at Pippa. "And I trust you, Pippa. You've done a fantastic job of keeping Imani safe this year. And I know she can be a handful." She looked at Imani, and the two shared a look.

For a second, Pippa's heart squeezed.

It reminded her, much, of the look she used to share with her father. To know and be known, and understood.

She missed that.

Princess Gemma sighed and closed her eyes, shaking her head. "Gunner is..." She opened her eyes. "He's John's most trusted officer. Served as his private security officer for years. We trust him implicitly."

"I share your confusion, ma'am. But..." Pippa glanced at Imani. "I also believe your daughter."

"So do I." She reached out and took Imani's hand. Then she gave Pippa a fierce look. "You trust this man?"

The words sank inside, found her bones. "With my life. With Imani's life."

Princess Gemma got up then and walked to the window. "And he'd take her where?"

"I haven't asked him yet, so I don't know. But I will keep you informed."

The princess wrapped her arms around herself as if holding in the what-ifs, the spirally sense of crazy. Pippa got it. She was barely keeping up herself.

"Okay." Princess Gemma turned. "Okay. I'll allow this man—"

"Fraser Marshall, ma'am."

"Yes. To assist in the personal protection of Imani until John and I figure out what is going on. As long as you are there."

"Every moment, ma'am. And thank you." She took a breath. "Can I ask another request?"

"Please."

"Don't tell anyone except His Royal Highness where we are going. Or with whom. If someone is after Imani, I don't want them to know where we are."

"Of course." She reached out and took Imani's hand. "You keep my daughter safe. That is your only job."

"With my life, ma'am."

The princess nodded, then she stood and embraced Imani. Whispered something into her ear.

Imani nodded as Pippa went to the door. She checked her watch. Please, let them not be too late. "We need to get going."

"What are we going to do?" Imani said as she slipped out behind Pippa onto the gangway.

"Pick up your backpack. Then go down to the bottom deck and wait for me."

"What are you going to do?"

"Probably something very stupid."

Imani smiled. "I like it."

Oh blimey. But she dropped Imani off at her room, then continued down to Creed's room.

The royal guard still stood outside the door, so clearly Fraser hadn't yet arrived for his rescue.

What if he wasn't coming? The thought swept through her even as she affected a smile. "Take a break. I need to talk to the American."

She still pulled some rank, but admittedly, when the younger man nodded and left, she stood for a moment outside Creed's room, undone.

Here went nothing.

She opened the door.

Creed sat on a chair in the room, his hands still tied. He looked at her, his jaw hard. "What?"

She put a finger to her mouth, then walked over to him. "Let's get you out of those cuffs."

He raised his hands, the flexicuffs dangling from his wrists. "You learn a few things when you have active military brothers." Then he got up. "Is Fraser outside?"

"Is he coming?"

"I thought…" He took a breath. "I don't know."

"Me too," she said. "C'mon."

She opened the door and checked the gangway. "Listen, if anyone comes, don't panic."

Creed nodded, his mouth a grim line.

"Or you could go over the side."

"I don't swim."

That was a problem.

Please, Fraser, don't let me down.

But why not? She'd betrayed him. Hard. And maybe he hadn't heard her small clue about the lifeboat—she knew he couldn't get Creed off with just the Jet Ski.

Not and take her and Imani along.

Voices, from the lower deck, and she froze, her hand on Creed behind her. He, too, stilled.

The guards moved back into the garage, and she kept moving.

From across the deck, Pippa spotted movement in the darkness.

Imani. She scurried across the deck and crouched next to the tender, in the shadows.

Pippa brought Creed down the stairs, then yanked him into the shadows underneath.

Two guards stood at the stern of the yacht, staring out into the dark water. And beyond that, the tender that Pippa had secured, floating in the darkness some twenty feet behind the yacht. One of the small rescue tenders. She'd deployed it after Fredrik and his crew had left for Geneva, leaving behind the yacht contingency.

Just a handful of guards, and in the darkness, while they'd been securing the prince and princess's return, they hadn't seen her unhook the box that held the raft.

Hadn't seen it inflate in the darkness.

Not large, it held four people. But it would get them to shore, hopefully without alerting anyone.

Probably it was a crazy plan, but even if Fraser didn't show up, she had to get Creed off this boat. Because if he'd also seen Gunner that night and the man was a murderer—and frankly, she still had a hard time letting that sink in—then Creed wasn't safe either.

Now, however, her plan seemed downright foolish. A dash across the deck would mean a dash through the light, and there was no way they were getting to that tender without being caught.

"You sure you can't swim?"

"Pretty sure," Creed came back. "But I can float. Give me something to hang on to."

She had to like the young man's chutzpah. "Okay." This, she could do. The yacht—from her memory of the specs—stored life preservers under the cushioned seats in all the decks.

"Stay here."

She climbed the stairs, then flicked off the lights on the deck and walked across to the benches lining the front area. Opened them and felt around.

Nothing but towels.

Bollocks.

Below, a man had come out from the bottom deck, looking up at the darkness. "Anyone up there?"

Pippa scooted back, crouching, her heart thumping.

They had to get off this boat before Creed's guard returned.

Then, suddenly, a splash sounded on the far side, near where Imani had crouched.

No—that girl! Pippa rushed to the rail, as did the other guards, who flashed their lights on the surface of the water.

In her worst fears, they found Imani, overboard. And then there would be explaining to do—

But, nothing.

Pippa scooted over to the stairs and took them down.

"Creed!"

He was gone.

She stared at the water over the edge, and stilled.

Fraser's head stuck out of the water, just barely visible above the waves and chop. Imani and Creed crouched in the raft.

He looked at her. Nodded.

He considers you his partner. The words rushed over her.

She was down the stairs, over the edge, and in the raft in a moment.

He disappeared under the water.

What—

But they were moving. Away from the yacht, into the darkness, in silence. He surfaced again, some ten feet from the raft, a line in his hand, then dropped it and vanished.

They bobbed there in the water, in the darkness. Where—

A few moments later, the sound of a Jet Ski buzzed the air. She could barely make him out in the darkness, but her eyes had adjusted, and the frame of him, solid and sure, stirred something forbidden inside her.

Partners.

He pulled up next to the raft, fished the rope from the water, and tied it to the ski. Then he looked at her in the darkness. "You're really doing this."

She nodded.

"Okay then. Hold on." And then he smiled.

And suddenly, she didn't feel like such a traitor.

In fact, she just might be one of the good guys.

"HELP ME UNDERSTAND WHAT IS HAPPENING HERE."

Fraser was wet, cold, and confused.

He hid a shiver, his body still frozen from his dunk into the Med. Thankfully, his backpack, secured in the rental car, held dry clothes for him to change into. Still, he smelled like the sea, briny and waterlogged.

Pippa now sat in the passenger seat of the Panda, Creed and Imani in the back seat as they drove through Italy, along the coast, towards Tuscany. The mountains still arched to the east, the sea to the west, barely a star in the sky as clouds had moved in.

He still couldn't shake free of the moment when he'd looked up and seen Imani racing to the lifeboat, leaping in.

The math had begun to add up then, but he'd just reacted. He was already in the water, detaching the raft from the boat and securing it to the Jet Ski. But he couldn't risk the motor alerting the guards, so he'd towed it along the side of the at-anchor yacht to where he'd seen Creed hiding in the shadows.

Creed hopped overboard, into the raft, and Fraser might have taken off if Pippa hadn't also appeared.

It took another heartbeat—during which she also evac'd into the raft—for him to add it all up.

Pippa was running. With Imani.

He didn't ask why. Not even when they got to shore and he loaded them up in the Panda.

Not even when he called Ham, back in America, and asked for a safe house, some place to lay low while he figured out his next move.

Ham had sent him to Tuscany, to the home of a mutual friend.

Now, after they'd put a good twenty miles between them and Santa Margherita, it seemed like a good time for answers.

Pippa stared out the window, her hand to her mouth.

"Pippa?"

She turned to him. Her hair had fallen from her bun, and she seemed...tired.

Or overwhelmed?

"Are you okay?"

"I'm trying to remind myself that this was a good idea." She looked at him, then glanced at Imani in the back seat. He looked at the couple in the back seat via his rearview mirror.

Imani leaned against Creed, her back to him, her eyes closed. He had his arm around her and stared out the window.

So, everybody seemed shell-shocked except him.

And he'd like to know why.

"Imani thinks the person she saw—the murderer—was Lauchtenland's captain of the royal guard. Gunner Ferguson."

It took a second. "Wait. I met him."

She looked at Fraser. "Yes. But Imani knows him and got a good look at him, and she swears it's him."

"What do you think?"

"I think...people can see many things when they're afraid. But Gunner has always been a patriot, so who knows but he had intel about the man he, um, murdered. Gerwig might have been a violent RECO terrorist."

"You have terrorists in Lauchtenland?"

"There are terrorists in every country. People who would advance their agenda without regard for fellow man. Maybe Gerwig had another agenda."

"I thought he was a physicist."

She sighed. "I don't know what is going on. And that's why I knew we had to leave." She looked at him again. "With you."

He drew in a breath. "You knew I'd never let Creed be brought back to Lauchtenland."

She nodded, her face lit slightly by the dash lights. "I knew you."

He didn't know why those words sank in, fell on fertile soil. He made a noise deep inside, not sure what it meant.

But not hating, either, the way she looked at him.

"I know it's a lot to ask," she said softly, "but will you help me keep Imani safe until we figure out what is going on?"

He met her eyes and nodded.

She reached over and touched his hand. Squeezed. And left it there for a good five minutes as they drove into the night.

"It'll be okay, Pippa. We'll figure it out."

He turned east just north of Pisa, headed toward the town of Lucca, and followed the GPS directions that Ham texted him.

The clouds had settled over the sky, the air smelling of rain when he pulled onto the road that led to what appeared a winery in the hills. The drying, skeletal stalks of harvested vines lined up in rows alongside the road as he cut through the night with his lights.

"What is this place?"

"It's a safe house. Or maybe just a safe place. Ham told me to lay low here, and he'd figure out how to get us out of the country."

"Ham?"

"Hamilton Jones. He's my boss—a former SEAL team leader who now runs Jones, Inc., a global search-and-rescue-slash-private-security team. He has contacts all over the world, and he's working on a way to get us back to the US."

He turned onto a private drive. "My folks are in Europe for the next two weeks. My best idea is to take you back to Minnesota."

"Won't they know where to look for us?"

He looked at her. "Okay, Pippa, I'm going to be honest with you. Other than a break-in at the hotel, we're not even sure someone is after Imani. I mean—it was dark, and maybe she didn't see what she thought."

Pippa drew in a breath. Looked out the window. "I thought of that. This might all be overkill. But..." She turned back to Fraser. "What if we're wrong? One moment left unguarded is all someone would need—"

"Yes. Okay." He couldn't stop himself from touching her hand. But her voice had risen, hardened, and the fact she'd asked him for help seemed a nice leap from him tagging along. So, "We have a security system around the winery. And it's home ground, so we have home-field advantage."

Pippa nodded.

He pulled up in the grounds of a two-story stone house that looked like something out of the Medici era. Tall cypress trees cordoned off the drive, and the main house was connected to a smaller house by a terrace.

All looked quiet.

Then an overhead light splashed on. He put out his hand, pressed it to Pippa's arm. "Stay here."

She gave a small laugh and reached for the door.

Right. He stepped out of the car just as a woman walked out of the doorway. Early thirties, maybe, with solemn, dark eyes. She didn't carry a weapon, but he had the sense that maybe she didn't need one, either, to protect herself.

"Fraser Marshall?" She came up to him, five feet away.

"Yes, ma'am."

"Ziggy Mattucci. Welcome to Estate Mattucci."

Tall, thin, with long black hair that snaked down her back in a thick braid.

"Fraser," he said, shaking her hand. "And this is Pippa Butler, from Lauchtenland."

Creed had gotten out of the car, pulling Imani with him.

"This is my brother, Creed, and Imani—"

"Her Royal Highness Princess Imani of Lauchtenland," Pippa said, coming around to stand beside them.

He looked at her, back to Ziggy. "Right. Her Royal—"

"I know Imani. Although I'm not sure we met." Ziggy held out her hand. "I was in Lauchtenland a couple months ago. I think you might have helped my friend RJ get ready for her wedding."

Imani grinned. "Yeah. I remember you. Pippa, you remember RJ and York?"

"Hard to forget York," Pippa said, her mouth tight.

Ziggy looked at her then. "Oh, you don't know. York is... okay, it's probably classified, but I can assure you it's not what you think."

Pippa frowned at her.

"Never mind me. Are you all okay? Roy said you needed a place to hide?"

"Just for a day while I sort this out," Fraser said. "You know Roy?"

"We're friends, yes. Work together sometimes."

And that suddenly made terrible, perfect sense. The tightness in his gut released. If she worked with Roy, she knew how to handle herself. And, probably, keep them safe.

"Creed." Ziggy shook his hand. "Any relation to Winchester Marshall?"

"The actor?" Creed looked at Fraser. "Really?"

"He's a cousin," Fraser said. "Although we haven't seen the Melbourne Beach Marshalls in years. Win and I recently connected, however, so...but how do you know Win?"

Pippa had retrieved her backpack along with Imani's from the back of the car. Fraser also pulled his out and put it over his shoulder.

"Win stayed with us a couple months ago. Scouted our place for a location for a movie he's producing." She nodded toward the house. "Come inside. Our perimeter has cameras and a security system, but you never know."

They followed her inside to a large living area with terracotta tile, a plaster fireplace, and overstuffed leather chairs. Beyond that looked like an eat-in kitchen.

"We have guest rooms upstairs. Take whatever ones you'd like," Ziggy said. "Anyone hungry? My mother made fresh pasta before she and Santini left on holiday."

He couldn't remember the last real meal he'd eaten, and maybe she saw that, because Ziggy smiled, nodded. "I'm not a great cook, but I can whip up Alfredo like nobody's business." She headed into the kitchen.

Pippa stood there, looking at Fraser. "Where are we?"

He couldn't stop himself from stepping up to her. "Just breathe. And trust me."

She stood there for a minute, then nodded. Then she turned to Imani. "Let's get you settled."

Imani had been holding Creed's hand but now let go and followed Pippa up the stairs. Fraser, too, went upstairs and found a quaint set-up for a bed and breakfast, with plank flooring and small rooms with ensuites, linen curtains, and overstuffed beds. He took the one at the top of the stairs and noticed that Pippa took the one down the hall—next to Imani's, of course. Creed followed another set of stairs to an attic room.

For a long moment, Fraser simply wanted to sink into the fluffy queen bed. Instead, he pulled out his wet clothes from his backpack and put them over the rack in the bathroom to dry.

He stopped by the window and noticed that the perimeter of the house was lit up. A beautiful pool, enclosed by cobblestone, filled the back terrace. Beyond that, a fountain spilled water into a tiny grotto.

Reminded him, in a way, of his parents' place. A slower, more patient way of life.

No wonder he'd never fit in.

He found his way downstairs and into the eat-in kitchen.

Cozy and Italian, with blue-and-orange patterned tile, white cupboards, and a plaster hood to match the fireplace in the next room.

Ziggy stood at the range, stirring up a pot of creamy white sauce. A strong scent of garlic stirred the air.

"I found some sausage, too, and put that in. Cut up the bread while you're here."

He spotted a crusty loaf of bread and a knife. Grabbing it, he used a towel to hold it, put it on a board, and began to slice through.

"So, how do you know Ham?"

"Jones? I don't. But Roy knows him, and he called me. I just happened to be here watching the place while my folks are on holiday in Croatia."

She set a plate of goat cheese on the table. "How do *you* know Roy?"

"I was on an op with him not long ago." His hand slid off the knife, and he flexed it, working it.

"You okay?"

"Just a recent injury. Yep."

She said nothing, kept stirring. "So, what kind of trouble is the princess in?"

"We're not sure. She witnessed a murder go down in Geneva and has been on the run since. She seems to think it was one of the royal guards. Gunner Ferguson."

"Gunner? No. I met him. Straight shooter. He's an old buddy of Roy's."

He looked at her. "Gunner knows Roy?"

She nodded.

He set down the knife. "Could Gunner know about this place?"

She had stopped stirring. "I don't know. Probably not, but... it's a small world, clearly."

"Clearly." He ran his hands down his face. Went to the window. "You said you had security on this place?"

"Yeah."

"Show me."

She turned off the heat from the pan, then picked up a cloth to wipe her hands. Met his eyes. Then, "This way."

She stepped toward a door in the kitchen and popped in a code. The door opened, and he followed her inside to a small office.

A panel of screens showed all angles to the house along with wide angles of the fields. "I know it seems like a lot, but we have some expensive wines along with a history of needing security. And I have a tunnel in the basement." She indicated a door. "It leads out to a cave behind the winery."

He stood there, staring at the cameras.

"Get something to eat. And get some rest. The security will alert to anyone who broaches the perimeter."

He didn't know why, but in his gut, he couldn't deny the fist that had formed.

No. He walked out to the kitchen where Pippa, Creed, and Imani had returned for dinner.

"This smells amazing," Creed said.

"Eat fast, because we're leaving."

Pippa stared at him.

Behind him, Ziggy dunked fresh linguini in boiling water.

He grabbed a piece of sourdough bread, put it in his mouth, and headed upstairs. In his bedroom, he stared out at the deepening night and called his boss.

"I'm going to need an extraction, ASAP," he said after he gave him an update.

"Working on that with Roy right now," Ham said.

"About that. Could be that we have a man named Gunner Ferguson after us. He's from Lauchtenland and apparently knows Roy." He ran his hand across his mouth. "I think the safe house has been compromised."

"You don't know that. Hunker down until morning. I'll figure out an exfil."

"I don't know, Ham—"

"Listen. You're tired. Hungry. And you're working off sketchy intel. Let me do some legwork."

Only after he hung up did he see Pippa standing in the doorway. She wore a tight-lipped look. "Are we in trouble here?"

He walked over to her. "I don't think so. But I'm not sure—"

"Stop. Time for you to breathe." She pressed her hands onto his chest. "Listen. You're tired. We're tired. And I talked with Ziggy. We have this watch. You get some sleep."

He gave her a look. "Pippa—"

"You don't always have to be the one in charge, Fraser."

Huh.

Then she smiled, something warm in her eyes. "Get some sleep, tough guy. I'll let you know if we need you."

Then, weirdly, she pressed a kiss to his cheek.

And he again was left with *what on earth was going on?*

TEN

All her training, all her years of keeping her focus...

And she'd simply abandoned it all in one blinding moment. Or two. First, when she'd jumped into the raft on the very thin edge of treason.

Then, four hours ago when she'd stepped up to Fraser and...kissed him.

On the cheek, but still.

What was that?

Pippa sat in the terrace off the pool—beautiful, all of it, with the starlight trying to break through the cloud cover, sparkling here and there on the pool. The scent of cypress and vineyard and flowers hinted the air. Although Ziggy said she'd keep watch on the cameras, there was nothing like being on the ground, listening, every cell alert to trouble.

Although, every cell might be alert thinking about how Fraser had looked when she'd walked in on him in the bedroom.

Standing in the darkness of the room, he'd seemed both a force to be reckoned with and then, when he'd turned, when he'd looked at her, had suddenly seemed positively, weirdly undone. Captain America fraying, just a little, at the seams.

Even after the train crash, he'd been put together. Wounded, maybe, and a little shell-shocked, but he'd put himself back together in moments, taken charge and...

And she hadn't in the least felt like she had to step in.

Sure, it could be the aftereffects of being tased a third time. Or maybe it was the way she'd simply thrust the care of Imani, and really, herself, into his arms. But he'd picked them up without a hiccup.

As she'd stared at him, for some reason, something Jonas had said to her rushed into her mind. *One of the guys he was with was killed. And the doc he was protecting got shot. I think he feels like he has something to prove.*

Which meant not leading a murderer to their front step.

No wonder he was breathing funny.

I think he looks at you as a partner, so I'm hoping you have his back too.

Indeed, she did.

She wasn't sure what had happened next, or how, but she did remember the crazy moment when she kissed his cheek.

Which, even now, felt weird. Because she wasn't a cheek-kissing person.

Or a kissing person, really. She couldn't remember the last time—

Movement, a shuffle of a foot.

Ziggy had given her a 9mm Magnum, and now Pippa picked it up. Crept out to the edge of the covered terrace.

More scuffing, coming toward her.

She held her breath and rolled out, her gun out, straight arms. "Stop."

Fraser stood in the wan light of the corridor between the house and the terrace. He put his hands up. "That's not a taser."

She flicked the safety back on and lowered it. "Nope."

"Guess you're serious."

She cocked his head at him. "When am I not?"

He emitted a small noise from his chest. "Right."

He smelled good—freshly showered, although not shaven—as he came toward her. He stopped at the edge of the corridor, stood beside her, and stared out into the night. She hadn't really realized how tall he was. At least five inches on her five foot seven. And bigger, his girth and chest outlined by his black T-shirt.

Every inch the operative he'd left behind.

"What are you doing up?" Her voice sounded weird. A little too breathy. Sheesh.

"I thought I'd spell you. It's been four hours." He turned, then reached down and closed his hand around the Magnum, his voice close to her ear. "My turn."

She didn't know why, but having him this close, especially after her crazy cheek kiss—what was *that?*—it just sort of shut her down.

He eased the gun from her grip. Stepped away. "You okay?"

Wow, he looked good in the light of the porch, toned and strong and...no. *Pippa. Go to bed.*

But she just stood there.

Because he just stood there. His eyes held hers, and she could taste her heartbeat, the strange hot cord that lit between them.

"Pippa?"

"I'm sorry I got you into this. I...just didn't know—"

"Hey." He stepped forward and put his hand on her face. "I'm all in, okay? Until we know Imani is safe and that Creed is safe, until we figure out who is after them and why—I'm in this."

Maybe it was the earnestness of his voice, or maybe her own fatigue.

Maybe it was even her stepping out of herself for another crazy moment, but suddenly she leaned forward and—

Stilled. One inch from his mouth. "Do you hear that?"

"Nope," he said, and closed the gap between them.

And then she really left her body. His lips were firm, decisive, and there was no question in his kiss. He tasted of his hunger. Thirst. As if he'd been thinking about it for a while.

Holding back.

Not anymore. Kissing Fraser was like kissing a storm, engulfing, pulling you in, taking over.

To her surprise, she found herself surrendering. No fight, just a strange, delicious need. As if she, too, had been thinking about it. She softened her mouth and kissed him back with everything inside her.

He made a soft noise from deep inside again, his hand wrapping behind her neck to pull her in, and something changed between them.

The hunger slowed to a deeper need. To know. To belong.

She wound her arm around his neck, her hand on his bicep. And didn't protest for a second when he slowly backed her against the wall, the hard planes of his chest and stomach against hers.

Fraser. She barely knew this man.

Except, maybe she did. She knew his wounds, at least the recent ones, and the people he loved, and what he'd die for.

She knew him at his dire moments, and even in his innocent sleep.

She knew that this man meant it when he stepped into a fight, shouldered her fears.

Meant it when he kissed her.

Oh...and maybe the breadth of that should have her pushing him away, but...but he tasted good, and she couldn't remember ever kissing anyone with the deep longing that washed over her like a hot wave.

What was it about this American that awakened something inside her that she didn't even know how to name?

As if he knew her too.

A tiny siren sounded deep inside, but she pushed it away, and Pippa slid her other hand around him and pulled him closer, not hating for a moment that something was clearly, definitely, deliciously out of sorts—

He broke away. "Wait."

For what? But maybe, yes, she should just *Slow. Down.* Because her heart wanted to leave her body, her breaths rushing over themselves. And she was dangerously close to forgetting—

Wait. "I do hear it." She stilled. Then, just like that, shoved him away.

Oh. Blimey, she'd let herself get way too distracted—

He let go too, but rounded and put his back to her. "A motor. In the distance."

She was already heading inside, to the kitchen.

To Ziggy's secret portal.

The woman with the silky dark braid sat on a chair, her gaze on the screens. "It's here," she said, pointing to motorcycle coming up the drive. "He's still a mile out, but…"

"We should go." Fraser had followed her. "Get Imani. Lights off."

On it. But as she turned, she couldn't help but notice that one of the screens happened to show the corridor where she and Fraser had just—

Calm down. It was a moment. Just a moment of terrible distraction.

And if Fraser hadn't—

Not now. She raced upstairs.

"Imani—get up." She banged her door open.

The girl sat up, her hair askew, blinking. She reached for the lamp, but Pippa caught her hand. "Get your stuff. We're leaving in one minute."

She headed to her room, grabbed her backpack and shoved

her jacket inside. Then she pulled the charging cord out of the wall, grabbed her phone, and shoved it inside.

In twenty seconds, she was back to Imani's room. The princess was still trying to clear her head, stumbling around. Pippa slid everything Imani had stacked on a nearby chair into the bag, the same with the items on her bedside stand.

Then she zipped it up, put it over her shoulder, grabbed the girl's shoes in one hand, Imani's hand in the other, and headed out the door.

"What—I don't—"

She'd probably stopped at the sight of Creed already heading down the stairs, Fraser standing at the top.

He held the gun, something dangerous in his eyes, even in the darkness.

"Go to the safe room. There's a tunnel there."

Pippa headed through the kitchen, then to Ziggy's room. She already had a door open at the far end of it. The cool breath of earth swilled up from the entrance. Ziggy slapped a flashlight into her hand. "Follow it to the end. You'll emerge at a cave. Go through it and wait on the other side."

"For what?"

"For me," Fraser said, standing at the door.

"Fraser—"

"Stay alive. All of you."

Then he closed the door.

You too. The thought rattled through her, weakened her. A distraction for sure.

She shook it away, took the flashlight from Ziggy and flicked it on. Shone it down the stairs to the tunnel.

This, she knew how to do. "Let's go."

HOW GUNNER HAD FOUND THEM SO FAST, FRASER HAD no idea, but as he crouched behind a tall cypress beside the drive, trailing the beam of light up the road, he could only think of one thing.

He'd screwed up. Something he'd done—or hadn't done—had brought Gunner or his henchman to Ziggy's doorstep.

Something he hadn't seen, hadn't heard...

It was Nigeria all over again.

Stupid—*stupid*. He could hardly breathe, a band around his chest, tightening as the light grew closer.

The motor thickened in the night, and Fraser tried to sort it out. If Gunner really was after them and he had a cohort, probably he'd sent said cohort to hunt them down. Unless, of course, he'd activated the entire Royal Guard, in which case there might be a dozen or so former marines descending on the place.

So, option one, given the lone motorcyclist.

He held his breath, and for a moment, the wind stirred, and he was back on the terrace, Pippa in his arms.

Not sure what had happened there.

Okay, probably he could attribute some of it to the restless four hours of sleep after she'd kissed his cheek. After she'd looked at him like...well, he didn't know what to think about it. Just that she'd smelled good, and that with her hair almost down, he had just wanted to wind his fingers through it. And probably that had been on his mind too much when he'd gotten up and showered and finally headed outside to clear his head and maybe find his footing.

Not. At All.

She'd been standing in the wan light, her blue-gray eyes almost smoky in the night, and for a second, she'd looked like she was going to kiss him.

And the hunger for her had just risen inside him. The fact that she trusted him despite his wounds, and maybe around her, he felt just a little needed, and suddenly he'd just—dived in.

Probably he should have asked, but it'd seemed like she didn't mind, at all.

It seemed, actually, that behind Miss Pippa I-have-it-all-neatly-tied-up Butler was someone he liked even more, someone who dove in and undid him a little, clearly all-in, and maybe he would have found himself even more in over his head if it weren't for whatever was coming up the road.

Ziggy had moved outside the house also. He'd seen her steal out of the house and secret herself on the other side of the drive.

The motorcyclist drove right into the yard. He wore a helmet.

Fraser emerged from the dark, gun out. "Stop. Hands out."

The man lifted his arms up, hands out. "No danger here. I'm on your team."

Fraser advanced on him. "Take off your helmet. Slowly."

The man unstrapped his helmet, eased it off, held it out in one hand.

"Really, Fraser. It's me. Roy."

He lowered his gun even as the man turned.

Roy Benjamin. He wore a pair of jeans, a leather jacket, his dark hair a little longer than the last time he'd seen him, back in Florida a month ago.

Ziggy came out of the shadows, also lowering her gun. "Why didn't you call me?"

"Sorry, Zig. I didn't expect the armed reception." He parked the bike and got off. "Ham sent me. Said you needed an extraction. I've got a flight out set up for you in the morning, but the runway is a little off-the-grid."

Then he met Fraser's gaze. "Ham says you know something about a murder that went down in Geneva a few days ago. I'm going to need details."

A beat, then, "Why?"

"Because the man who was killed was working with the Russian mob. And we need to know why he was killed."

"The physicist?"

"Yes. I need to talk to Creed. And that princess he's with, see what they know."

And then suddenly, Ziggy's words were in his head. *Gunner? He's an old buddy of Roy's.*

He looked at Ziggy. "I need to find Pippa."

"She's already in the tunnel."

"Mind if I take your bike?"

"Keys are in the ignition," Roy said, all friendly-like.

And maybe he was jumping to wild conclusions. Roy, after all, was a former SEAL.

But Roy had also worked black ops and wet work and all sorts of out-of-bounds missions for the past five years, and who knew what he was into.

And what his true allegiances were. So Fraser nodded at him, all friendly. "We'll be right back." Then he turned to Ziggy. "Make sure he wasn't followed."

He mounted the bike and turned the key. Started the bike. Remembered Ziggy's words about the tunnel and how it connected to the cave.

Then he turned the bike around, gravel flying, and headed down the path.

As he was driving, it came to him.

Her cell phone.

He'd seen Pippa shove it into her backpack and hadn't given it a thought then, not until he'd been standing out here in the yard for five whole minutes, his brain shuffling through the hows and what-ifs.

He'd been an idiot to forget that, but certainly, if the Royal Guard could track a royal necklace, one smartphone shouldn't be a problem.

Stupid—stupid. He should have killed it the minute she got into his car back in Portofino.

He spotted the cave with the big wooden doors over the entrance. Probably used for tastings now, but once upon a time, it could have been used to store the wine.

Maybe even, during the World War II occupation, used to hide partisans, resistance fighters, and probably he was letting his imagination get the best of him.

Happened sometimes when he was in Europe, a land with such rich history, the rise and fall of monarchies, royal deceptions and betrayals.

He stopped at the entrance, got off the bike, and pulled open the wooden door. Darkness, thick and unyielding, filled the space.

But there, in the distance, a pinprick of light.

"Pippa!"

The light stopped, shone back at him.

He closed the door behind him, took out his cell phone light and flicked it on. Then he followed it down the cavern.

Pippa shone her light on the floor, moving it away as he came up to her, winded. "You okay?" Her voice was sharp, also winded.

"I don't know. The man on the motorcycle was Roy."

"Roy? From the Caleb Group?"

He blinked at her. "How do you know that?"

"He was in Lauchtenland a while back, hunting down an assassin—it's a long story. Why is Roy here?"

Fraser met her eyes. "He knows Gunner."

A beat, a breath. "That's...that's not good."

"I know."

She stared at him, her jaw tight.

"I don't know what to do here, Pippa. He also says that Ham sent him with a way out, but Ham never called me." Speaking of— "Give me your phone."

"What?" And then her eyes rounded. "Oh. Bollocks."

"Yeah. If we're wondering how Roy found us so fast…"

She unzipped the front pouch of her backpack and pulled it out. Held the light for him as he opened up the back and pulled out the sim card.

He then ground it under his boot and handed her the phone back. "Sorry."

"No. You're right. I'm a bloody fool." She closed her eyes, shook her head.

Okay, she was being a *little* hard on herself.

She glanced at Creed and Imani. They stood near a door on the other side of the cave tunnel. "Now what?"

And for the first time, he had…nothing.

All around him, blackness, save for the tiny light Pippa held in her hand. Creed and Imani breathing quietly just a few feet away.

"What if we open that door to find Gunner and the Royal Guard on the other side?"

And now his brain was really playing with him, because, "What if Ziggy, being Roy's friend, is in on all this, and I called—"

"Stop." Pippa stepped up to him. Met his eyes. "What does your gut say?"

"I don't…I don't know."

"Fine. What do you feel, in here?" She fisted her hand and thumped his chest. "What is the truth you know?"

It wasn't a gentle touch, something romantic, but something he might expect from Ham, or North, or any of the guys who always had his back.

"I trust Ham."

"And Ham…who does he trust?"

"He trusts Roy. He served with Roy." He met her eyes. "Gunner and Roy might be mates, but it's not the same as surviving together. Being teammates. No, Roy wouldn't betray Ham."

"Ham wouldn't betray you."

No, he wouldn't.

He met Pippa's eyes, then Imani's. "Stay here. And if anyone but me comes in…" He handed Pippa the 9mm. "Sure shot."

She nodded. "Please be right."

What she said.

He ran back out along the tunnel to the cave entrance and pushed open the door.

Roy sat against his bike, his hands folded, his feet crossed. Ziggy sat on a boulder near the entrance, her arms folded over her chest.

Fraser half closed the door behind him and came out.

Roy looked at him.

A beat passed between them.

"Ziggy told me about Gunner." Roy.

"Mm-hmm."

"It's hard for me to digest. I know the man. We overlapped in some training while we were both in the military."

Fraser nodded.

"And even a couple months ago, when we connected, I'd tell you that Gunner was a patriot."

"I'm sure he is."

"If he did kill Gerwig, I think we need to reserve judgment."

"And who, then, broke into their hotel room?"

Roy uncrossed his ankles. "I have a theory. And it involves a man we've been tracking for a while. A rogue operative named Alan Martin."

This name, Fraser knew. "The guy involved with the plot to kill the president."

"He escaped a couple months ago from federal prison, and according to a member of the Caleb Group, he and a man named Abu Hassiff, along with the Petrov Bratva out of Russia, were involved in a plot. It included the director of the CDC, and the purpose was to disable the president and release a deadly variant of smallpox in America."

Fraser had turned a little hollow. "Abu Hassiff?"

"Yes."

"Boko Haram terrorist."

"The same. He was killed in a boat accident in the Med during that op."

Fraser leaned over, catching his knees, almost light-headed.

"Fraser?" Ziggy said, and he heard gravel crunch as she got up. He put out a hand. "Just a sec." He breathed it out, the last of his nightmares stirring free into the night.

Then he stood up. "What does this have to do with Gerwig Buchen and his murder in Geneva?"

"We think Martin isn't finished. I originally thought he'd been the one to kill Buchen. This news about Gunner is...disturbing."

And Fraser didn't know why—maybe it was his tone, although granted, Roy was an operator. He knew how to lie.

Still, watching him sit there, his hands still folded, a posture of non-aggression, made Fraser loosen just a notch.

"Why would he kill Buchen?"

"We're not sure yet. But Gerwig was one of Lauchtenland's leading nuclear researchers. Haxton had a sister relationship with the Swiss Federal Institute of Technology in Lausanne, and he runs the research reactor there."

"As in nuclear materials?"

"It gets worse. According to Logan, who is the head of the Caleb Group—"

"I know Logan."

"Right. He says that there was a break-in at the research reactor in Lausanne a few hours after Buchen's murder. Plutonium was stolen."

Fraser stilled. "Plutonium. How much?"

"We don't know. And we're not sure the events are connected. But we are sure that Alan Martin was in Geneva on the night of the murder. He showed up at your brother Ned's hotel room the next day. Blood spatter from the site is his."

Fraser stared at him. "How did you...what—?"

"A housekeeper called the police, and samples were taken, put in the system, and flagged by Interpol, and thus, the Caleb Group. I was stateside visiting a friend. I landed in Amsterdam last night, checked in with our team, and then Ham called me about your little adventure."

"You have a team in Europe?"

"How can we keep the world safe if we're not prepared?"

He didn't want to know. Just, "And Gunner Ferguson? How is he involved?"

"This is the first I've heard of this, so...I'll have to start nosing around."

"Gunner's team—or at least Fredrik, his brother—thinks Creed was in on it. Apparently, a man named Konrad Vogel connected with him on a tourist junket."

"Okay. We'll look into him too." He stood up. "But first, I promise you, Fraser, I'm here to get you and your princess—"

"She's not my princess."

"She's my princess," said a voice, and Pippa stepped out from behind the door. She held the gun, easy, at her side.

"I'm not a princess!" Imani stepped out behind her.

"Sorry, sweetheart, but yes you are," said Fraser.

"—to safety," Roy finished.

Imani closed her eyes and shook her head. "Fine. Whatevs. Can I please put my royal head down on a royal pillow and get some royal sleep?"

"Yes," Pippa said, just as Fraser smiled and nodded.

"I'd like some royal breakfast," Creed said as they headed along the road toward the house.

Pippa looked at him. Not a smile. But not a glare either.

Then she clicked on the safety, put the 9mm in her belt, and followed Imani down the road.

And he hadn't a clue what to think about that.

All he knew was that finally, the tight band around his chest had eased.

Maybe he hadn't screwed up and gotten them all killed.

This time.

Eleven

Maybe, probably, for sure, this had been a very bad idea. Because what in her head had told her that Fraser— and she—alone could protect Imani out here in…booniesville?

Even though Fraser had certainly made a good run of it.

Pippa stood on the patio of the Marshall family winery, staring out at the stretch of harvested vines—far as her eye could see, really—trying to see where Fraser was pointing to in the fading sunlight.

"Where's the camera?"

"It's on the edge of the barn—there." He stood behind her, cupping his hand over his eyes against the falling sunlight.

She traced the edge of the massive red barn—very quaint, with its sign, Marshall Fields Winery, over the double doors— and finally spotted it at the corner, facing the drive to the barn. "I don't know. At Hadsby Castle, there isn't one inch of ground that isn't monitored."

"I know. But that camera catches the drive to the barn and the house, and even a portion of the gazebo. And the one on the house secures the entire backyard."

"And what about the other side of the house?"

"We have one on the roof that faces the road and two on the front the house. I promise you, Pippa, the grounds are covered."

She handed him back the binoculars. Nodded. "It's just… everything here is so…big. You have vast tracks of land, the barn is the size of a small apartment building in Dalholm, and your house could hold a futbol team and the entire Blue extended family."

He laughed, and even that was big, powerful, and filled her entire body.

Fraser had changed since returning home. As if he'd settled into himself, taking charge in a way that should have given her confidence. After all, he'd spent the past four days installing more cameras, setting up a security room in his father's office, and creating round-the-clock surveillance for as much of the space as he could.

So maybe it was herself she didn't trust.

Hadn't trusted ever since she let herself—sheesh, she'd practically launched herself—into Fraser's embrace.

She'd thought about that kiss, that very overwhelming, disturbing, distracting kiss, way too much.

Whereas Fraser hadn't actually said a word about it. Like—nope, nothing to see here. He hadn't even sat by her on the plane over the pond, a private jet sent by his friend Ham.

Who had the necessary resources, apparently, to usher her into the country and right past passport control and customs. Interesting.

So really, no one knew they were here, tucked away in some tiny town in the great prairie of southern Minnesota. Frankly, for the last three days, when she'd woken in the big queen bed at the end of the hall—the one she insisted on sharing with Imani (and not just because it had its own fireplace)—she'd had to blink a few times and get her bearings. It helped that the smell from downstairs roused her to reality.

Fraser, frying up sausage or bacon and eggs.

She'd go for a lovely spot of tea and jam, really. But not a tea bag to be found.

She'd poured a lot of milk into the coffee and tried to pretend.

Fraser had finally gone out today and brought home tea bags, bread, and jam. And for Imani, frozen pizza and a box of Captain Crunch.

For the love.

But she wasn't here to protect Imani's teeth or cholesterol levels, and probably her slim, twenty-year-old body was years away from worrying about death by sugar, so she said nothing as the girl showed up in her pajama pants and a T-shirt today around noon, and ate right out of the box by handfuls.

So maybe she might be a little dazed and out of her element too. She'd picked up another cell phone—unregistered—and had spent hours watching YouTube.

Or playing video games with Creed.

Although, a few times Pippa had spotted her on the porch swing outside, a faraway look on her face.

As long as she didn't leave the grounds—and maybe that was Imani's problem.

Hard to run when the nearest town was ten kilometers down the road.

"The right gun, the right sniper, could find her from a mile away, and we'd never see him. In Lauchtenland, we have a perimeter all the way around the Hadsby grounds that alerts us, not to mention constant patrols and dogs and—"

"Hey. We have Sherlock here." Fraser had walked over to where a black lab lay on the patio, big brown eyes considering him. His thick tail thumped. "Neil take good care of you, buddy?"

She smiled at the way Fraser petted the dog, both hands rubbing his whole body. The dog finally rolled over, and Fraser scratched his belly too.

Sweet.

In fact, this wasn't exactly prison. Fraser had ordered in Chinese food or pizza, and last night he'd grilled burgers. Imani had devoured it like she'd been on a forty-day fast.

The girl clearly missed America.

The only one suffering here seemed to be Pippa.

So, what was her problem? She stared back out at the horizon.

Fraser looked up from where he'd finished petting Sherlock.

"It's my job to worry." And the last thing she needed was to get distracted by a way-too-handsome American. Hello.

If it hadn't been Roy coming up the drive, but rather a cavalry of royal guards...

No more kissing. *Ever.*

"It's my job too. Listen." He turned her. "Imani is going to be just fine. Ham and Roy and the Caleb Group are looking into all the pieces. We just have to be patient."

"I don't do patient well."

He laughed. "Me either."

She looked up at him. He had shaved when he returned to America, but a dark stubble still raked his jawline. The denim shirt, rolled up at the sleeves, only deepened his blue eyes, and when he smiled...or laughed...

Or breathed...

Oh, she noticed him.

"Maybe you trust me a little here, Pips."

"Pips?"

He waggled his eyebrows.

"I'm not a Pips."

"Not royal enough?"

Oh, he could make her smile, despite herself.

"Maybe Phillipa is better. That's pretty royal."

"I'm not a royal." She turned, put her back to the pillar. She liked the patio—stone floor, a massive fire pit with Adirondack chairs around it. Last night, Fraser had suggested a fire, but the longer Imani was outside, the more she was a target, so...nope. "Although I did meet the queen once."

"Once? That's it?"

"It's not like she walks around chatting up the security. But my father worked at Hadsby, and one summer, while his boss was on holiday, he was in charge. I happened to be in his office—it was toward the end of the day—and suddenly, the queen walked in."

She looked out at the darkening sky. The sun had begun its descent, and it bled orange and gold along the horizon. The autumn air was mixed with smoke and leaves and the scent of a nippy breeze—so different from her island, but oddly fragrant.

"I was drawing, curled up on the sofa with a pencil, my notebook open, and I remember just looking up at her, shocked. She was wearing a dress, of course, and her pearls, and I remember wondering where her crown was. I'd never seen her in public without a crown of some sort. And then I remembered who I was and my manners, and I dropped my notebook on the floor and stood up and curtsied."

"I would have liked to see that."

"The queen?"

"The curtsy."

"I have a perfect curtsy. We all learn it and practice it, just for those moments." She could almost smell the moment, the worked leather of her father's temporary office, the polished wood floors, the old carpet. And the queen's perfume. Floral. Regal.

"I stayed down until she told me to rise. And then I realized that she'd picked up my notebook. I was drawing a tree through the window—I remember that because she told me that it was a linden tree and that it had been planted by her great-great-great-grandfather. And that if I looked closely, I might see that fairies lived there. I was twelve, so I didn't believe that, but I nodded anyway."

He had sat on the edge of the firepit, braced back on his hands listening. It flexed all the muscles on his tanned arms.

She ignored them. "But what was amazing was that she asked me if I wanted to be an artist when I grew up and I said no, I wanted to be a guard. A royal guard. And she paused for a moment and then told me that, someday, she looked forward to having me in her service. And then she handed me back my notebooks and said but if I wanted to, I could also be a protector of the fairies. Then she left, and I never talked to her again. But I'll never forget it. I felt...I don't know..."

"Royal?"

"No. But seen, maybe."

He had gotten up. Started to stack wood into the firepit. "Back in BUD/S, you didn't want to stand out, ever. But after I'd passed my SQTs, one of the instructors, a man named McCoy, came up to me after a training op and told me that I had good instincts. It stuck with me." He crunched up paper. "It stays with you—to be noticed by people you esteem."

For a moment, she was standing in the crowd, meeting eyes with her father.

"Pippa?"

"Nothing."

He was quiet for a long moment. Then he smiled. "Maybe you were wrong. What if fairies did live there? Don't you believe in magic?"

She considered him. "No. I believe in facts and realities. I don't go for make-believe or happy endings or even, if I'm being honest, faith in things you can't see."

His mouth made a tight line, and he nodded.

"Sorry. I don't know where that came from. Just..."

"I get it. More than you know." He finished with the paper. Walked over to the wood pile. "Ham says that even when we don't see it, God is still doing good in our lives. That we just have to stand firm in our faith. Like what you said in Italy—the truth we know."

The truth we know. She'd said that to him in as a reflex. "My mother used to say that to me."

He lit the fire, and it ate the paper. A tiny curl of smoke lifted into the sky, and the flames cracked and popped. "The truth I know is that God isn't a fairy tale. And that He doesn't make mistakes. And that my feelings, or fears, don't change the fact of His love for me." He blew on the flames, and they burned higher. He stood up and held out his hands to the flames. "My dad says that the greatest enemy of hope is forgetting God's promises."

She stepped closer to the flame. "How can I believe in a God who breaks His promises?" She didn't know where that came from, but she wrapped her arms around herself. "We were faithful church-goers, but after my dad died, I couldn't get past being angry that God wasn't there. I felt abandoned."

"Unseen."

She glanced at him. Lifted a shoulder.

"I don't know why your dad died—in the great cosmic scheme of things, Pippa. But I do know that the chief aim of darkness is to make God look worthless. To make faith seem worthless."

"Isn't it? It's like believing fairies are in the tree."

"No. It's not. Faith is what holds us together. It's our foundation when the world is shattering around us. It's the belief in a bigger picture. A bigger reason. It's the hope that we have when we realize we are not enough."

She stared at him. Then away at the fire, eating at the wood. "I have to be enough. Because if I'm not, then…" She blew out a breath. "Then evil wins. Again."

She didn't even hear him move. Just suddenly, he was beside her.

And then she was in his arms, pulled against his warmth, the strength of him.

And, okay. He wasn't sweeping her off her feet or anything. He was just giving her something to hold on to.

To trust in, besides herself.

She let herself lean into him, just for a moment. *It stays with you—to be noticed by people you esteem.* She closed her eyes.

"Evil won't win. It never really wins. It only looks that way from the ground. But that's what it feels like when all we trust in is ourselves." He pushed her away, his hands on her shoulders. Met her eyes with his, so blue she could lose herself in them if she wasn't careful.

"We're going to figure this out, Pippa. We're not going to let anyone get close enough to hurt Imani. Or Creed. And even if we're not enough, God is, okay?"

Pippa stared at him.

Behind her, the flames popped, sizzled, grew, eating away at the chill in the air, and at her feet, the wind stirred the decaying leaves. Scattered them across the patio like jewels.

"Okay," she said softly. "Okay."

She'd stopped holding his hand.

And Creed got that—really, he did. But it sorta felt like maybe she didn't need him anymore.

Not that she had, but back in Europe, she'd looked at him with this sort of earnestness in her hazel eyes that illuminated all the golden streaks, and he'd...

He'd thought she liked him. Crazy, but that's where it was.

Had started considering himself in the running for the affections of a princess.

Except she didn't seem like a princess so much as she sat

cross-legged on the sofa in the den, working the controller of the Xbox and racking up points in the current version of *Don't Starve Together*. So far, in the past three days, they'd died four times.

Not that he cared. She had this cute way of biting her lower lip when she was trying to figure out a problem.

And when she laughed, it was like starlight, sweet in the darkness of the past week's terror.

He still woke at night, sweating, remembering being tased.

And of course, that only stirred up deeper memories. Running. Gunshots.

"Aw. Dead again." Imani put down the controller.

"I told you—you can't eat the raw red mushrooms when your health is so low." He picked up a slice of cold pineapple pizza from a plate. "Wanna play again?"

She shook her head. "I wish I had my phone."

"You do."

"No, I mean, I wish I could call people." She wore her hair pulled back in a headband today, and one of his University of Minnesota Golden Gophers sweatshirts that only did beautiful things to her eyes.

What was his problem? They were just friends, and that wasn't a terrible thing. He just had to get that through his head.

"Who do you want to call? Maybe Fraser will let you use his phone."

She lifted a shoulder, then picked up the remote and changed the input to television. Turned it to YouTube.

"Imani?"

"I had this friend named Justin."

Justin?

"We went to high school together in Hearts Bend, in Tennessee. Used to hang out at my mom's farm. Played basketball, listened to music. Watched shows. You know."

Yeah, he did know. All the things he liked to do with her. And now he hated the burn in his gut. "Your mom had a farm?"

"Yeah. She took in wounded animals." She gave a little laugh, which sounded less like humor and more like irony. "I was one of them."

"A wounded animal?"

She made a face. "My mom died when I was born. And my dad was killed in a car accident when I was fourteen. I lived with my grandparents for a while, but even they didn't want me—"

"Imani."

"No, really. I was way too much for my grandma, and I was a foster kid and pretty jaded when Gemma took me in. But it's hard to be jaded around Gemma. She is...well, she loves big. She took me in and loved me back to a place where I could love too. We hung out all the time."

Oh. And then he couldn't help himself. "And you loved Justin."

Why had he said that? Because she looked at him, and a faint blush filled her face. She drew in a breath. "Oh. Um..." Then, "I mean, we never really...nothing really happened. One kiss, before I moved to Lauchtenland. But now he's dating Penny, my other friend, so..." She lifted a shoulder.

Not dating. But she hadn't answered his question, had she.

So, there was that. And, no biggie, because he didn't really think he had a chance.

Not with a princess of Lauchtenland.

But over the past three days, she'd seemed more just like a regular girl who...

"You play basketball?"

She brightened up. "I can totally take you."

"Horse?"

"Bring it."

He found a basketball in the garage, topped it off with air, and she was out on the side basketball court, wearing her tennis shoes, stretching out. He'd flicked on the outside lights, the night falling around them, and now bounced the ball a couple times, then left his feet for a three-point shot.

It hit the rim and bounced off.

She grabbed the ball, bounced it twice, then put it up in a sweet layup.

"Is that H?"

"Nope." She walked over to the top of the key. And then, with a form that could be called sheer beauty, rolled the ball off her fingers and sent it in a perfect arc for a swoosh through the net.

"Oh, I'm in trouble."

She grinned as she retrieved the ball and shot it back at him.

He bounced it, found his place at the key. Eyed the basket. "Do I have to swish it?"

"No—"

It slid through the net, no backboard.

"You were holding out on me." She took the ball.

"Luck."

"Sure." She did a back layup, hooking the shot in.

He mimicked her.

"This could be a long night," she said. Then she lined up with her back to the basket.

"What are you doing?" He stood at the edge of the half-court, watching her. The stars were out, the air smelling loamy, the scent of a fire nearby. Maybe Fraser had built one in the pit.

"This." She met his gaze, then simply flipped the ball over her head.

It hit the backboard, then dropped in.

"Oh, for cryin' in the sink."

She grinned.

He hadn't a hope of getting that. It hit the backboard and shot off into the woods.

"I'll get it," Imani said and took off.

He was already fetching it.

She swiped it up, then faked him out and took off for the basket. Oh, so they were playing one-on-one now. He chased after her and went for the block as she closed in on the basket for a layup.

Her shoulder bumped him as she shot, and he fell back.

She landed and caught his wrist. The movement pulled her toward him and suddenly, they landed against the house, her in his arms.

"Foul!" she said, her hands on his chest.

"On you," he said.

She laughed but didn't disentangle herself. Just stayed there, her gaze in his.

And suddenly, everything inside him turned to heat and fire, his throat thickening.

Especially when she leaned forward and, just like that, softly, gently, kissed him.

He closed his eyes, every sense wanting to savor this moment. To taste her lips, to feel the curve of her in his arms, to smell the night on her skin, to hear the thunder of his own heart as he opened his mouth and kissed her back.

He didn't want to scare her with the sudden rush of desire, but he couldn't stop himself from curling his hand around her neck, holding her there, deepening his kiss.

She stepped closer.

He had to be dreaming. Had to be caught up in some crazy fairy tale, because a guy like him, with his own scars, his own wounds, didn't deserve a girl like Imani.

Princess Imani.

His breath hiccupped. And for a second she pulled away. "Um...you okay?"

"I'm okay," he said, and lowered his head again.

Maybe the peasant did get the princess. At least here in Minnesota.

He wound his arms around her waist and pulled her against himself and stopped trying to talk himself out of the greatest moment of his life.

"What is going on here?"

The voice sliced through all the happy-ever-after feelings and jerked Imani back. She turned in his arms.

Oh boy. Pit Bull Pippa stood on the court. "What are you doing out here?"

He wanted to snap back something along the lines of *what did it look like?* but Fraser walked up right about then. He raised an eyebrow.

And perfect. Fraser already thought of him as a hoodlum. And sure, he'd shown up to scoop him out of Europe, but they hadn't exactly talked about it like bros.

He was still the foster kid in need of rescuing, apparently. By the look in Fraser's eyes, he was just as much trouble as Fraser expected.

"We were just playing basketball," he said lamely.

Imani had twisted out of his arms and clearly had a different take on the situation.

"What, are you spying on me now?"

Pippa held up her hands. "It's not called spying when I'm trying to keep you alive."

"Look where we are!" She spread out her hands. "In the middle of nowhere, America. Who is going to find me here?"

"I don't know. But it's my job to make sure they don't. And you playing basketball in the dead of night on a court lit up like a bullseye doesn't help. Imani, I know you hate this, but you need to work with me."

"I do hate this. I hate every second of being...trapped. I want to go home." She stormed off the basketball court, heading inside.

Pippa followed her.

Creed just stood there.

Fraser picked up the abandoned basketball. Bounced it a couple times. "Seriously?"

Then he shot it over to Creed, who caught it. "You should talk. I see the way you look at Pippa."

Fraser's mouth drew in a dark line.

Oh, he'd done it now.

"We have a job to do here. You and me. And we can't do it when we're kissing them."

You and me?

He didn't know why those words found soil, dug in. He swallowed nodded.

Fraser nodded, looked away, then back at him, and his expression had gentled a little. "Keep your head, Creed. We don't get to keep them."

Then he followed Pippa into the house.

Right. He knew that.

Really.

Keep your head, Creed. We don't get to keep them.

His own words from last night rattled around in his own head as Fraser stood on the ladder and again inspected the wiring to the camera above the barn door. The feed kept cutting in and out. Yesterday, Neil had shown up, and it wasn't until he was inside the barn that Fraser caught him on video.

Which freaked him out more than a little. He'd sat up last night in the quiet of the living room, watching the back entrance, the lights, monitoring the feed on his phone.

Seemed to be working, so he'd let himself sleep on the sofa—fell like a rock into a dreamless night until a squirrel set off the motion detector at six a.m.

He'd woken with a jolt only to find the feed to the barn out, again.

Poor squirrel nearly lost its life. Now, Fraser reconnected the wires at the base of the mount, added the wire nut, and tucked it back into the device. His father had mounted the security system years ago, but maybe they needed new equipment.

Pippa came out of the house as he was climbing down. "It looks like you've got it sorted. The feed came up."

"Good." He pulled the ladder away from the house, an eye on his grip as he carried it inside the barn. Neil had been by earlier, and all seemed well with the wine.

And his father had called last night, asking if Creed got home okay. Yep. No problem there. He'd fill him in when they returned in a couple weeks. They'd left France and were headed to Austria. More wineries to tour.

He listened for the strangeness in his father's voice that Jonas had mentioned, but he wasn't picking that up.

Or maybe it was just eclipsed by the sudden, crazy awareness of Pippa every time she walked into the room or took his place in his dad's office, watching the screens. Or the way she stirred her coffee so precisely, and even the way she smelled.

He could get very used to having her around. She thought like him—they'd turned over motives for Gunner over scrambled eggs and sorted through Gerwig Buchen's past, looking for clues as they watched Creed and Imani play video games.

Weirdly, she felt like an extension of himself.

A teammate.

A teammate that he couldn't stop thinking about kissing. He'd seen the line she'd drawn after the near fiasco in Italy, even if she hadn't spoken it, and save for his embrace on the patio—which had been more of a mutual moment of support than anything romantic—she hadn't made any moves in his direction.

So, yeah. Keep your head there, Captain America.

She'd called him that last night, right before she went upstairs to check on Imani, then turned in.

And it had sat there. Eating at him.

We don't get to keep them.

Pippa had followed him into the barn. "Wow, there are a lot of barrels here." She stood looking at the racks and racks of the new wine.

"We have more bottles aging in the back."

"It's a waiting game with wine, isn't it."

"Yep. And you just hope and pray you didn't damage the fermentation process in some way. Or somehow cork the wine."

"What's that?"

"It's when you bottle it with a contaminated cork and ruin the wine. A fungus can grow on the cork, and it makes the wine smell moldy and blunts the flavors. It can ruin an entire year of work."

She'd walked over to the barrel, put her hand on it. "The House of Blue make their own wine. They have a massive cave they store it in. Back during World War II, they used to hold dances and grand events in the cave."

"They were involved in the war?"

"Oh no, we were neutral. But the Germans flew over us to get to Great Britain, so we had a blackout. We also have a very small standing army, so we had to remain neutral. That's part of the reason why Hamish Fickle and his RECO party want to join the North Sea Coalition—so we'll have the protection of the larger countries."

"And through the various treaties, Great Britain, the US, and NATO."

"We don't want you marching through our country and setting up a base, but, yes, I suppose if we were attacked, our small but fierce military might appreciate backup."

She smiled at that, and he wondered if they were still talking about politics and Lauchtenland.

She wore her hair up, of course, but it was looser today, and a few strands fell around her face, framing it. He nearly lifted his hand to push them behind her ear.

The air thickened around them in the silence. He swallowed. "I think America would feel privileged to come to your aid."

She blinked then and looked away, then back to him. Her blue-gray eyes seemed almost dark in the shadows of the barn. "I don't know how to thank you for all you've done, Fraser. I've literally thrust myself and Imani into your care without really asking, and you...you simply stepped up into the fray. I..."

"It's my honor to help protect the princess. And her body-guard. Pipsi."

She shook her head but laughed. "Whatever."

"Now you sound Minnesotan."

"No, to be Minnesotan, I'd have to say things like *yooo betcha* and *soory*." Her accent left the words twisted.

"It's not so bad here."

"No. I sort of like it." She ran her hand along the barrels, walking the length of the building. "I like the colors of the leaves and the smell in the air and your addiction to campfires—although I'm waiting for one of those American s'mores—"

"You betcha." He'd followed her.

"And I'm starting to like the silence and the deep black of the night, the beauty of the stars. Everything is so close together in Lauchtenland, the city lights bleed out into the night sky."

He'd caught up to her as she now stood in front of a massive sliding glass door. "That's a lot of wine."

"About fifteen hundred bottles a year." They lay stacked end to front in tall racks. "Would you like to taste my father's best recipe? It's called La Crescent Gold."

She turned then, looked up at him. "For a guy who doesn't want to be a vintner, you know a lot about wine."

"No, I know a lot about the work of growing grapes. I don't know anything about how to make a great wine. But yeah, I worked these fields growing up, along with Jonas, Iris, and Ned, although we'd find him in a row, eating the grapes more than picking them."

"Are they good?"

"Sour. Strong. Not like the grapes you find in a store. But still good, in their own way."

He walked towards the tasting room. A small room with a long table and leather-backed chairs. Pictures of his family, going back generations, hung on the walls. He opened the door, and she followed him in. Stopped at a picture. "Is this you?"

"If you're referring to the tall, grubby kid in the back, yes." He stepped up behind her. "That was taken on a family camping trip to a nearby lake. We fished and swam all day, and that night was the first time I slept under the stars. The next day we went river rafting down the St. Croix. We tied all our rafts together like one big blob. I thought it was the coolest thing."

She turned to him. "It was. It is. To have a family like this. To be there for each other, like you were for Creed."

He lifted a shoulder. "Yeah. I'm not sure Creed looks at it that way. I think he feels like I'm a bit too bossy. Maybe critical."

"It's hard to be the one left out. Standing on the sidelines. Watching."

She was standing so close he could see the tiny variations in her eyes, the hint of gold around the irises, the layers of blue.

She smiled, and oh boy, what was he thinking? "Want some wine?"

"Nope," she said softly. "Any wine and I won't be able to think straight."

He stilled. Swallowed. "Pippa?"

She wrinkled her nose. "The thing is, Fraser, being here with you has me...breathing, I think. I know it's crazy, but you...you make me feel..."

"Safe?"

"Maybe strong. Maybe not alone. And seen. Maybe...well, I was thinking maybe that's what faith might feel like, right?"

He nodded. "That's exactly how faith makes you feel. When you put it in the right person. When you put it in God."

She gave him a hard look, then turned away.

"What?"

"Just...something my dad said. Right before he died." When she turned back, her eyes had filled. "After the attack, there was just...chaos. And the PM was still alive, so a bunch of guards rushed the stage and grabbed him, and my pop was there, still alive too, but...anyway, they sort of forgot him in all the rush, and I somehow got up there with him."

Fraser so wanted to reach out, to pull her to himself, but she had her hands wrapped around her waist.

"That's when he told me not to forget my name. Not to forget who I was."

She looked at Fraser. "All this time, I thought he meant the Butler name, you know? Our tradition of being royal guards, but what if..." She looked away. "My middle name is Fay. It's Old English for...faith. And maybe...I don't know. My parents both had great faith. My father used to recite Isaiah 43:1 when he would leave."

He shook his head.

"'But now thus saith the LORD that created thee, O Jacob, and he that formed thee, O Israel, Fear not: for I have redeemed thee, I have called *thee* by thy name; thou *art* mine.'"

Thou art mine.

The words swept over him, through him, and shuddered into his bones.

"I've been working pretty hard to make sure that our family name was redeemed. But maybe that's not the legacy here."

He nodded, slowly. "What is the truth you know?"

She also nodded. "Exactly." And then she smiled. "I was thinking...I don't miss Lauchtenland quite so much."

Oh.

But her gaze was roaming his face.

Wait.

"Pippa—" he whispered. "I don't get to keep you." But his hand had found her cheek.

She leaned into it.

Forget what he'd said to Creed. Maybe he could keep her. At least for now.

She stilled. "Someone is coming."

He pulled his hand away. "I hear it too."

He pulled out his phone. The motion sensor hadn't alerted yet, but he spotted it—a pickup coming down the road.

Except he knew that pickup. "It's Ham."

"Your friend?"

"Yep." He met her eyes.

Yeah, there was desire there. He swallowed. Oh, the timing. But maybe this was God intervening to save him from disaster. He walked out to meet Ham's truck.

His friend pulled up in the drive and got out, lifting his hand. "Thought I'd come and check on the Royal House of Marshall."

"Funny," Fraser said.

"I brought sustenance and news." Ham pulled out a bag of fresh corn, another of groceries. "You cook, I'll tell you what we know about your friend Gunner."

TWELVE

Maybe Imani was right.

Pippa should just…calm down.

Take a moment to breathe.

Let herself be, as Imani put it—*If I can be a princess, so can you.*

What?

She hadn't really let the words settle down and find root, not until she'd found herself in the tasting room with Fraser.

Not until he'd stood so terribly close to her that she'd nearly forgotten her name.

Not until he'd met her eyes and said he didn't get to keep her.

Except, what if…what if he did?

And then for a second, her crazy conversation with Imani after she'd chased her into the house last night took root.

"I don't want to talk about it." Imani had headed upstairs to their shared room in the farmhouse.

Pippa wasn't here to be her mother, so no, this wasn't going to be about the kiss—er, *snog* that she'd walked into.

Hello.

And Imani was a twenty-year-old adult who could make her

own choices, although Pippa wondered just how Princess Gemma might feel about Imani's choices.

Bother, and there went her Lauchtenland traditions, but what could she say? Yes, the writ had changed to allow Prince John to marry someone not from Lauchtenland—not to mention not of royal blood—but Pippa had always sort of thought of the royals as...

Well, royal.

She followed Imani into their room, where the woman sat on her bed, knees pulled up to her chest, acting very not-royal.

And as Pippa stood there staring at Imani, who stared at the wall like she might actually be a prisoner, it occurred to her.

As much as she tried, Imani wasn't a princess. She wasn't of royal blood. Wasn't a true Blue.

But that didn't make her any less important to the Crown. Or to Pippa's duty. Except maybe she got it then—how Imani might feel having a royal title thrust upon her.

Being suddenly in the limelight.

Maybe her gap year wasn't about seeing the world but... escaping. Which had landed her here. Under lock and key.

Pippa sank down on the bed opposite her. Folded her hands. "Your Royal Highness—"

"Please. Don't." Imani held up her hand.

Pippa took a breath. "Imani. I'm sorry for interrupting you. And, perhaps, for embarrassing you."

Imani lifted her head. Looked at her.

"Creed is..."

"I know. An American."

"Brave. And kind. And I see how he looks at you." She drew in a breath. "And if he's anything like Fraser—"

"Exactly like Fraser. Brave and strong and just wants to protect me. Except he's sweeter. Fraser is...such a grump."

"He's not a grump. He's just trying to keep us all safe. And playing basketball in a lit up court in the middle of darkness is like pointing a neon light down upon you, a target for any shooter."

Imani looked at her. "You like him."

That's what she got out of Pippa's rather controlled—thank you—comment about her recklessness?

Imani had uncrossed her legs, turned, and put them on the floor, leaning over to Pippa. "You like Fraser."

"I...we're friends."

"You're not just friends. I mean, probably, yeah, but...that's why you asked him to protect us. Because you trust him."

"Uh—"

"And you don't trust anybody. Ever. But yourself."

That hurt. But maybe... "I would like to trust you. And I would if you didn't always act like I'm your jailer and sneak out on me. I have a job to do, and you...you don't make it easy."

Imani stared at her, and something in her expression changed. "No, I guess I don't."

She got up. Walked to the fireplace. No ashes, no wood, no grate, but a slew of candles had been set in the opening. "I'm sorry."

Pippa stilled. What?

"Truth is, I...I don't want to be a princess anymore."

Pippa had no words. Who didn't want to be a princess?

"I mean, sure, it was cool at first. But mostly I wanted Prince John to be my dad, you know? And being a princess is...great. When you get to go to dances and dress up and...I don't know— go to the head of the line at the theater with your own box. And once I went backstage for a Brett Young concert, but that was before I was a princess, and it was because I knew Buck, so that didn't count—"

"Imani."

She turned.

"Being a princess isn't just about the dresses and balls and... special treatment. It's a...position. A belonging. A state of being. You're the daughter of the prince—and maybe not by blood, but by choice. Being a princess is being set apart. It's being renamed and seen as special. And because of that, you have the right to expect protection. Special favor. And for the prince to send his best to protect you. Or someone who at least tries very hard."

Imani smiled. "No, you're the best."

"I don't know. But—"

"You're trying very hard."

"I am."

"Why? You don't even like me."

Pippa looked at her. Blinked. Then, "Actually, I like you very much. I like your spirit. And your courage. And...frankly, this year, if I'm being honest, I've very much enjoyed seeing the world with you. Riding an elephant, not so much, but many of the other things."

"C'mon. You liked the pistachio arancini in Rome."

"I did."

"And seeing the Acropolis."

"Magnificent."

"And climbing Machu Picchu was cool."

"Exhausting, but...one of the top ten moments of my life."

Imani sat back down on the bed. "And because of me, you met Fraser."

She sighed. "Yes. But...we're from two different worlds. He has his life, and I have mine."

"Not right now. Right now, you have the same life, in the same place. And maybe that's worth figuring out. My mom said the same thing about Prince John when he came to Hearts Bend. That there was no future for them. And look at them now. Married, happy. You don't know how life is going to turn out. Maybe you'll even end up as a princess."

Pippa let herself laugh. "I'm not a princess."

"Why not? Like you said—it's not about clothes or dances,

or even royal blood. It's about being seen as special, a state of royal favor. If I can be a princess, so can you."

Pippa had laughed again.

But the words had stirred inside her despite her efforts to forget them, and she couldn't help but hear, with them, Fraser's words from the night before. *It stays with you—to be noticed by people you esteem.*

Maybe that's what she longed for, really. To be seen by someone she loved.

Like her father had seen her. In a crowd, picked her out. Esteemed her enough to meet her eyes and smile.

And then, of course, died right in front of her eyes. So there was that.

But before he'd died... Somehow, her conversation with Imani, and with Fraser earlier, only stirred up the deeper memory.

The one she kept locked away in fear that it would run her over, leave her wrecked.

"Phillipa Fay. I love you. Don't forget who you are. Don't forget your name."

Wow, she missed him. But in a way, Fraser reminded her of him. Undaunted. Driven. But sweet—Imani just didn't know him the way she did...

"As for Creed, I have no advice for you. Just, be smart?"

"Don't worry. My mom covered all that stuff."

Phew, because Pippa had no idea how to broach the topic of romance when she didn't even understand her own heart.

All she knew was that the more she spent time with Fraser, the more she...well, wanted to spend time with Fraser.

"But maybe I'm not the only one who needs the talk?" Imani said.

Pippa's eyes widened.

"Like I said, we're not in Lauchtenland. Not right now. And maybe you just...see what happens."

She'd almost gotten a taste of that in the, um, appropriately named tasting room. She didn't know what she would have done if Fraser had kissed her.

Okay, wrong. She knew exactly what she'd have done. Or had wanted to do.

So maybe it was a very good thing that Ham had shown up with steaks and corn on the cob. As they unloaded Ham's groceries, he gave Fraser an update on the Jones, Inc. team. Sounded a lot like the camaraderie her father had had with his fellow royal guards.

She walked into the office to check the cameras. Yes, the barn camera was back online. She synced it with her phone, just to confirm, and returned to the kitchen.

Fraser was leaning against the counter, his arms folded across his chest, nodding.

She had the image of those arms around her in a shadowy enclave in Italy, and a shiver went through her.

Ham looked up at her from where he was seasoning the steaks on a board.

"So, what do you know about Gunner and the murder of Gerwig Buchen?"

Ham wiped his hands on a towel. "I'm not in charge of the investigation, but Roy did call me. He and the Caleb Group are tracking down the images on the cameras. My cousin RJ, who is also their analyst, is on it. She also pulled the cameras from the lobby of the hotel where Creed and Imani stayed, and she's pretty sure that the man who came after them in their room was indeed Alan Martin."

"The rogue spy that they're tracking."

"The very same. Like I said, he has ties with the Petrov Bratva—the Russian mob. So we're activating a contact in Russia for more on that. In the meantime, RJ also pulled all the video footage from the Four Seasons in Geneva. There's lobby footage as well as loading-dock footage and key card records.

Everything we have puts Gunner Ferguson inside the Four Seasons the entire night of the murder."

Pippa came over to a tall stool and sat down. "He was at the hotel?"

"In his room, the entire time. He left once, around nine p.m., but cameras have him in the lobby, talking to the concierge. He never left the hotel, and returned to his room not long after."

Fraser ran his hands down his face. Turned to her. "That's good, right?"

She stared at him. "Wrong. Who ran after Imani in the park?"

Fraser's mouth just tightened.

He said nothing as they cooked up the corn on the cob and threw steaks on the grill.

But as the sun settled into the twilight, as the aroma of dinner settled into the night, she started to breathe.

If it wasn't Gunner, then whoever it was couldn't track them. Because only Princess Gemma knew where they were.

Which meant maybe they were safe.

She could calm down. Breathe.

And, as Fraser built a fire, enjoy the view.

Fraser loaded up marshmallows on a stick, and she learned how to cook them to a golden brown, then how to make s'mores.

Ham finally left, and Creed and Imani went inside, leaving only Pippa and Fraser by the fire. A nip had settled into the air, and Fraser brought her a blanket.

She stood up. Took the blanket. "Thank you," she said softly.

He nodded. And then drew in a breath. "I have bad news for you."

OH, MAYBE HIS JOKE HADN'T GONE OVER QUITE LIKE he'd wanted.

Oops. Because Pippa stared at him, her eyes widened in a sort of horror. "What bad news?"

He made a face. "You'll have to stay awhile."

She blinked at him.

Yep...wow. So, not quite so funny. And maybe for her it *was* bad news. Maybe he'd let that whole *I don't miss Lauchtenland quite so much* statement, and the way she'd looked at him before Ham showed up, linger too long inside.

Maybe she hadn't been about to kiss him. Sheesh, what kind of—

"Yeah, you're right, that is *terrible* news."

He stilled, and then she smiled.

Oh. *Oh.*

But just as abruptly, her smile fell. "Wait—do you think that's bad news?"

"What—no. I was joking." He wrapped a hand around his neck. "Apparently, bad joke."

She laughed then, and it loosened all the knots inside. "Calm down, Captain. I'm on board with sticking around. But now, at least, I can get ahold of Gunner and tell him what is going on with our runaway princess."

"I don't think she's running anywhere without Creed." He picked up the blanket on her chair and put it around her shoulders.

"That's the truth. They had a *moment* there."

"I talked to Creed. I told him that we had a job to do, and we couldn't do it while kissing the princess."

She nodded then, and sighed, and he had no idea what that meant. "Yeah, you're right." She walked out toward the edge of the patio and stared up at the sky, arched black and glittering with stars.

He frowned, but behind it stirred again the memory of the way she'd looked at him in the tasting room.

He came out to stand beside her. "You okay?"

"Yeah. I was thinking about Ham and your team and something Imani said to me."

"What's that?"

"She thinks I don't trust anyone." She sighed. "Maybe I don't. Or didn't." She looked at him then, something raw in her expression, before she turned back to the stars. "Hard to trust when everyone out there is a threat."

"Not everyone," he said softly.

A beat, then, "No, not everyone."

He met her eyes, and his heart gave a thump.

"Maybe we should go back before she loses her heart to a Marshall." She said it softly, and he almost had to hold his breath to hear it.

"Is that a possibility?"

"I think so." She was still looking at him. "Do you think he could fall for her?"

His pulse was in his ears. "I think it's a distinct possibility."

She pulled the blanket tighter. "And then what?"

A beat fell between them, a moment of silence.

And in it, crazily, he saw himself with Pippa. Maybe not here, maybe in Lauchtenland, but together. Working together. Laughing together. *And maybe, if you're honest, you want more.*

Clearly, the silence stretched too long, however, because she turned away from him, nodding to something.

Whatever it was, he couldn't stop himself from reaching for her, turning her to face him. "I don't know. They figure it out? They...trust each other? They decide to live happily ever after?"

She met his eyes.

He did want more. He didn't know what it looked like on the other side, but having Pippa here had made him almost feel whole again. Like he wasn't a liability, but trusted.

Needed.

And then, just like that, she stepped toward him, rose up on her toes, and kissed him.

It took him a second. Just a split second, because his impulses weren't that off, but in that second, he knew.

This was where he was supposed to be. Right here. With her. And if he'd been healed, he'd have been back on assignment with Jones, Inc.

Maybe this time-out, as Jonas had put it, had been exactly what he'd needed.

Ham's voice was in his head. *God hasn't forgotten you. There's a plan. You just don't know it yet. But when you're ready, He'll tell you.*

He was listening. And if this was God's answer, he was all-in. Because wow, she tasted good, her lips soft, willing.

Pulling her to himself, Fraser kissed her back.

She caught his face in her hands, softening her mouth to his urging, then slid her arms around his neck and hooked them, holding on.

His arms tightened around her waist. She wasn't so tiny that she felt fragile, but tall and capable and keeping up with him as he urged his kiss deeper.

He had to slow them down. Because he hadn't kissed a woman—well, he didn't really remember the last time, and in the back of his mind, he didn't want to take them to a place where he couldn't walk away with honor.

Or walk away at all.

And that truth just sort of exploded inside of him, shrapnel slicing through his heart.

He loved this woman. Or at least was on the way. Loved her determination, the way she could keep up with him, even kept him guessing.

Loved that she loved her country...

And that slowed him down enough to lift his head. He was breathing hard as he said, "What's going on here, Pippa?"

She swallowed. "I...I don't know."

"Should I stop?"

"*We*. Should *we* stop. Because I kissed you first."

Right. But he'd been sort of in his head and... "I don't want to...overwhelm you."

"Oh, I'm already overwhelmed here, Captain." And then she smiled, something sweet and slow and perfect. "Please, over-whelm me more."

Aw...

"I do promise not to tase you again."

It took him a second, but he simply laughed. "Sweetheart, I think it's too late."

Then he leaned in again.

Somehow, they ended up with him in the Adirondack chair, her curled into a blanket, sitting on his lap. Her fingers touched his face, and his held the edges of the blanket, pulling her in. He'd slowed them down, however, kissing her face, her neck, her lips, meeting her eyes, asking, and then kissing her again.

Pippa. The sense of her, here in his arms, the quietness of the moment despite his desire, the peace that settled inside him...

He pulled away. Searched her face, words forming in his heart—

"Pippa!"

The voice, shouted from inside the house, made him jerk. Pippa's eyes widened even as she fought to disentangle herself.

He helped her up as Imani ran out onto the patio.

Pippa was already on her feet and headed toward Imani. "What?"

Imani wrapped her arms around herself. "I saw him! I saw him!"

"Who?"

She was shaking. "The...man. Gunner. He was here. I saw him."

"Where?" Fraser was already dousing the fire.

"Outside. I was in the bathroom—I kept the light off like you said—and I saw him over there." She pointed toward the gazebo.

"Okay, calm down," Pippa said, coming toward her. She put her hands on Imani's shoulders, turned her and pushed her into the house.

Glanced back at Fraser.

He was one step behind her. He closed the door, locked it, and pulled the curtain. Then he headed toward the office.

The camera should have picked him up. Probably she was just scared, seeing things.

There was nothing on the screens—back of the house, front of the house, the porch, the basketball court, the barn—

The barn. He looked at the camera.

Nothing moved. Not the leaves on the ground. Not—wait. In the corner of the screen, he spotted a shot of himself with Pippa, standing on the patio.

"Pippa! Get her upstairs!" He grabbed his 9mm Sig Sauer from his desk and shoved it into his belt, along with a walkie. Then he grabbed another walkie and a pair of night vis glasses, rounded out of the office, and headed toward the den.

Pippa had Imani around the shoulders, was headed upstairs. He shoved the Sig into her hand, the walkie in the other. "Lock the door."

Then, although the curtains were drawn, he shut off all the lights inside—and outside—the house.

A body stood in the den door. Creed. "What can I do?"

"Get down on the ground." Fraser reached for him and practically shoved him on the floor.

"I can help!"

"How? Just stay—"

Creed took off for the office on all fours.

Fine. At least he'd be safe there.

Fraser crouched below the family-room windows, then rose and stared out into the night.

Nothing of a human body glowed in the darkness, but he did spot a cat scare and leap away.

He focused on the space around it.

Wait. Movement by the woodpile near the edge of the patio.

He grabbed the radio. "Pippa. I have movement outside. I'm going out there."

Two clicks. Affirmative.

He clipped the radio on his belt again and headed toward the sliding door. Slipped outside. Closed it.

Crouched behind the fire pit.

No movement—maybe the target had relocated. He crept along the house and toward the drive. No target. And he heard nothing but the wind, his own heartbeat.

Static over the line, then, "Fraser—where are you?"

Creed! He grabbed the radio. "Not now." Then he turned it off and clipped it back on his belt.

A skittering noise from the basketball court, in the back of the house. Fraser worked his way toward it, hiding behind the trash can corral, peering into the space.

Leaves, maybe, across the pavement.

He rolled out, kept his gun out—he'd switched hands and had been practicing with his left, but even now it felt unwieldy. He switched it back to his right, leaning hard into muscle memory.

"Fraser!"

The voice came from behind him, and he turned to see Creed waving from behind the trash corral. What the—

He motioned for him to get down, but Creed shook his head and, to Fraser's horror, ducked and came running for him.

It all happened in slow motion. A man emerged from behind the big oak near the driveway, also wearing NVGs. He pointed his gun at them—Creed, Fraser, he didn't know. But he pulled off a shot.

Missed.

Creed was running straight for him.

Fraser aimed, again fired.

Missed, but this time the man turned, started to flee.

"Fraser, look out!"

Creed leaped for him.

A shot sounded, somewhere behind them.

Creed landed on him, and Fraser barely caught him as they slammed into the ground. The NVGs were knocked off, his breath nearly blown out.

He lay there a moment, Creed on top of him, gasping for air.

What—

Still fighting, he rolled out from under Creed and turned.

A man stood in the yard, illuminated by the moonlight.

He raised a rifle, sighted Fraser. Or maybe Creed—Fraser didn't know as he fought for his feet, searching for his weapon.

There—on the pavement. He lunged for it, but his hands were slick, and the gun slipped away.

He glanced back at the shooter.

A gunshot cracked the air. Fraser wanted to jerk, waiting for the heat of the shot, but—

But the man crumpled in the grass, shaking, then still.

What—

Fraser pushed to all fours, then back on his haunches. Looked around. Then up.

Pippa stood at her open window at the far end of the house.

And then, behind him, Creed started to howl.

He looked down at his slick hands.

Not his blood.

Thirteen

Pippa understood hysterical.

Understood why Imani completely lost it and raced outside to Creed's shouts.

He'd been shot in the leg, bleeding hard onto the pavement. If it hadn't been for Fraser's quick thinking—clamping down on the bleeding with a tourniquet—maybe he would have lost that leg. Or his life.

So she even understood Fraser's actions as he ran out to the man in the grass to secure him—or maybe finish him.

Her shot had been dead on, even in the night, even with the 9mm. Even with her own panic sluicing through her when she spotted the shooter get a bead on Fraser, or maybe Creed—*probably* Creed. She didn't wait to sort it out.

Simply opened the window and shot.

She never tracked down the other shooter. After the EMTs left, Fraser had found tire tracks on the dirt road that led into their long drive. So, note to self—install cameras on the road.

If they stayed. Because suddenly the Marshall place felt compromised, and even here, at the Waconia hospital, some forty miles from Chester, Pippa hated the lack of security. The sense that at any moment, the second shooter would round the corner into the waiting area of the ER and finish off Imani.

So, yeah, Pippa got hysterical. She just wasn't giving in to it.

For her part, Imani had clamped down on her tears after the EMT team arrived from Chester and sent Creed screaming away in an ambulance.

Fraser drove them to the hospital, his phone on speaker to Ham, who was galvanizing his Jones, Inc. team and meeting them at the hospital.

Creed had already been taken to surgery when they arrived.

And that's when, only after the quiet settled in, Fraser spun out into his own version of hysterical.

He went deathly quiet.

Painfully, eerily silent.

Fraser stood, his arms folded across his chest, his legs planted, his jaw tight, so much torment in his expression, having his own personal meltdown.

Imani sat on a couch, her legs up, her hands around them, blood still on her shirt, looking wan and broken.

Pippa didn't know what to say.

What to do. How to help. So she'd gotten Imani a diet coke from the vending machine. And checked on Creed's progress—still in surgery. And now she just held up a wall, watching the two people she cared about individually unravel.

The elevator opened and Fraser looked up, took a breath.

Pippa leaned off the wall and spotted Ham and another man—solid, blond hair, a warrior type—heading toward them.

Fraser leaned up and outstretched his hand. "Ham. Jake. Thanks, guys."

Ham met his hand, then Jake, and Fraser gestured to Pippa. "Jake, this is Pippa, Imani's bodyguard."

Jake didn't ask questions, just gave her a grim nod.

"I just got off the phone with Logan, who placed a call to the

Chester sheriff. They have the body already in the morgue, with an identity. You ever heard the name Konrad Vogel?"

Pippa had stepped up to them, a strange heat washing over her. "Yes. He was a person of interest in the Geneva shooting."

Ham glanced at her. "Any idea how he could have found you?"

She shook her head, glanced at Fraser. His mouth formed a tight line.

"How's Creed?"

"The bullet nicked his femoral and shattered his thigh bone, so not great," Fraser said, and a muscle pulled in his jaw.

Ham nodded. "Have you called your folks yet?"

Fraser ran a hand behind his neck. Shook his head.

"Right. Okay, we're here now. Go get some coffee. Jake and I will stay with Imani." He glanced at Pippa. "You too."

She wasn't going anywhere.

Fraser, too, didn't seem to be leaving. He walked to the window. "The other shooter is still out there. I shot twice and missed."

Silence. Then Fraser turned. Met her eyes, then Ham's. "I'll go call my Dad. Let me know if Creed gets out of surgery."

Then he stalked away down the hall.

The stairwell doors slammed against the wall.

Pippa looked at Ham.

"We got this," Ham said.

She glanced at Imani, back to Ham. Then Jake. Who gave her another grim nod.

"Five minutes," she said, then followed Fraser down the hall.

She found him, his hands looped behind his neck, pacing in the small landing on the first floor. And then, as she stood on the flight above him, watched as he turned and slammed his fist into the wall. His right hand.

He backed up, shaking his hand, looking at it.

Then he formed a fist again—

"Stop!" She ran down the stairs and grabbed his wrist. "That doesn't help." The look her gave her should have turned her cold. Instead, she met it. "This wasn't your fault."

He blew out a breath, then tore his wrist from her grip, shaking his hand. He'd ripped a couple knuckles, fresh blood forming.

"You can't feel that, can you?"

"Now I can. A little." He rubbed his hand. "I wish I were in agony."

"Damaging your hand more won't make it heal any faster."

His eyes narrowed, then he turned away. "It's never going to heal." He leaned over and braced both hands on the well of the window. "And tonight, I nearly got Creed killed."

"No. That was on Creed."

"Yeah, what was he doing out there?" He'd stood up. "I told him to stay inside—"

"You turned off your radio. He was going to warn you about the other shooter."

He stared at her. "That's how you knew."

"Mm-hmm. He saved your life."

Fraser blinked at her. "*You* saved my life."

"I did my job. Who knows who he was aiming at."

Fraser's shoulders rose and fell. And with everything inside her, she wanted to reach out and put her arms around him. Hold on.

And maybe not for him, either. But because she suddenly warred with her own brand of hysteria.

Fraser had nearly been killed. Right in front of her eyes. And the thought nearly took out her knees. She even pressed her hand on the windowsill.

"Pippa."

She looked up at him.

"I think maybe you guys need to go back to Lauchtenland."

She blinked, the words bouncing off her. Yes, she'd thought it, but to hear him say it...

"I don't think I can protect you here." He drew in a breath, cleared his throat. "Now that Gunner has been cleared, I think you need to bring Imani back to the protection of the Royal Guard."

Oh. She stilled, rocked.

He wanted her to leave?

Except, he was staring at her, a storm in his eyes.

And just like that, she was back in Lauchtenland, watching her father's gaze on her. Seeing in it the same storm.

Because suddenly, she got it.

She wasn't a distraction but the focus. And maybe he wouldn't have seen the shooter—not with so many people and places and threats—

But he'd seen *her*. Seen her looking back with pride and love in her eyes.

Phillipa Fay. I love you. Don't forget who you are. Don't forget your name.

Phillipa. From Phillip, the one who loves.

He'd looked at her because he loved her.

And her heart sort of exploded.

Maybe she wasn't a princess by blood, but the love of her father declared her so. Because he saw her as his. Special. Set apart for his favor.

And deserving of his protection.

And just like that, she *knew*—

Her father had known what was going down that day. Had known there would be chaos and shooting and had been torn, in that moment, between saving his daughter and saving the Crown.

Which meant what? That he'd been part of the RECO movement? No, that couldn't be right. He'd been a patriot to his core. Had died protecting the king consort Edric.

Still, for a second, the choices burned inside her.

The Crown, or her heart. Because as she stood there, caught in Fraser's gaze, she could hardly breathe with her affection for this man. He'd believed in her. Made her feel strong. And safe.

And...oh, she should just admit it.

She loved him. Loved the way he stood by the people he cared about. Loved that he was unwavering in his loyalty.

Even loved his stupid humor.

Her eyes filled.

His breath stuttered even as he reached out his hand, touched her face. "I just can't have anything happen to you, and...I'm not enough. I'm just...not enough to keep you all safe."

Oh. Fraser. She put her hand to his. "Of course you're not."

He stilled.

"If you're enough for the task, your faith isn't big enough, right? That's why you have a team. That's why you have God. You're the one who said it. Faith is what holds us together. It's our foundation when the world is shattering around us."

"I said that?"

"Or something like that. Or maybe...maybe my father said it. But I think it's right."

He swallowed.

Then he stepped away from her. "I need to call my dad. And you need to call Gunner and take the first flight out of here."

Then he turned and pushed through the doors to the lobby.

And she couldn't help but feel as if warm blood ran through her fingers while she watched something of the man she loved die.

The door closed, the stairwell quiet, only the thump of her heartbeat remaining.

Oh, Fraser.

Then she headed upstairs.

Ham and Jake were standing in the lobby area, both nursing

a cup of coffee. She walked up to them but paused when she noticed the couch empty. "Where's Imani?"

Jake motioned to a nearby room. "Creed is back from surgery. Imani's in there with him."

She looked at the two men. "And why aren't *you* in there with them?"

Ham set down his coffee, frowned. "Because a royal guard of Lauchtenland is already in there?"

She stilled. "What?"

"Tall guy, good-looking. Said his name was Ferguson. Showed us credentials."

She pressed a hand to her chest. How had Gunner gotten here so quickly?—but it had been a few hours since the attack. And didn't Ham say he'd called Logan? "Did Logan call Roy?"

Ham glanced at her. "I don't know. But maybe."

She blew out a breath, hearing Fraser's words. *"I think maybe you guys need to go back to Lauchtenland."*

But maybe it was for the best.

She ignored the terrible keen in her heart and pushed inside the room.

No Imani. No Gunner. Just Creed, asleep in the bed, his leg thickly bandaged.

She stepped back out into the hallway. Walked down to the waiting room. "She's not there."

Ham frowned. Got up. "Really?"

"It's just Creed in the room."

He frowned.

"Where's Jake?"

"Went to call his wife. Terrible reception up here. I think he's outside, or in the lobby downstairs. Would she have gone with Gunner?"

Maybe. "She did want to call her mom, and her phone doesn't have a sim card, so she could have used Gunner's." Made sense, really.

And it wasn't like Imani stuck around to ask permission.

But it did feel a little off, what with the recent events.

"I'll go sit with Creed until you get back," he said, reading Pippa's mind.

She nodded and headed to the elevator.

The lobby was lit but empty as she walked through it. Although, as she headed outside, she did spot Jake sitting in a window well at the end of the hallway. She lifted a hand.

He returned the gesture.

She didn't see Fraser, either, but maybe he'd gone outside, even into his truck, to make his call.

Faith is what holds us together. It's our foundation when the world is shattering around us.

For some reason, her words pushed at her as she exited the hospital. She fully expected to see Imani sitting on the bench near the planter, or maybe even leaning against one of the pillars.

Nothing.

The wind had stirred up the night, leaves blowing across the parking lot. She stepped out into the shadows, under the glow of the lamplight, the whisper of wind in the trees, shivering.

Something wasn't right. She felt it, maybe under her skin, maybe in her soul, but that same feeling she'd had in Geneva.

Outside the VIP club.

"Imani?"

"Pippa." The voice, however, wasn't Imani's. Male.

She followed it out to the road in front of the parking lot. A man stood just outside the ring of light, his hand on Imani's arm, him positioned behind her.

Imani lifted her hand. "Over here."

Weird. Was Gunner trying to leave without her?

The thought gripped her that maybe...what if...was he *firing* her?

She picked up her pace, drew closer...then slowed.

Broad-shouldered, lean, and looking enough like his brother that, especially in the shadows, he could very easily pass as Gunner Ferguson.

"Fredrik?"

"I knew you'd show up."

"What are you doing here?" She came closer.

And that's when she saw Imani move toward her, then jerk.

Fredrik had her by the arm, still behind her.

Did he— "What's going on here?"

Even as she asked, she pulled the 9mm from her belt. "Let her go."

"Stop."

She stood close enough to see the tears that streaked down Imani's face. "Sorry."

"For what?" Pippa said.

"Everything."

Oh, Imani. "Your Highness, this is not your fault." Pippa looked at Fredrik. "I'm not sure what your play is here, but you do know that you won't get away. This is the end for you. And I can't let anything happen to the princess."

"She's not a princess. I think we all know that."

"She is to me."

Imani blinked at her. Swallowed. *Breathe, Your Highness.*

She just needed him to move, just a smidgen, to get a decent shot. And probably he knew this. "So it was you Imani saw in Geneva. Why, Fredrik? Who was Gerwig Buchen to you?"

He shook his head. "You're so blind, Pippa. Blind with loyalty. Blind with tradition. You'll never understand that we are meant to be a free people."

He was a *RECOist.*

"Does Gunner know you're a traitor?"

"Gunner is too caught up in his pomp and circumstance to see the real world. Put the gun down, Pippa, before this happens right here, in the parking lot."

"What happens?"

"The end of the monarchy as we know it. Because when the daughter of a traitor kills the princess—an American princess, no less—and then herself, she'll land in a diplomatic tussle with one of the world's last great powers. And then we'll see if the people want a monarchy."

She stared at him. "This is political?"

"Everything is political, honey."

"My father wasn't a traitor. He loved Lauchtenland."

"Sure he did. Which is why he let the PM die. And you're following right in his path."

She stared at him. "What are you talking about?"

He smiled. And then he held up his gun, his hand moving to wrap around Imani's throat. "Cute little Glock you have here. Sad you had to leave it in Geneva."

Yes, very sad. She ground her jaw. Met Imani's eyes.

A little spark had gone back into them.

"We're leaving. Or I'm putting a bullet in your princess's spine."

"No, we're not," Imani said. Then, just like that, apparently everything Pippa had taught her seemed to click in, because she landed her boot on Fredrik's foot, slammed her elbow into his gut, brought her fist down into his groin, then turned and jammed her left hand into his nose.

And hopefully pushed the gun away from her body just as it went off.

Fraser held the phone to his ear, calculating the time difference, hoping against hope that the call went to voice mail.

Nope. "Fraser?"

"Hey, Dad." He paced the unlit sidewalk on the side of the building, not far from the door where he'd exited. The wind had raked up, and a chill shivered through him. The scent of rain hung in the air, and the dark sky hid any stars, the cover thick with clouds.

He might have heard thunder.

Or maybe it was just his own words to Pippa, landing on his heart. *"I think maybe you guys need to go back to Lauchtenland."*

He was a jerk. But even she could see he was right.

Hadn't she even said it? *"Of course you're not. If you're enough for the task, your faith isn't big enough, right?"*

Right.

And sure, he had a team, but clearly, he was a liability. His stupid arrogance had nearly gotten Pippa and Imani and Creed—Creed, *oh, Creed*—killed.

"What's going on?" His dad brought him back to the moment.

Fraser ran a hand across his forehead. "Dad, uh, so...okay, I need to level with you about...that last couple weeks."

Silence, and Fraser closed his eyes.

Another beat.

"Whatever it is, son, know that I trust you."

"Probably you shouldn't," he said, and wasn't sure where that came from. "I've totally screwed up and..." He opened his eyes, his throat closing.

Sheesh, he'd never had a hard time talking to the old man. But then again, he'd always been, well, Fraser.

The oldest.

The protector.

The SEAL.

The one who got it done.

"I did mention that we have insurance on the wine."

"It's not the wine. The wine is...it's fine. Because, you know, Neil is watching over the wine, Dad."

Another beat. "Okay—"

"It's Creed. He's alive, but he's been shot."

This time the silence was so long Fraser looked at his phone to check the connection. And then, "Dad?"

"I heard you. I had to sit. And now I'm on speaker with your mom."

Perfect. "Hey, Mom."

"Son. Just take a breath. What's going on?" She seemed calmer than both of them, but then again, she'd endured breast cancer, twice, and was probably the source of his SEAL genes. Or at least half of them.

"So, it's a very long story, but Creed has been..." He sighed. "So, after you left him in Geneva, he met this girl..."

It took a bit in the telling, although he left most of it out— like his run-in with Jonas, and Iris's strange absence, and the tasing of himself and Creed, but left in the bit about Pippa and Imani staying at the farmhouse, and the murdered physicist in Geneva. Then, "I'm not sure how they found us, but the house was attacked, and Creed was trying to help, and somehow we got our wires crossed, and..." He ran a hand across his face and found his cheek wet. "Creed was shot. In the leg. He's in surgery now."

"Will he lose the leg?" His mom.

"I don't think so...he lost a lot of blood, but the EMTs from Chester had him to the hospital within the hour, so..."

"Fraser. This is not your fault." His father.

He drew in a breath. "I missed him, Dad. Twice."

"The shooter?"

"No." He was shaking his head, looking at his feet, crushing a leaf. "A different shooter. Pippa got the one who shot Creed."

"I see," his father said.

"So he's still out there?" his mother added.

He was nodding when he heard a shout, maybe Imani's name, in the night.

Or it could be the wind. "Yes."

"And could he be coming after you or Creed, or Pippa or Imani?"

More voices, maybe. He turned, but they seemed far away. "Yes, maybe, but...I..."

"Fraser, what's going on?" This from his mother, and it seemed she'd picked up the phone to speak into the mic. "You don't sound like yourself."

And he didn't know why—maybe it was the last twenty-four hours, but it might be the past twenty-four weeks, since he'd been taken hostage, but— "I'm not myself!" He didn't mean to shout, and now schooled his voice. "I...don't know who I am. I can't move my hand, and...I don't know, I'm stuck. This Abu guy is dead, and I still have nightmares that he's going to sneak up on me. Take me hostage or maybe someone I love, and..." He shook his head. "I just...I feel like my life is over. That every-thing I worked for is...dead. And with it is the guy I used to be. And I don't know who this new guy is. All I know is...I think God is done with me."

There. He said it. The truth. Whether he'd screwed up, whether he was being punished or just benched... "My career is over. And that's all I had. All I am."

Another beat, and he could just see his parents, shaking their heads, disappointed. And not that he'd been the kind of man to need his parents' smiles, but...

Okay, he liked being the family superstar. Liked being the one his parents named in a sentence first. Fraser, our oldest, former SEAL, special ops warrior.

Whatever.

The last thing he expected, however, was...wait, "Dad, are you laughing at me?"

"No, Fraser. Never. I'm just...actually, I think this might be the most important moment in your entire life."

And now he wanted to throw the phone. "I did mention that Creed is in surgery."

"I know. And we're praying for him. But we've also been praying for you. And the first thing you need to hear is that God is not done with you yet."

His jaw tightened. "It feels that way."

"I know. But the good thing is that feelings do not define truth. God's word defines truth. Don't try to bend the truth to justify your feelings. Instead, stand on the truth you know."

The truth he knew. "I'm not sure what that is right now."

"That truth has never, will never change, despite your feelings. God loves you. And no one, not even your parents, will love you as much as God does."

"It doesn't feel like love."

Silence.

"Right. Feelings aren't truth. It's just…what now? I've spent my entire life…doing something. And now…"

"And now you have to simply be."

He looked up, to black sky. And weirdly, Jonas was in his head. Again. *This time-out God has given you is His way of showing you that you need Him more than you need a grand purpose.*

"I don't know how to *be*. I've always had a purpose."

"Son. A purpose is a good thing. But it can be an idol. God is not a purpose. He's a person. And maybe He's saying, 'I love you for who you are, not what you can do.'"

"I sort of want to be loved for what I do."

"No, you don't."

He drew in a breath.

More voices, again behind him, lifting into the night. Sounded angry.

"Here's the truth. If you ever thought you were enough, then you were making yourself, your abilities, an idol. And you *will* fail yourself."

Right. He lifted his hand, looked at his bloody knuckles. "I think I already have."

"Then maybe, right now, God is rescuing you from yourself. God isn't done with you yet, Fraser. You just need to get out of your own way, stop looking for your glorious purpose, and lean into the God who loves you. And then you'll truly learn the meaning of the verse that says 'I can do all things through Christ, who strengthens me.'"

Behind him, a shot cracked the air. He stepped off the sidewalk.

Could be a car, maybe. "Thanks, Dad."

"Text us when Creed gets out of surgery. And tell him we're praying for him. We'll get the first flight out."

"Dad, hold your roll there. Don't cut short your trip—"

"We're on a plane, Fraser. See you soon."

"Okay." He hung up and ventured out into the parking lot.

The hospital had three lots, and this one was half empty, save for a handful of cars. He guessed it might be for employee parking.

Turning, he headed toward the stairwell entrance. Of course, the door was locked.

Perfect. And at this hour, probably the only entrance was through the ER.

He pocketed his phone and headed down the sidewalk, his father's words, along with Pippa's, in his ears. *You're the one who said it...Faith is what holds us together. It's our foundation when the world is shattering around us.*

He *had* said that. And meant it.

But maybe his father was right. He'd spent so many years depending on his abilities, his own grit that...well, he hadn't needed God a whole lot.

Just needed his team.

But maybe that was God, providing for him. Watching his back.

And now, maybe it was just Him and Fraser, their own team. And Pippa, maybe.

He didn't want her to leave. The thought tore a hole through him, and he couldn't believe he'd actually said the words.

But maybe...what if...he could go with her?

Oh, please. And do what?

There he went again, trying to fix everything.

A scream broke the night.

He had left the sidewalk, treading through the grass nearly to the ER entrance, and now, he ran toward the sound.

He spotted the source standing in the front parking lot in a patch of shadow, straight ahead. The man was looking away from him, toward—

Pippa. Who held a gun on him.

But more importantly, Imani struggled on her feet, a man jerking her hair, a gun at the base of her neck.

Wait.

Fraser knew this man.

Fredrik. From the boat.

Fredrik, who had tased Creed.

Fredrik, who, in Fraser's humble opinion, looked a lot like his brother, Gunner.

Ah, and now he got it.

It helped that Fredrik told Pippa to put her gun down. "Last chance. In the end, it doesn't matter what happens to me. Because the news will read that you shot the princess and then tried to kill me to cover it up."

What?

Fredrik jerked Imani's hair again.

She grunted, and Pippa raised her hands.

And right then, Fraser saw it. The nightmare.

As soon as she put the gun down, Fredrik would kill her, Fraser knew it in his soul. And then he'd kill Imani.

Fraser calculated the distance—five, maybe seven feet.

And Pippa was a sure shot.

Still, Imani could get killed.

Oh God, help.

And right then, the wind swept through the trees, thunder cracked, and a streak of lightning broke the sky.

Now.

More than a whisper, the voice rumbled through him, igniting every muscle, steeling every bone.

Now.

Fraser took off. Two steps, and he launched himself at Fredrik.

Pippa shouted.

Imani screamed.

Fredrik turned.

A gunshot, but Fraser felt nothing as he landed on Fredrik. The two scrubbed into the pavement. Fraser rolled, came up, grabbed Fredrik, made a fist with his right hand and—

Shouted, more of a roil of heat and agony.

Blood. So much blood from his mangled right hand.

And then Fredrik clocked him.

He fell back, and somewhere in his groggy periphery heard Pippa shout.

"Run, Imani!"

Fredrik bounced to his feet—

Oh no he didn't. Fraser might not have a grand purpose, but God did make him tough, right here, right now.

Help me, Lord.

He kicked out Fredrik's feet, then pounced on him.

His right hand might be disabled, but he had plenty of angry in his left. He broke Fredrik's perfect nose and added a back-hand that made Fredrik howl.

But Fredrik had two hands. And he grabbed Fraser around the neck and squeezed.

Fraser clamped his hand on the grip, his breath cutting off.

Fredrik rolled them, but Fraser got his legs around him and pushed.

Rolled on top of them. And then he got an elbow into Fredrik's face, and the grip loosed.

He gulped in air.

Fredrik hit him in the solar plexus and he gasped. Fell back.

And just like that, Fredrik was on him, a knee in his chest, a gun to his heart. "You stupid arrogant American—"

A shot.

And just like that, Fredrik jerked away, off him.

Crumpled on the pavement.

Fraser looked over.

Pippa stood in the lamplight, tears on her face, her jaw tight.

"Took you long enough," he said.

"You wouldn't hold still."

He might have formed a smile before the darkness slid over him.

FOURTEEN

She'd left her post.

Betrayed her country, maybe.

Pippa stood at the window of the University Hospital, her forehead pressed to the cold pane, watching the sun rise over the cityscape of Minneapolis, and prayed that she hadn't just done something stupid.

"Coffee?"

She turned to Jake handing her a fresh cup and, without a tea bag in sight, sure. "Thanks."

"Is he out of surgery yet?"

Jake shook his head and went over to sit down in the waiting-room chairs.

Three hours of surgery. She blew out a breath. The tiny out-of-city hospital didn't have the specialist they needed to repair Fraser's hand. If they even could.

However, the ER staff had been able to stabilize him and send him by ambulance to downtown Minneapolis. Meanwhile, Fredrik was life-flighted to the same hospital for surgery and recovery under the security of the local police.

She had no doubt that Gunner and a cadre of royal guards

were on their way to Minnesota, having had a conversation with him on her ride to Minneapolis in the wee hours of the morning.

She couldn't bear to tell him that she'd left Her Royal Highness Princess Imani, behind.

Frankly, she'd nearly stayed at her post. But Imani had looked at her as they packed up Fraser for his ride and said the words Pippa had ached to hear for a year.

"I'm not going anywhere. I promise."

Pippa believed her.

It helped that Ham had agreed to stay behind and not leave her side, no matter what royal guard showed up. So Pippa had given him her gun, and her faith, and left her post.

And followed her heart.

Jake had driven her to the hospital, meeting his wife Aria in the lobby as they came in. Apparently, her boss, Lucas Maguire, a cardiothoracic surgeon, had met Fredrik's life-flight and had taken him into surgery.

Fraser was already on the operating table under the care of a specialist that Aria had called.

"McKenna Graham is a master of reconstruction. If anyone can save his hand, it's her," Aria had said before she left to scrub up and observe.

Save his hand. Yes, that sentence reverberated inside Pippa.

That, and her own words to him only hours before. *Faith is what holds us together. It's our foundation when the world is shattering around us.*

Please, God, save his hand. She'd said it while staring out the window as the sun rose over the skyline of Minneapolis. And then again when, as she searched for a bathroom, she found a chapel.

She wandered inside, took a chair, and sat, staring at the cross at the altar for a long time.

See us, God. See him.

She finally lit a candle and then returned to the waiting area to find Lucas there, giving a report on Fredrik. Stable. But still unresponsive.

She hoped he lived. Prayed it, really, because he held the key to the bigger picture.

She still didn't understand why he'd kill a physicist from Lauchtenland.

Now she stood with the rest of the team—Fraser's team had slowly arrived. Orion and his wife Jenny, and Ham's wife Signe, and a woman named Scarlett, and even a couple of warrior types—a man named North and another named Skeet.

Ham, however, had stayed back at the Waconia hospital with Imani. And Creed.

Taking over her job as royal bodyguard.

What. Was she. *Doing?*

But she'd been second-guessing herself, unraveling in the parking lot—or at least feeling like it—from the moment Imani's escape attempt went south.

Oh, she'd executed it correctly, but Fredrik had recovered fast—too fast—and grabbed poor Imani's hair before she could run.

Nearly ripped it out of her head as he yanked her back to him.

Her scream tore out Pippa's heart. And right then, too, she got it—why her father had given his life for the king consort, Prince Edric.

Because she loved Imani. Not as a daughter, or even as a princess, but...as the person she was charged to protect. Loved her enough to surrender, in hopes that the princess might live.

But for Fraser's courage, his act of sacrifice, they might both be dead. As it was, the shot that took out Fraser's hand nearly took out her heart when she saw him fall.

And then there'd been the part where Imani took off

running, and Pippa knew that she should follow her. Make sure she was safe.

But she couldn't move, her gaze trained on Fraser as he fought Fredrik for his life. It took a full second for her to raise her gun.

And then she couldn't get a decent shot, and all she could think was *this isn't a taser*.

Instinct made her pull the trigger.

Instinct and fear and fury.

The shot hit Fredrik in the chest, and he nearly died right there on the pavement from a pneumothorax.

Would have, if Imani hadn't run inside and alerted Jake and the ER.

As it was, he'd nearly died twice on the table as they repaired the shot to his lung, according to Dr. Maguire when he emerged with the report.

Whatever.

Pippa was more focused on the results of the *other* patient. The one who was still in surgery.

"You should sit down. You've been up all night," Jake said.

Her entire body buzzed, awake. "I do better pacing."

Jake grinned. "You're so much like Fraser."

Huh. Maybe she was. She sort of hoped so. And at the same time, maybe that was trouble.

Both of them, running into danger. For some reason, his voice, soft and teasing as he'd broken into his sister's home in Como, sifted back to her. *I go down, you go down.*

Yes. Her eyes filled.

"C'mon," Jake said and urged her to a chair.

She sank into it. Stared at her coffee. She gave it a sip, made a face, but it did fill her bones with something bracing. "I still can't believe how close the princess came to being murdered."

"But you were there. And Fraser was there. You both deserve a medal."

She looked at him. "I'll be lucky if I don't get fired."

Jake just looked at his coffee. "Listen. I know what it feels like to make mistakes. To feel like you blew it. But I have learned that God is all about second chances and happy endings."

Huh. "I'd like that, but—" She stood up as Aria walked into the area. "How's Fraser?"

Aria wore a pair of scrubs, her surgical hat—her dark hair tucked back inside—and a mask, which she pulled down. "He's out of surgery. Doctor Graham will be here in a moment, but...I think there were miracles in that room today."

A few of the team members punched the air with their fists. Jenny and Orion embraced. Pippa gave into the heat in her eyes and wiped her cheek.

Aria hugged Jake, and right then, Pippa decided she'd made the right decision.

Dr. Graham appeared a few minutes later, holding her surgical cap in one hand, a cup of coffee in the other. Mid-forties, with dark red hair braided and pulled back, she was tall and thin and wore a slight smile. "We were able to repair the damage and reset most of the bones in his hand. The others we repaired with pins. But better, I also got a good look at the nerves. They'd been damaged by his previous injury, and I was able to go in and start over. I reconstructed the connections to his fingers and even grafted in a cadaver nerve. It will take a while, and no guarantees, but I'm hoping for a satisfactory recovery."

"So, he'll have use of his hand again?" Pippa asked.

"With physical therapy and prayer, it's a good hope." She smiled at Pippa. "Are you Pippa?"

She nodded.

"He's awake and asking for you."

Pippa dropped her coffee into the trash and followed Dr. Graham to Fraser's room.

He lay in the bed, his eyes closed, his hand in a cast past his elbows, wires trailing from his fingers to a machine nearby.

"It stimulates the nerves and keeps the blood flowing. It'll speed up the healing," Dr. Graham said. She smiled at Pippa. "He said something about a princess. Are you…"

"Yes, she is."

She looked at Fraser, who had opened his eyes—still a little drunk on morphine, clearly.

"I—"

"She's extremely special," he said.

She rolled her eyes.

"Welcome to Minnesota, Your Highness," Dr. Graham said, and grinned as she walked out.

"What are you playing at?" she said and came up to him. Slid her hand into his good one.

His hand gripped hers. "Just realizing that I…" He made a face. "I know what I said, but I don't want you to go, Pippi. I like it when you're around."

She didn't correct him, especially because his eyes twinkled.

"I agree."

He blinked.

"I'm not going anywhere, champ."

He made a face. "I don't think I can protect you."

"Maybe I protect you, tough guy. I talked with Gunner. He agrees that until we figure out what Fredrik is up to and understand the bigger picture, I need to keep Imani away from Lauchtenland."

"Really?"

"Someone needs to stick around and watch your back, for pity's sake."

His smile was slow and long, and he tugged on her hand. "C'mere."

She gave him a look.

"Please," he said softly.

She stepped closer.

He let go of her hand and touched her hair, then cupped her cheek. "You have completely derailed me, Natasha. And I didn't see it coming."

Oh. She leaned down and pressed her forehead to his. "Yeah, well, sometimes people get the drop on you, even on the best of days."

He smiled then, wrapped his hand around her neck. "Kiss me."

"You're a little bossy."

"I know." Then he pulled her to himself. His kiss was sweet, chaste and tender, and in it, she tasted the man she loved.

The man she'd traveled the world to find.

"YOU'RE A LUCKY GUY."

Doc Franzen stood beside Creed's bed and pulled the cotton cover back over his leg. "The stitches are healing well, and from the X-rays, the bone screws are set right. We'll get you casted tomorrow, and then you can go home. But I think, with physical therapy, you'll be back on your feet by the new year."

Creed tried to hear him, to agree with the smile on the older man's face, but... "Will I run again?"

Because, shoot, all he could think of—after asking if Fraser was alive—was the fact that his leg had nearly been blown off.

Okay, that was an exaggeration, but it felt like that, the way it was encased in a thick bandage, the pain that seemed to scream up his leg into his entire body.

If Imani hadn't been sitting by his bedside when he woke up, he might have burst into tears like some eight-year-old.

Still sort of wanted to, honestly, but he refused to let himself unravel in front of her. Especially since it was probably only a matter of time before the Lauchtenland guards dragged her back to her palace.

He didn't want her last memory of him being him blubbering. He dug deep for a smile as he waited for the doctor's answer.

"It's up to you. I'm not sure you'll be running any races, but yes, I think in time you'll be able to pick up the pace."

He kept his smile all the way until the doc left the room.

Imani had been standing behind him and now walked over and took his hand. He couldn't look at her, though, and put his gaze to the window, where the rain spit upon it.

His throat tightened.

"You'll run again, Creed. Really." She squeezed his hand.

He looked at her and resisted the urge to yank it away, to yell, maybe throw something. But she hadn't been the one who'd...who'd done something stupid.

If only he'd listened to Fraser and stayed put, like he said. Instead, he'd tried to be a hero.

And Fraser had been shot anyway. Not at the time, but later, after the second shooter found his way to the hospital.

Imani had told him the entire story, including her own failed attempt at escape—which, to him, seemed the height of courage—up to the moment when Fraser risked his life to save her. And got his hand nearly blown off.

Wow. Now there was a hero.

He leaned his head back in the pillow and tightened his hand in Imani's. Sighed.

"Do you want something to drink? Maybe something from the vending machine?"

Poor woman had been here for two days, meeting his every need—food, drink, channel changer, *Wordler*. She'd even slept on the fold-out recliner next to the bed.

Which meant her bodyguard, a royal guard flown in from Lauchtenland, was planted outside in the hallway.

Pippa the bulldog had apparently opted to stake out Fraser's room. Now there was a lucky dog. Because although Imani had stuck around, she hadn't tried to kiss Creed, or otherwise make a romantic move, since that night under the basketball hoop.

Clearly, coming to her senses. And now, he was a...well, he wouldn't say cripple.

But he wanted to.

"No. I'm not hungry."

She gave him a look. "Now you're pouting."

He stared at her. "I'm going to college on a scholarship. Which is now useless. My entire life has been destroyed, thank you."

She drew in a breath. Recoiled.

"Sorry. I just—"

"No. You're right. Your life has been completely derailed. Wrecked. And it's because of me." She let go of his hand. "Because I pulled you into this—"

"Imani, I didn't—"

"No. You're right. I...I should go—"

"Stop."

She had already turned away, but something in his voice— he'd even surprised himself—seemed to still her.

"Don't run."

She turned back around, her eyes wide.

He took a breath and reached out his hand. "I shouldn't have said that. I just meant...yes, maybe I was pouting. But listen. I get it." He sighed. "But I *really* get it. Maybe I didn't tell you, but I was a foster kid before the Marshalls took me in, and...it wasn't easy. I wanted to run, more than once. But I kept thinking...what if I stay? What if I don't let my fear tell me that this is going to really hurt? What if I believe that maybe this could be a good thing?"

"You nearly died because of me."

"No. This is not your fault. None of this is your fault. I nearly died because I didn't listen to my brother."

"But you saved my life."

The voice made him look up toward the door, where Fraser stood, Pippa behind him. He wore a clean pair of jeans and a short-sleeve shirt, a jacket over his shoulder, loose, and under that, a massive sling on his arm, a pad at his hip to hold it out from his body. His hand was casted, each finger individually, and it ran all the way past his elbow. Tiny wires extended from each finger.

A few scrapes still showed on his face, a cut healing, but the whiskers across his chin seemed to cover anything else.

Still, he looked rough.

"Hey," Creed said.

"Hey, little bro," said Fraser, and for some reason, Creed's stupid eyes burned again. Because Fraser came in and smiled at him and walked over to the side of his bed. Then he lifted his arm. "We match."

Creed laughed and then, oh no, his laughter dissolved to something of sobs. Shoot—but he couldn't seem to stop it.

Fraser sat down on the bed. "Aw, kid. You're going to be okay."

Creed swiped his hand across his face. "No, I mean—yeah, maybe, whatever, but—you nearly died. And it's because—"

"Are you serious right now?" Fraser palmed Creed's chest. "Because you saved my life. If you hadn't come outside, then the second shooter would have shot me in the back. As it was, you saw him, yelled—you *saved our lives*, Creed."

The pressure of his hand on Creed's chest, the warmth sank right through him.

"But that's what brothers do, right?"

Creed nodded, wordless.

Fraser patted him on the chest, then got up. "So guess what? We do get to keep them."

He blinked at him for a second, a long second, and then, "Wait—what?"

Fraser turned and looked at Pippa and then Imani. "They're staying. At least until we figure out what's happening in Lauchtenland."

Creed met Pippa's gaze. "Really?"

"Somebody needs to look after you two. You're pitiful." But she smiled.

Imani took his hand. "I guess I'm not going anywhere."

And then she leaned down and kissed his cheek.

Making him the luckiest guy on the planet.

And then Fraser winked at him. "Anyone want a pizza?"

"YOU CAN COOK?"

"I'd hardly call this cooking," Pippa said, setting down the waffles. "It's fried batter."

Whatever. Just seeing her move around his kitchen made Fraser smile. Even if she did cut up his food.

More, he'd started to get feeling in his pinky finger. More than the needles and stings. Real feeling, and he couldn't stop rubbing the tip of his finger where it protruded from his cast.

A real miracle.

Pippa noticed as she sat down, because she reached over and wrapped her fingers around the pinky. "It's working."

"It is indeed working."

It's working. Last night, as he'd lain in bed in the quietness of his room, he'd realized...

This was enough.

Weirdly, perfectly, enough. To be alive, to wake up in the morning and find Pippa still here, to watch Creed mend, smile, laugh as he and Imani played video games.

To see Imani safe and starting to unwind out of her cocoon.

To breathe in and out and watch the sun rise and set behind the drying vines, to pet Sherlock in front of the flickering fire in the outside hearth. Or watch his marshmallow brown as Pippa sat across from him, trying not to burn hers.

To hear her stories of Lauchtenland, her childhood, and see in his mind's eye a girl with long dark braids, and to share his own stories of a wild and perfect childhood on the Marshall farm.

Yes, this life was enough.

God was enough, right here. Right now.

Now. The word spoken in the wind. It hung onto him, filled his bones.

Now. Not tomorrow. Not the grand purpose.

Now, right here, with God, enjoying His presence. Him.

"What are you grinning at?" Pippa had let go of his hand.

He picked up the syrup. "Just...nothing. And everything."

She cocked her head. Then smiled and nodded.

On the table, her cell phone buzzed, and she picked it up. "Movement from the barn sensor."

He drew in a breath.

"It looks like a truck. Maybe Ham's truck?" She handed him the phone.

The familiar F-150 pulled into the drive. "Yeah. And someone's with him."

He finished his food, and Pippa cleared the plates by the time the doorbell rang. He answered it.

"Gunner," Pippa said from behind him.

Right. He remembered the man from the hotel. Tall, blond, wide-chested, although he was out of uniform, wearing black jeans and a leather jacket.

"Hello, Pippa," said Gunner.

Ham stood with him. "How's the hand?"

"Getting there. Come in."

The two men stepped inside. Behind them, the day was breaking over the far horizon, a hint of chill in the air.

Maybe tonight he'd make a fire in the hearth. Pull Pippa into his embrace and just watch the flames flicker.

Pippa was wiping her hands. She wore her hair down today, dark and shiny. And a pair of yoga pants, a white oxford rolled up to the elbows.

Bare feet.

And he couldn't help but think of the woman he'd met in Geneva. Uptight. Armed.

Yeah, she'd tased him all right. Sent a shock right through to his heart.

"Sorry I haven't been around sooner," Gunner said as Fraser closed the door behind them. "I've been arranging to bring Fredrik back to Lauchtenland for recovery, interrogation, and trial."

Pippa's mouth made a tight line. "Have you gotten much out of him?"

"No. But we've gone through his computer, his apartment, and already started our investigation at home. Apparently, he'd been involved with RECO for some time. Gerwig was a mate from uni, back in the day. I didn't know that."

"Does he have any connection with Hamish Fickle?"

"None, other than Fickle is also RECO. We've kept the incident out of the press for now, so no one knows, including Fickle. We have people on him, watching."

"I can't believe Fredrik would..." Pippa shook her head.

"He was my brother," Gunner said. "So I share your disbelief."

Ham glanced at Fraser. He had his own sad story of betrayal, so Fraser got it.

"What's going on?" Imani came down the stairs. She stilled when she spotted Gunner.

"Hello, Your Highness."

She walked over and stood behind Pippa.

"I'm so sorry for what my brother did to you. You were wise to run. And even wiser to trust your friend Creed. I'm so sorry for what happened to him."

She offered a bare smile. But Fraser saw her slip her hand into Pippa's.

"I have something for you," Gunner said. He carried a satchel and now pulled out of it an envelope. "It's from your mother. It's airline tickets to Hearts Bend, when you're ready."

He handed over the envelope.

She took it. "Thank you."

"We'll probably be sticking around here for a while," Pippa said, glancing at her.

Fraser raised an eyebrow when Imani said, "Anything you say, Pippa."

Huh.

"Are those waffles for Creed?" She pointed to a stack on the counter.

"Yes. And you. Fix him a plate."

Imani grabbed a plate from the cupboard and filled it, adding syrup.

"I have something for you too, Pippa. I didn't want to leave without giving it to you."

He pulled out a large white envelope from his back. "It's from Her Majesty Queen Catherine."

She blinked at him a moment, then opened the envelope. She drew out a folder and opened it. "It's the Golden Rose."

"Indeed, it is."

Fraser walked over to her. "What's the Golden Rose?"

"It's like your Medal of Honor, our highest award."

Her hand covered her mouth, and when she looked at Fraser, her eyes had filled.

"What?" He came over to her.

"It's for my dad," she said.

Indeed. Inscribed on the certificate was the name Sir Phillip Butler III.

"I don't understand."

"Read the note," Gunner said.

She set down the folder and opened the note. Fraser read over her shoulder.

To Phillipa Fay Butler, from the Office of Her Majesty Queen Catherine,

It has come to my attention your gallant actions regarding my beloved granddaughter, HRH Princess Imani. Your bravery, sacrifice, and loyalty is exactly what I have come to expect from the House of Butler.

It did, however, bring to mind the tragic events of your father's sacrifice for our country, and I asked my secretary to look into the events. I discovered, to my dismay, that he was never awarded the honors due his name and actions.

My beloved husband, HM Prince Edric, recalls that day as one of terror and gratefulness. More, upon reading the investigation report, it is clear that your father took the place of a RECO-affiliated guard that day.

He very well knew of his sacrifice before he made it.

This, above all, deserves the honor he was denied until now.

We shall have a proper Golden Rose ceremony upon your return. Until then, my deepest gratitude for your sacrifice and your continued service in Her Majesty's Security Detail.

HM Queen Catherine

Pippa looked up at Fraser, then Gunner.

Gunner stood to attention. Saluted her.

"Thank you, sir."

"I look forward to seeing you on Her Highness's service when you return."

She set down the paper. Looked at Fraser. "Thank you, sir, but no."

"No?" Gunner raised an eyebrow.

"I have a job, sir. To protect Princess Imani. Where she goes, I go. I...like I said, I understand her. And she needs a special kind of bodyguard."

Imani had finished plating her food and was heading for the stairs. She looked over at Pippa. Smiled. Nodded. Mouthed, a *thank you*.

"I see." Gunner looked at Fraser, back to Pippa. "But after she returns to Lauchtenland?"

"After that..." She looked at Fraser, smiled. "We'll see."

And with those words, Fraser's heart nearly left his chest.

"And what are you going to do?" Ham said to Fraser.

He pointed to his cast. "Eat waffles, and maybe watch paint dry."

Ham considered him a moment. Then nodded. "Okay then."

"Mm-hmm."

Ham closed the door behind himself and Gunner, and Fraser turned to Pippa. She was wiping her face. "Wow."

He picked up the letter, read it again. Set it down. "He knew he was going to die."

"Maybe. Maybe that's why he looked at me."

"Maybe that's why God had you there that day."

She met his eyes. Held his gaze.

"The truth I know now—that I'd forgotten for a while—is that we are never more loved than by our God. Our refuge and strength," he said.

She nodded. Whispered, "'Fear not: for I have redeemed thee, I have called *thee* by thy name; thou *art* mine.'"

He touched her face. "Yes. And maybe mine too?"

She leaned in and touched his forehead. "A little bit glad I tased you?"

"A little bit," he said. Then he kissed her.

And prayed it took a long time for the paint to dry.

"I would have picked you up at the airport. You should have called." Fraser stood next to the Uber as his father unloaded their suitcases. His mother had come around, wearing a ball cap, a pair of jeans, and a jacket, wearing the four days it had taken them to get home on her expression.

"We left you a message when we got to London," his father said as he added their backpacks to the pile in the driveway. "But that was two days ago, and we didn't know when we'd get in, with our flights cancelled from London to Minneapolis."

The answering machine. Fraser hadn't thought to check it after he arrived home from the hospital yesterday. He reached for a backpack in the pile.

"Oh no you don't," said Pippa, coming out of the front door. She'd been at the monitors, watching, and had alerted him to the unknown car coming up the driveway. He guessed she'd tucked her Magnum back in her belt when she spotted him embracing their interlopers.

"Hi," she said, sticking out her hand to his mother. "I'm Pippa Butler."

His mother, Jenny, pulled her into a hug. "Fraser briefed us when he called after Creed got out of surgery. Apparently, you all have had quite the adventure."

"Sorry to descend on your place—"

"We're glad to have you," his father said. "Garrett Marshall." He shook Pippa's hand. "Stay as long as you need."

She pulled the backpack over her shoulder and grabbed the handle of a suitcase. "It might be a bit, given that we still don't have any leads. Unfortunately, Fredrik, the only connection to what's going on, is still unconscious after his transfer back to Lauchtenland."

His father grabbed another backpack and the other suitcase. "How's your hand, son?"

Fraser realized he'd unconsciously wrapped his good arm around his cast. "Pain is subsiding. And I'm getting some feeling back."

"Praying hard," his father said, and gave him a smile.

Yeah, him too. But, "I'm okay on the sidelines for a bit."

His father glanced at Pippa, now hoisting the bag into the house after his mother. "I'll bet." He winked.

Fraser couldn't help a smile. Yep.

They went inside and Creed met them, on crutches.

"Aw, Creed," his father said. "It'll be okay." He pulled him into a hug.

"That's what Fraser said." Creed gave him a thin smile.

Fraser met it, nodded.

Behind Creed stood Imani, getting a hug from his mother.

Creed introduced Imani to their dad, who also gave her a hug. "So, the epic trip to Europe turned out to be a little more epic than you thought," he said as he let her go, looking at both of them.

Creed managed a wry smile. "Sorry."

"I'm just glad you're okay and all of this is over," his mother said.

His father had walked into his office.

"Can I bring these upstairs?" Pippa asked, referring to the bags.

"Oh, Pippa, you—"

"Fraser, come here." His father's voice interrupted his mother's objection.

Fraser glanced at his mom, Pippa, then headed into the office.

His dad was leaning on the desk, next to the recorder, wearing a grim look.

He pushed play on the ancient machine.

Ned's voice. "Hey, um, Fraser—tried to get ahold of you, but you didn't pick up. Hope you got Creed home okay. I just wanted to let you know that I think I tracked down Jonas, and there's a plan to extract him. And I think we found him in time. As long as he didn't get too close, you know? So I guess we'll see. I just wanted to give you an update. Don't tell Mom and Dad—they have enough on their plate." A pause, during which Fraser looked at his father. Oddly, the old man swallowed, then looked away.

What was that?

Then Ned continued. "Maybe I wasn't supposed to say anything, but I don't have time to record another message… just…stay put. I'll call you if I need you, but for now, don't worry…I promise I'll find Jonas and bring him home."

A click, and then the message began to play his father's message from London.

His father pressed End.

Looked at Fraser. "What's happened to Jonas?"

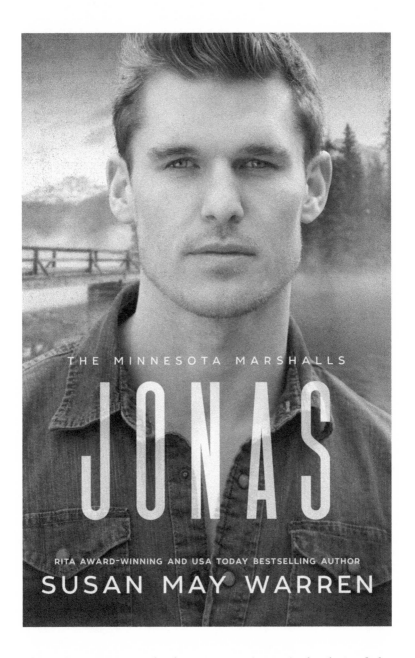

THE MINNESOTA MARSHALLS

JONAS

RITA AWARD-WINNING AND USA TODAY BESTSELLING AUTHOR
SUSAN MAY WARREN

The epic romance and adventure continues in book 2 of the Minnesota Marshalls. We have a sneak peek for you...

JONAS

The Minnesota Marshalls || Book 2

CHAPTER 1

He had to get off this mountain.

Because, if Jonas read the skies correctly, a doozy of a storm was headed his direction.

And Jonas Marshall, with his PhD in atmospheric science, always read the skies correctly. Or at least, with a 99.8 percent probability.

The other point-two percent were simply those God moments that no one saw coming. But then again, that's when people died.

So yes, barring a divine intervention, the altocumulus clouds that had chased him most of the morning, now morphing into dark gray, ragged nimbostratus clutter, would turn this day hike into a soggy, freezing fight for survival.

"C'mon, we need to go."

He said this to his buddy Nixon, who held his cell phone up, taking a panoramic view of the Julian Alps. "Just another minute."

The wind cut through Jonas's Gore-Tex jacket, and he shoved his hands into his pockets against the chill. But he got it.

He could take just another moment to soak in the glorious view from atop the 2,864 meter high Triglav Mountain. Craggy granite spires, high pockets tufted with white, rumpled the horizon from here in Slovenia to Italy to the west, and across the Austrian border to the north and east.

Gray cliffs fell down to green valleys pooled with moraine-blue lakes and countless spectacular waterfalls. Feeding them were roiling rivers that twined through a thick northland forest, ripe with cedar and pine and the sense of a world untouched.

Probably it was, because Slovenia was largely hidden from the popular tourist hotspots. Jonas had only found it because of Tarek—and, of course, the footage from Walter 01, one of his weather dirigibles, a solar powered, directed balloon soaring over the northern border.

Walt hadn't quite captured the scale of the mountain, the crisp, thin air, the heady feeling of flying as he stood at the top.

Sort of felt like he could just take a step off and soar.

Sometimes, lately—especially since the accident—he wished it.

Shouting in Slovenian turned him, and he spotted a kid, maybe age twelve, sticking his head into the giant white canister at the apex of the mountain.

"Can't believe that kid made it up here." He said it to himself, mostly, but Nixon made a noise, even as he kept filming.

"Next time you invite me to visit, maybe let's not do it on summer holidays," Nixon said.

"Right." He expected the holiday crowds down in the Alpine town of Kranjska Gora, on the banks of the river Sava, where Slovenes escaped with their families for the August holiday. But families and day adventurers clogged the trail through the Krma

Valley, despite the technical challenges near the top, with him having to use carabiners attached to cables.

A tiny red flag on the apex of the canister whipped wildly in the wind.

Get off the mountain. He wanted to wave his hands and yell, but probably they had hours left, and maybe he shouldn't be the crazy American on top of the mountain scaring everyone.

But still.

"Nixon—"

"Got it." He pocketed his camera, grinning at Jonas. "Wait until Geena sees this."

Jonas tried to keep his smile, nod, but he just...aw. "How is she?"

"She's good. They have her hooked to a machine that moves her legs, and she sent me a video just a couple days ago of her upright and 'walking.'" He finger quoted the last word with one hand.

Everything inside Jonas burned. "That's great."

"You'll see. She'll be walking again this time next year."

He searched Nixon's face for guile, but only found honesty in his friend's brown eyes. Or maybe faith.

"Here, let's take a selfie." Nixon held out the camera and stepped up to Jonas, lifting it high to catch the breathtaking terrain behind them.

Jonas managed a smile, the camera and sunlight glinting off his mirrored sunglasses.

"She'll love that," Nixon said. "I'll send it when we get to the mountain hut." He pulled on his backpack.

"No internet there, Nix. You'll have to wait until we get off the mountain."

Jonas also shouldered his pack, glad to see the family with the kid had already left the top. Still remaining were a young couple and two women who'd just arrived at the peak.

He walked by them wanting to offer a "Don't stay too long," but opted to keep his mouth shut.

Mostly because he couldn't speak the language, but also because it wasn't his...nope, he couldn't stay silent.

He stopped and turned to one of the women, her brown hair pulled back in a long tawny braid down her back, her eyes shielded by aviator sunglasses. "It's going to rain. Don't stay long."

He wasn't surprised when she just ignored him. But her friend, shorter with a pixie cut to her dark hair, looked past her. "Thanks."

Hmm.

The couple was leaving, so he followed Nixon off the mountaintop, clipping into the line that led down the ridgeline.

An hour later, he'd descended nearly a thousand feet and found himself sitting inside the small gathering room of the Kredarica mountain hut, rain pelleting the windows, shivering as a man stoked a fire blazing in the black stove in the middle of the room. Around him, the family he'd seen shared sandwiches, and the couple had heated up some soup, all of them eating their dinners at the rough-hewn picnic tables. Many were still shivering.

"You were right," Nixon said, handing him a cup of tea, then scooting in beside him. "That mountain is socked in. Hope those women got off it."

He did too.

"Good call to book a night here."

"Sorry about the shared room."

"Hey. It's a hostel. I expect bunk beds. As long as I don't wake up to some kid drooling on me."

Jonas laughed, picked up his tea. "Could be worse. We could be sleeping in a car under an overpass."

Nixon's smile tightened into a thin line. "Yep."

And oh, the air between them stilled, tightened. Nixon

looked away. Jonas stared at his cup. Why had he said that? Because of course, yes, they'd been there, done that, but in the case he hadn't been referring to, their car had been thrown by a twister, landed upside down in the ditch, and they'd been trapped in the freezing rain for hours, waiting for help.

While Geena nearly died. So yeah, maybe Jonas should keep his stupid mouth shut.

"Water's boiling," Nixon said and got up, heading for the makeshift kitchen where their freeze-dried soup sat on the counter. He filled the soup as Jonas retrieved the buns they'd purchased in town, now slightly crushed. Some cheese, hot soup, and crusty bread. Yes, it could be worse.

"Tell me again what this grant is about?" Nixon blew on his hot chicken soup.

"Lightning. Storm patterns."

"You finally got to use your balloons." Nixon was back, grinning at him, the Geena specter at least diminished.

"Dirigibles, and yes. I've upgraded them since the last design. Now they're controlled by drones, powered by air and sun, and can stay aloft for weeks. They're programed to fly in a selected area, so we get real data points for specific areas. The black boxes send data down to my app, but it's sketchy here in the mountains, so I have to constantly check on them."

"Have any accidents?"

"One. Came down in a field north of our office in Ljubljana. No one was hurt, but it was a mess."

"How?"

"Wind sheer." He dunked his bread into his soup.

"How much longer on your contract?"

"Another month or so in country, then a few months in Oklahoma sorting out the data. Then maybe...I don't know."

"No more storm chasing?" Nixon had finished his soup and picked up his phone, scrolling through the pictures, occasionally showing Jonas.

Jonas said nothing, watching the family now taking out a deck of playing cards. Outside, the rain roared, and in the distant, low rolls of thunder.

He expected that there might be snow up at the higher elevation.

Yeah, he hoped the women had made it off the peak.

Eventually Nixon let the question die, showing Jonas pictures of the trek up and yesterday's walk around Kranjska Gora, and then Nixon's trip to Venice, Italy just over the border, and then Rome, where he'd finished a gig shooting a commercial for a clothing brand.

Probably a good thing Jonas had gotten out of the storm chasing biz. Gave Nixon a chance to spread his wings.

And that way, nobody else got hurt because of him.

The door blew open, and a man came in, soaking wet, breathing hard. "We've got an accident on the mountain."

Everyone stilled. Apparently, he wasn't the only English speaker in the room.

Jonas found his feet. The man shivered, came up to the heater, still breathing hard. "Big winds. Blew a couple women over."

"Who's hurt?"

"I don't know. I heard them shouting, but it's raining too hard to get to them."

Jonas looked at Nixon, who blew out a breath. Nodded.

"How far up the trail are they?"

"About two hundred meters from here."

"Anyone got climbing gear?" Jonas asked the room.

Silence again. He shook his head and headed toward the door.

The man stopped him. "You go out there, you'll fall off the mountain too."

Jonas brushed his hand away, feeling Nixon step up behind him. "I know how to live through a storm."

The man held up his hands in surrender and stepped back. "Suit yourself."

Jonas zipped up his jacket, pulled up the hood, and stepped out into the gale. The black sky obscured any hope of reading the clouds, the wind moaning.

For a second, his stomach hollowed, and a tremor went through him.

Jonas! Don't let me die!

"You sure about this?" Nixon, grabbing his gear up behind him, steady as usual, as Jonas led him into danger.

"Never pin a weatherman down on his forecast."

Nixon grinned, white teeth against a dark night. "You got this."

Oh boy. But Jonas put his head down, the wind fighting him as he headed up the path.

Yeah, he really needed to get off this mountain.

Thank you for Reading

Thank you so much for reading *Fraser*. I hope you enjoyed the story. I also want to thank my writing partner Rachel Hauck for letting me steal her princess! Check out her True Blue Royal series to dive into the world of Lauchtenland!

If you did enjoy *Fraser*, would you be willing to do me a favor? Head over to the **product page** and leave a review. It doesn't have to be long—just a few words to help other readers know what they're getting. (But no spoilers! We don't want to wreck the fun!)

I'd love to hear from you—not only about this story, but about any characters or stories you'd like to read in the future. Write to me at: susan@susanmaywarren.com. And if you'd like to see what's ahead, stop by www.susanmaywarren.com .

I also have a monthly update that contains sneak peeks, reviews, upcoming releases, and free, fun stuff for my reader friends. Sign up on www.susanmaywarren.com.

Susie May

About Susan May Warren

With nearly 2 million books sold, critically acclaimed novelist Susan May Warren is the Christy, RITA, and Carol award-winning author of over ninety novels with Tyndale, Barbour, Steeple Hill, and Summerside Press. Known for her compelling plots and unforgettable characters, Susan has written contemporary and historical romances, romantic-suspense, thrillers, rom-com, and Christmas novellas.

With books translated into eight languages, many of her novels have been ECPA and CBA bestsellers, were chosen as Top Picks by *Romantic Times*, and have won the RWA's Inspirational Reader's Choice contest and the American Christian Fiction Writers Book of the Year award. She's a three-time RITA finalist and an eight-time Christy finalist.

Publishers Weekly has written of her books, "Warren lays bare her characters' human frailties, including fear, grief, and resentment, as openly as she details their virtues of love, devotion, and resiliency. She has crafted an engaging tale of romance, rivalry, and the power of forgiveness."

Library Journal adds, "Warren's characters are well-developed and she knows how to create a first rate contemporary romance..."

Susan is also a nationally acclaimed writing coach, teaching at conferences around the nation, and winner of the 2009 American Christian Fiction Writers Mentor of the Year award. She loves to help people launch their writing careers. She is the founder of www.MyBookTherapy.com and www.LearnHowto-WriteaNovel.com, a writing website that helps authors get published and stay published. She is also the author of the popular writing method *The Story Equation*.

Find excerpts, reviews, and a printable list of her novels at www.susanmaywarren.com and connect with her on social media.

- facebook.com/susanmaywarrenfiction
- instagram.com/susanmaywarren
- twitter.com/susanmaywarren
- bookbub.com/authors/susan-may-warren
- goodreads.com/susanmaywarren
- amazon.com/Susan-May-Warren

Also by Susan May Warren

THE MINNESOTA MARSHALLS

Fraser

Jonas

Ned

Iris

Creed

SKY KING RANCH

Sunrise

Sunburst

Sundown

THE EPIC STORY OF RJ AND YORK

Out of the Night

I Will Find You

No Matter the Cost

GLOBAL SEARCH AND RESCUE

The Way of the Brave

The Heart of a Hero

The Price of Valor

THE MONTANA MARSHALLS

Knox

Tate

Ford

Wyatt

Ruby Jane

MONTANA FIRE

Where There's Smoke (Summer of Fire)

Playing with Fire (Summer of Fire)

Burnin' For You (Summer of Fire)

Oh, The Weather Outside is Frightful (Christmas novella)

I'll be There (Montana Fire/Deep Haven crossover)

Light My Fire (Summer of the Burning Sky)

The Heat is On (Summer of the Burning Sky)

Some Like it Hot (Summer of the Burning Sky)

You Don't Have to Be a Star (Montana Fire spin-off)

MONTANA RESCUE

If Ever I Would Leave You (novella prequel)

Wild Montana Skies

Rescue Me

A Matter of Trust

Crossfire (novella)

Troubled Waters

Storm Front

Wait for Me

MISSIONS OF MERCY SERIES

TEAM HOPE (Search and Rescue series)

Waiting for Dawn (novella prequel)

Flee the Night

Escape to Morning

Expect the Sunrise

NOBLE LEGACY (Montana Ranch Trilogy)

Reclaiming Nick

Taming Rafe

Finding Stefanie

THE CHRISTIANSEN FAMILY

I Really Do Miss your Smile (novella prequel)

Take a Chance on Me

It Had to Be You

When I Fall in Love

Evergreen (Christmas novella)

Always on My Mind

The Wonder of Your

You're the One that I Want

THE DEEP HAVEN COLLECTION

Happily Ever After

Tying the Knot

The Perfect Match

My Foolish Heart

The Shadow of your Smile

You Don't Know Me

A complete list of Susan's novels can be found at
susanmaywarren.com.

CPSIA information can be obtained
at www.ICGtesting.com
Printed in the USA
BVHW031324160223
658645BV00002BA/471